LIVING ON LIGHTNING

By
Don Green

Donald R. Green
3201 Southwood Drive
Philomath, OR 97370
U.S.A.
www.consultco@comcast.net

To my parents, Emmett and Esther Green, who with love, patience, fortitude, and bravery, struggled to lift themselves out of poverty into prosperity during the Great Depression and provide for two children.

PREFACE

In the early 1930's, a boom in power line construction was followed by a sharp increase in the demand for power line maintenance. At that time, work on live lines was one of the most dangerous jobs in the United States. According to the Internet open encyclopedia, Wikipedia, approximately 1 in 3 linemen were killed by electrocution on the job between the 1890's and the 1930's. Due to the high fatality rate, there were usually job openings for men willing to be linemen. Emmett Green was desperate for a steady, well paying job to support his family. In spite of the danger in those early days of line work, he accepted a job in as a lineman in 1934. He was part of a multitude of desperate men seeking jobs. Youth, strength, and the ability to perform physically hard work were qualities linemen needed to endure the heavy work of climbing poles. They often had to work in uncomfortable positions straining to install heavy items such as steel tower legs, lacework (bracing), and insulator strings. High up on poles and towers in all kinds of weather, they had to tolerate extreme heat and cold. Linemen at that time had to be either brave or naïve to remain cool headed and focused while working only a few feet from hot wires that could trade instant death for a moment of inattention. Many brave men survived; many naïve men did not. This story includes many of the adventures and narrow escapes endured by Emmett during his long struggle to survive and free himself from the grip of poverty.

Much of the power line work in the early days was done by "boomers", linemen that roamed all over the United States working in impromptu temporary crews called "gangs". A line gang would be assembled to perform a specific construction or maintenance job, after which the gang would be dissolved and the men would go their separate ways roaming the nation to find work in other temporary gangs being assembled to perform specific jobs. Men who worked in boomer gangs rarely got any formal training in line work, but started as "grunts" working on the ground watching experienced linemen. When a grunt felt that he had learned enough to pass himself off as a lineman, he would try to do so. Often he would barely be qualified in one branch of line work, such as erecting steel towers, but would accept a job working on live lines as a lineman in a gang, frequently with fatal results.

By 1934, when Emmett entered line work, power companies and contractors were increasingly establishing their own permanent home-based crews for construction and maintenance work. It was more conducive to formally train and qualify new linemen when a permanent group of men were retained instead of having a constant turnover of boomers. The high rate of death and injury in the early years of line work led to the formation of labor organizations to represent electrical workers and advocate for their safety. The most important of these organizations in the United States is the International Brotherhood of Electrical Workers (IBEW), which today has 760,000 members. Safety equipment, procedures, and training developed through the combined efforts of IBEW, power companies, skilled line workers, and engineers have made present-day line work a much safer career.

ACKNOWLEDGEMENTS

My warmest thanks to Simon Johnson, Professor Emeritus of English and the members of his creative writing class, for their gentle (and sometimes not so gentle, but always helpful) critiques; Donna Holloway, writer, for copy editing and for suggesting constructive changes in the story; Linda Olsen, English Teacher, for helpful suggestions and copy editing of an early draft; George Kastl, lineman, and Martin Burrus, retired lineman, for their expert advice and suggesting changes in parts of the story that deal with line work; and Robert Dunsmore and Marcia Biotti from the Staff House Museum of the Shoshone County Mining and Smelting Museum Inc., Kellogg, Idaho, for a helpful guided tour of the museum and describing some Kellogg history from the 1930's and 1940's.

I gratefully acknowledge the cover background photograph, used with the permission of Dr. Steven Horsburgh.

You Tamed The lightning

You tamed the lightning you men of old.
Tamed it into wires to be bought, and sold.
You risked your lives you men so bold,
In winter storms and freezing cold

Tame the lightning you men of today,
This marvel that helps us work and play.
Restore it quickly, without delay,
When it 's disrupted by a stormy day.

-Don Green

CHAPTER 1

BAD NEWS

It was late August 1932 when twenty-five-year-old Emmett Green started plowing a field on his leased farm in Oregon's Willamette Valley at daybreak. The peaceful, golden dawn, like so many others that summer, gave no indication of serious trouble. Now, at 2 PM, a brassy sun was beating down from a cloudless, blue sky. Shimmering heat waves rising from the fields distorted distant objects, making them appear to stretch, shrink, and dance. The shirt, which Emmett had worn earlier in the chill morning air, hung on a bush at the edge of the field near a one-gallon water jug. The jug had been full of cold drinking water when the plow first bit into the soil that morning, but now there was only a pint or so of lukewarm water left in it.

The plow was slightly bent and stubbornly insisted on pulling to the right, but it was no match for six-foot-three-inch Emmett's powerful muscles as he strained to keep the furrow straight. Perspiration was streaming down his suntanned face, stinging his eyes, and dripping off his nose. Brown blotches ringed with white salt deposits covered the legs of his blue denim work pants where sweat was soaking through, trapping dust, and evaporating. Although he wouldn't admit it to himself or anyone else, Emmett was hot and tired. Pulling back on the reins, he said, "Whoa Maggie, whoa Nellie." After the horses had stopped, he continued to pull on the reins and said, "Back—back—back." The horses backed up a little, slacking the traces. Emmett pulled a red bandanna out of his back pocket and wiped his face.

The satisfying earthy aroma of the freshly turned dark brown soil was now mingled with the strong, leathery odor of sweating horses. Emmett treated them more like pets than farm stock, and he didn't want to overwork them. He said, "Girls, I think we've had enough for today." Then he pulled the plow handles up to lift the blade out of the soil, unhitched the horses, draped the leather

traces over their backs, and retrieved his shirt and water jug. He
began walking toward his distant farmhouse carrying the shirt and
water jug in one hand and leading the horses with the other. At
that moment, a car drove into his driveway.

"Girls, I wonder who that is?"

As he walked through the oven-like heat in the field, Emmett
looked longingly at the distant purple mountain peaks that soared
majestically into the cool layers of air high above the valley floor.
He remembered when, as a boy, he had hunted in the cool
Douglas Fir forest near his parents' mountain homestead farm.
Emmett's face took on a dreamy, far away expression as he said,
"Girls, I sure would enjoy being up there out of this heat, but I
have a family now, and I have to provide a lot more than just meat
for our table."

A pump and watering trough awaited Emmett and the horses in
a shady barnyard near the house. He removed halters, bits, traces
and work collars from the horses, which immediately went over to
the trough and began drinking the cool, clear water. After
hanging the equipment on hooks nailed onto nearby trees, Emmett
took a tin cup from a hook on another tree. Using the hand pump
near one end of the watering trough, he filled the cup with fresh,
cold water. He reveled in delicious, cold wetness as the water
swept away the parched, dusty feeling in his throat. It seemed to
cool and sooth his entire overheated body. Just as Emmett was
filling the cup for a second time his landlord, Mr. French, came
walking rapidly toward him, accompanied by Emmett's wife,
Esther, who was carrying their blonde 21-month old son, Donnie.

Esther was an attractive 24-year-old woman of medium height
and above average strength and intelligence. She was wearing a
plain housedress that flowed around her as she walked. Ringlets
and waves in her dark brown hair gleamed as she passed through
spots of sunlight filtering through the trees. Emmett was alarmed
to see a dark cloud of worry in her brown eyes.

Mr. French was dressed in a cheap, black suit. He was a
heavy-set 60-year old gray-haired man who had been a farmer
most of his life and looked old for his age. He had acquired
several adjacent farms when he was younger and had run them
with hired labor. Now he was leasing the farms to tenants on a
shared crop basis. He also owned a small dry goods store where

he and his wife were now struggling as its sole managers and clerks to keep it going; times were bad, and not many people had money to spend on dry goods. The store was teetering on the brink of failure.

As Mr. French approached, he said, "Emmett, your lease expires next week and it's time to sign a new one." Then, stopping near Emmett, French spoke more slowly and hesitantly as he said, "I—hate to do this to you, but—I can't even meet the taxes and expenses on this place—with the 30% share of the crops you have been paying me for rent. I'll need 50%, or—I'll have to sell the place."

Emmett was shocked that the rent was to be raised so much in such hard times, and he felt a knot in the pit of his stomach. He thought about the lease for a few moments, then said, "There's no way I can make a living on only 50%. We're barely making it on the 70% we get now, and we don't have enough money to buy the place."

Mr. French looked sad as he said, "Then—I'm sorry, but I have an interested buyer. You'll have to move out in 30 days. I can't give you any longer and risk losing this deal. Things are so bad right now that buyers are scarcer than hen's teeth."

Emmett thought, My God, I don't have enough money to lease another farm and start over, or even rent an apartment. Esther and Donnie are depending on me, and now my livelihood is gone. How could this have happened? Emmett's mind recoiled as he tried to make sense of the situation. The color drained from his face and he felt sick as he realized that he wouldn't get any of the much needed benefit from his hard work plowing and planting during the past two months. He'd invested most of his meager savings in seed that he had already planted.

Due to his father's large family and past financial difficulties, Emmett had had to quit school and start work immediately after he finished the eighth grade. Now, he didn't know where he could find a job; unemployment was at 25%. There were ten men waiting in line for almost every job, especially if it required no more than an eighth-grade education.

Seeing Emmett's distress, Mr. French said "I know you've done a lot of work plowing and planting crops that won't be ready for harvest by the time you have to leave. I'll try to negotiate with the new buyer to give you 40% of the harvest from the fields you planted. That's the best I can do."

They all walked to French's car. After getting into his car, French rolled the window down. As he backed out of the driveway, he said, "I want you to understand how very sorry I am about this, but I just don't have any choice."

Emmett and Esther, who was still carrying Donnie, looked dejected as they waved goodbye. They went into the farmhouse, and sank onto chairs at the kitchen table. Esther put Donnie down on the floor to play. Gloom hung in the air like soggy gray clouds on a rainy day.

For a long time they sat in silence, each lost in thought. Finally, Esther broke the silence. "What are we going to do?"

Emmett didn't answer, but got up, went out on the front porch, and stared out across the fields in which he'd worked so hard for the past two years. Esther followed and stood beside him. Without saying anything, she put an arm around him and gazed out over the fields too.

Esther was surprised to find Emmett's side of the bed empty when she awakened before daybreak the next day. Knowing his state of mind, she was worried. At about 8 AM, Emmett returned in his worn 1922 Model T Ford. Esther was giving Donnie a bath in the kitchen sink.

Emmett came into the kitchen and said, "I went to Dad's place early to get our car, and to return his horses so he could use them today before it gets too hot. When I told him about our situation, he said we could move in with him and Ma until we get back on our feet. He has space in his new barn where we can store the hay that we move out of the barn here. He also said we can bring our chickens, and let our cow and sheep graze in a couple of his fields."

"Oh Emmett, that's good news! I was worried when I woke up this morning and you weren't here; but I guess I should know by now that you always face serious problems head on."

They began packing non-essential items of their meager possessions into cardboard boxes and burlap sacks. A couple of weeks later, when his father's horses and hay wagon were available, Emmett borrowed them and hauled the boxes and sacks to his father's place. Most of their possessions had to be stored in an equipment shed since Emmett, Esther, and Donnie would now be living in one bedroom. Later, Emmett began moving the hay to his father's barn. This took several days since his father's place was about 10 miles away and it was possible to take only one load a day.

It was late September with a gray, overcast sky when it was time to haul the last load of hay and essential last-minute household items. Emmett put a halter on the milk cow and tied the lead rope to the back of the wagon. Esther and Donnie went along on this trip, and sat on the back of the load so they could watch the cow. As they started moving, the wagon bounced them up and down cushioned by the hay. Donnie thought this was great fun and began giggling delightedly. His delight made Emmett and Esther laugh, and lightened the anxiety and sadness they were feeling. At that moment, the warm, golden light of the sun broke through the clouds and finished transforming the family's mood into one of hope and anticipation.

Esther said, "You know, I think we're going to be all right."
Smiling, Emmett said, "Of course, I knew it all along."

Later, Emmett's optimism faded when he returned to pick up their six sheep. Two were dead, and one of the others was badly injured.

"Damned coyotes," Emmett muttered to himself. "They tore these two up so bad that we can't even salvage the meat."

He lifted the four remaining sheep one by one into the hay wagon. Emmett had installed stake-bed sides on the wagon to keep the sheep from jumping out.

He climbed into the front of the wagon and picked up the reins. "O.K. girls, gidup," he said, giving the reins a flip. His gaze swept longingly over the farm as he left it for the last time traveling toward an uncertain future.

CHAPTER 2

AHEAD INTO THE PAST

The big, old farmhouse owned by Emmett's parents had been built in 1884, and it was devoid of any modern conveniences that had become available later. As Emmett and Esther moved into one of the four bedrooms they were grateful to have a place to stay, but they felt like they were stepping 50 years back into the past.

By 1932, ten percent of farm homes and most city dwellings had electricity and incandescent lighting. Many even had gas or oil heating. The old farmhouse had none of these. Water was obtained using a hand operated pump mounted at one end of the kitchen sink on a drain board. Heat, cooking and hot water were provided by wood burning stoves that had to be stoked every one to two hours, depending on the type of wood. Kerosene lamps were used for light at night, and the strong odor of kerosene permeated the entire house. Clothes were laundered in a hand-operated washing machine by pushing a lever on the side of the machine back and forth to move a plunger up and down inside the tub until the clothes were clean.

The first night, after moving into a bedroom in the old house, Esther and Emmett were dead tired and went to bed early. At last, finally having some privacy, they were able to freely express their feelings.

"Esther, I'm sorry it has come to this. I'm really worried. The way things are going, I don't know if I'll ever be able to earn enough to have a place of our own and give Donnie a good education."

"It's not your fault, Emmett. You've worked hard and done everything you could to provide for us. It's this awful economic depression. I'm glad we have a roof over our heads -- lots of families aren't so lucky. We've just had some terrible luck, so naturally you're depressed. We have our health, you're strong and hard working, and I know things will get better."

"I promise, I'll do everything I can to get us into a better situation," Emmett said forcefully, his voice tight with emotion.

"I know that, Dear. Now go to sleep so you'll be rested for your job hunt tomorrow."

The next day Esther was helping Ma with the housework when Mabel, one of Emmett's sisters, dropped by. She was the assistant postmaster at the Philomath Post Office. Mabel looked at Esther and said, "We need a clerk at the post office. Would you be interested?"

Esther said, "Yes, yes!" Then, after thinking about it for a few seconds, she said, "But I'll have see how Emmett feels about it."

"Of course, but I'll need to know in the next couple of days. Our clerk has given us a week's notice and we'll need to get a replacement soon."

Esther said, "Emmett's out looking for work, but he'll be back tonight so I should be able to let you know tomorrow."

"That will be fine."

When Emmett got home that night, he looked like he'd been dragged through a knothole. He was tired and discouraged.

"How did it go today?" Esther cautiously inquired.

"Not good. I applied at eight places for work, and the only job I could find was a temporary one at the Oregon State Agricultural College plowing a few fields for experimental crops. They want me to use a horse-drawn plow so they can compare the crops to those grown in tractor-plowed fields. Something about compaction of the soil. When they learned that I had a lot of experience using horses to plow, they hired me."

"That's good, isn't it?"

"Better than nothing I guess, but the job only lasts a week."

Esther said, "Oh honey, I'm sorry. I can see that you're tired out. Why don't you go rest? Ma and I will have dinner on the table in about an hour. By that time, your dad will be in from the field and we'll all have dinner together." Esther didn't mention the post office job. It was a bad time to bring it up while Emmett was so depressed; she worried that her easy success might make him feel even worse.

During dinner, Emmett explained the temporary plowing job.

His father looked perplexed. "I'm sorry, Son, but I can't spare the plow and horses right now. I have to finish plowing my own fields."

"That's okay, Dad. The college is furnishing the horses and equipment. The plow even has a seat that the operator can ride on."

"My, my, pretty fancy. You've really come up in the world," Emmett's father said with a little chuckle.

Ma was beaming, and Emmett's father asked her, "What are you so happy about?"

Looking at Emmett, she said, "How about that little wife of yours getting a job today!"

Emmett dropped his fork and stormed off to the bedroom.

With a pained expression on her face, Ma said, "Oh Esther, I'm sorry. I thought he knew."

"No, I didn't want to tell him when he was so downhearted. I'd better go after him."

When Esther got to the bedroom, Emmett was sitting on the bed, bent over with his elbows on his knees and his face buried in his hands. "I guess I'm not much of a man when you have to work to help support us," he said plaintively.

Esther sat down beside him. "The job doesn't pay nearly as much as yours. I won't take it if you don't want me to." Then, she told a little white lie saying, "But of course, we'd be letting Mabel down. She's desperate for someone to take the low paying clerk position at the post office, and they need someone willing to start right away."

Emmett sat up straight and put his arm around her. "Oh honey, of course it's alright with me. We don't want to let Mabel down."

Just then, Donnie woke up and stood up in his crib. Seeing Emmett, he started jumping up and down in his crib, saying "da-da-da-da-da," with a big grin on his face. His obvious delight lit up the room, lifting the gloomy atmosphere that had pervaded moments before. Emmett went over and picked him up, and the world seemed right again, at least for now.

CHAPTER 3

COPING WITH NEW JOBS AND HYENAS

The next day, Emmett drove his 10-year old, nearly worn-out Model T Ford to the temporary plowing job at Oregon State Agricultural College in Corvallis, and Esther walked 1-1/2 miles into Philomath, Oregon, to accept the post office job. Ma was pleased to be left in charge of Donnie.

When Esther got to the post office, Mabel handed her lists of customers' names for a number of mail routes. "This morning, familiarize yourself with the names on each of these routes. Then we'll put you to work sorting and organizing the mail."

Esther spent the morning doing her best to memorize the 100 or so names under the listed routes. After lunch, Mabel took her into the back room where several large bags of mail were waiting to be sorted and bundled. A narrow counter ran the full length of the room on one wall, and a grid of pigeonholes was mounted on the wall over the counter. Each pigeonhole was labeled with a route number and a mail carrier's name.

Mabel gave Esther more instructions. "These pigeon holes are for organizing the mail by route number. When all of the mail has been sorted, the mail in each pigeonhole is bundled with a rubber band for the route's carrier to pick up. Each mail carrier delivers mail to several routes. Efficiently pre-sorting and bundling the mail by route saves the carrier a lot of time so he can deliver more mail in a day. You'll find used rubber bands in the jar at the end of the counter where the carriers put them after each day's deliveries." Then, as Mabel moved one of the mail bags to the floor in front of the counter, she said, "Watch me sort mail for a while to see how it's done." She reached into the bag, withdrew a handful of letters, and placed each one into its proper pigeonhole.

After watching for only a few minutes Esther said, "O.K., I get the idea. Now, let me start earning my pay."

Mabel smiled. "It's not as simple as it looks, but alright, go ahead while I watch. Work from the route lists I gave you today. Place the letters, for persons not on your lists, in the bin at the end of the counter. Later, when you remember all the names on this

list, I'll give you more lists to work from. In the meantime I'll
sort mail that is not on your lists."

Esther started sorting at a frantic pace, knowing how important
this job was to her and Emmett's financial future. She had only
placed a half dozen letters into their pigeonholes when Mabel
shouted.

"Stop! The labels apply to the pigeon holes below the labels,
not over them".

Esther looked embarrassed and said, "Oh, OK," as she pulled
the letters out and placed them in their proper pigeon-holes. She
was so anxious to do well that she was nervous and made a
number of foolish mistakes. She was in fear of losing this badly
needed job since, contrary to the "white lie" she had told Emmett,
there were a number of out-of-work people that would have been
glad to have this steady job.

Meanwhile, Emmett was having difficulties with his new job.
The two-wheeled ride-on plow conserved the operator's energy;
however, it was a much larger plow, had tandem blades, and was
unlike any plow that Emmett had ever used. He had hitched two
college-owned horses to the plow, but he wasn't used to working
with these horses and they weren't familiar with him. When he
gave the reins a little flip and said "giddup," as he did to start his
father's horses, nothing happened.

A student stable boy passing by saw Emmett's difficulty and
said, "These horses were trained in the British tradition. They
don't know 'giddup' from 'hail Columbia'. You have to say
'WALK ON!'"

Upon hearing the loud command from the stable hand, the
horses immediately lurched forward, nearly dumping a surprised
Emmett from his seat on the plow. His legs flew up in the air as
he struggled to maintain his balance.

As soon as he recovered, he shouted, "How do you stop them?"

The stable boy had gone into the barn and apparently couldn't
hear Emmett's question. The horses were headed for a row of
plants, and Emmett shouted,

"Whoa!"

The horses kept pulling and were now too close to the plants to avoid them by turning. In desperation, Emmett pulled hard on the left rein and the horses responded by turning just enough to trample a long diagonal path across the row.

Now, desperate to find the proper command, Emmett shouted

"Stop!"

Nothing happened. The horses kept pulling.

"Stop, damn you!"

Nothing happened.

"Halt!"

Finally, the horses stopped.

Behind him, Emmett heard uproarious applause and laughter. A half dozen student stable boys had been tipped off by the one that had gone into the barn and they had lined up outside to see the show. One of them shouted to Emmett in a condescending tone. "Welcome to the world of British trained horses. Congratulations! You found the magic word faster than most of the other ignorant rubes who get temporary work here."

Emmett's mind flashed back to 1918 when kids at school had cruelly teased him about his "shell-shocked" older brother who had returned from World War I. They had taunted Emmett cruelly, shouting over and over, "Emmett's brother's a dummy, and so is Emmett, Emmett's brother's a dummy, and so is Emmett".

Enraged, Emmett tied the reins to the blade control lever of the plow and walked rapidly toward the "laughing hyenas". Seeing him coming toward them, this raging bull, this 6'3" mountain of solid muscle honed by years of heavy labor, the hyena stable boys scattered and disappeared into the safe, dark interior of the barn.

Emmett had visualized wringing all of their scrawny necks, but seeing them scatter, like cockroaches do when they are suddenly uncovered, he decided it wouldn't be worth losing this badly needed job. He was treated with respect in all future encounters at the school; the word had spread among the students that Emmett wasn't a man to "mess with".

As Emmett was finishing work that day, a man walked out of the Forestry Building and approached him. The man walked along beside the plow and said, "My name is Charlie Fisk. I've been attending a class in the Forestry building, and from a nearby window I could see you working out here all day. You didn't even stop for lunch. You must be tired."

"Naw. A little hard work never hurt anyone."

Then, Fisk said something that made Emmett's heart almost jump out of his chest. "I own a sawmill, and you are the kind of man I would like to have working for me. I don't have a position for you right now, but one of my men has given me a week's notice and is quitting at the end of next week. Would you be interested in the job? You would fill in on various jobs around the mill when people are absent, but most of the time you would drive a truck hauling logs from the forest to the mill."

Emmett had to fight his emotions to keep from appearing too eager and blowing his chance to negotiate.

"What does the job pay?" he asked, trying to appear nonchalant.

"For a good man like you, I can offer 30 cents an hour."

"I'd have to get 40 cents an hour," Emmett replied forcefully as he fought against the fear that he might lose the only job opportunity available to him in the foreseeable future.

"I can't pay more than 30 cents."

Emmett, somewhat rattled, said to the horses, "Gidup. Oh hell, I mean walk on."

"Now, hold on. I guess I can go to 35 cents," Fisk said, after walking a few more yards beside the plow which was now moving toward the barn.

Emmett again spoke to the horses. "Whoa. Oh hell, I mean halt." He was deep in the throes of emotion produced by the stress of playing the game of "job and wages poker" for this job he so desperately needed. He thrust his right hand out to Fisk and said, "Okay, it's a deal."

Fisk shook hands with Emmett and said, "Deal."

At that time in Corvallis, a handshake was as good as a written contract, and people even believed the campaign promises of politicians.

When Emmett got home that evening he was obviously elated and "walking on air". Ma immediately knew something had happened.

"What happened, Emmett? Your feet haven't touched the floor since you got home."

"Oh, nothing much — I just got a permanent job that starts right after I finish my temporary plowing job." Emmett watched Ma's face for the surprise he expected to see.

Ma, knowing that he was "playing" her, was careful not to show any strong emotion, and nonchalantly said, "Oh, that's nice".

"Nice! What do you mean nice! Do you know how hard it is to get a job these days? It's a miracle! A full-blown miracle! It's...."

Ma cut him off saying, "I knew you were playing me. You can't fool me Son. Remember, I've known you since before you were born".

Then she grabbed his hands and danced around him hollering "Wahoo! Emmett's got a job. Yippi! Hurray! Whoopi! — Is that what you were expecting to hear? Well, that's really how I feel Son. I'm very pleased that you found a job, and I'm proud of you."

A short time later, Esther trudged in from her post office job. She was obviously tired and downhearted. Believing that his success might make her feel worse, Emmett decided to wait for a better time to tell her about it.

"What's the matter, dear?" Emmett inquired.

"Oh, it was a rough day. I made a lot of mistakes at the post office, and the job only pays 20 cents an hour if I can even manage to hang on to it." Emmett put his arms around her, kissed her on the cheek, then gave her big reassuring hug.

At dinner that evening Ma remarked, "I'll bet you're really proud of Emmett".

Emmett shot a frowning glance at Ma, but too late as Ma continued. "A permanent job at 35 cents an hour!"

Suddenly, Esther's face brightened and she happily said, "35 cents an hour. That's wonderful!"

Ma looked embarrassed. "Oh, Esther, I thought you already knew. Sorry Emmett, I guess I let the cat out of the bag again. Don't you two ever talk to each other?"

Emmett explained. "I guess I misjudged the effect it would have on Esther. She was so downhearted, I was afraid my good news would make her feel inferior."

"Inferior! Emmett Green, everyone knows women are superior to men," Esther joked.

Everyone at the table laughed, and a mood of joy, confidence, and well being filled the room for the remainder of the meal.

A week later, Emmett started his new job driving one of Fisk's two log trucks, and the family settled into a routine with Ma caring for Donnie, Esther working at the Post office and Emmett leaving for work at 5 AM.

Three months went by quickly, then one evening Emmett came home excited and asked, "Esther, how would you like to have a home of our own?"

"What do you mean? How could we possibly afford one? You know we don't have much money."

"Fisk is having trouble meeting his payroll and... ."

"So how is that going to allow us to afford our own home?"

"As I was about to say before you cut me off, Fisk has offered to pay me partially in lumber at a big discount, and Dad has agreed to subdivide a small plot of land off one corner of his farm for us near the highway. He's going to let us have it cheap, and he won't require any payment until we can afford it."

"Fine. But how could we afford to pay someone to build the house?"

"I'll build it myself."

"What! How?"

"After work, on weekends and holidays. And my uncle George -- you remember, he's a master carpenter -- has agreed to oversee my work on the house, and he'll show me how to do anything that I don't already know."

"Oh, Emmett, you'll kill yourself working so many hours. When will you ever rest?" Esther said, with trepidation in her voice.

"Aw, a little hard work never hurt anyone. If it did, I'd have been dead a long time ago. Besides, I promised to take care of you when we were married, and if a man doesn't keep his promises to the woman he married, he isn't much of a man."

Then, with tears in her eyes, Esther said, "Oh Emmett, I love you so much. How did I get so lucky as to marry you?"

She might not have felt so lucky if she'd known what risks he would have to take now and later to fulfill his promise.

CHAPTER 4

THE LITTLE HOUSE BEFORE HARD TIMES

The next six months were brutal for Emmett. He left for work each weekday morning at 5 AM, and on his way home after work at 2:30 PM he stopped and worked on the house for 6 to 8 hours, only taking an hour off to eat dinner. On weekends, and rainy days when the logging roads were too muddy for trucks, he worked on the house from 6 AM to 10 PM with two hours off for meals and breaks. After dark, he worked by the light of a kerosene lantern to postpone the expense of an electrical hookup fee and monthly bill.

One night, when the house was about two-thirds complete, Emmett knocked over the lantern and started a small fire, which he frantically stomped on and finally ripped all the buttons off his shirt getting it off to smother the fire. His shirt was ruined, but he saved the house.

"What happened to your shirt?" Esther asked when he got home that night.

Emmett, didn't want to admit that he'd made a careless mistake. He said, "Oh, I was attacked by giant moths."

Esther knew him well enough to know that he'd made what he considered a dumb mistake, and that he didn't want to admit it. She got a mischievous look in her eyes and decided to have a little fun with him. She said, "You did something really stupid, huh?" She didn't realize that Emmett was so exhausted that he was near his breaking point. Until now he'd managed to fool everyone into believing that he was invincible.

Suddenly, Emmett got a deeply sad expression on his face. He started gasping and snuffling, and said "I al-lm-ost bur-ned th-the h-house down t-t-tonight," as his chest convulsed with great sobs. Emmett reeked of sweat from emotional stress and working beyond exhaustion. Esther looked more closely at his face. Even in the dim yellow light of the bedroom lamp, she could see that he had deep, dark hollows under his eyes, and he looked gaunt and thin. Esther's eyes immediately filled with tears as she realized that this strong man she loved was at his breaking point. Then, with her greatest tact and charm, she said, "Well, of course you did. You've nearly killed yourself with work far beyond what ordinary human beings could endure. I want you to take the next few evenings and the weekend off. I've been wanting us to take a picnic lunch to the beach and have some fun. Please tell me we can go."

By now, Emmett had recovered his composure and replied, "Okay, if you really want to go I'll take you. It's only 40 miles and the Model T should make it over there and back." Emmett looked relieved as he anticipated having some badly needed time to rest "just to please his wife".

It was unusually warm and pleasant for May on the coast, and a light breeze was blowing. Donnie was now 2-1/2 years old and was seeing the ocean for the first time. He was afraid of the water that kept lapping up on the smooth, wet beach toward him. At first, he toddled away as fast as he could to escape each wave. But his Mom and Dad seemed to be enjoying the waves rushing over their feet and ankles. They were laughing and splashing each other like a couple of children. Finally, Donnie tentatively ventured into the water up to his ankles. The water was cold, and made his ankles ache. As it advanced and receded it made him feel dizzy when he looked down at it. He fell down, soaking all of his clothes and giving him a bad scare. He was screaming when Esther rushed over to pick him up. As she spoke comfortingly to him, she wrapped her warm hands around his cold feet. This made him feel better and he stopped crying.

Esther said, "Gosh, I hope this hasn't made him afraid of water for the rest of his life."

"Naw, he's a Green. A little scare like that won't hurt him. Let's go eat. I'm starved."

They spread a blanket down in the midst of some sparse light-green beach grass in the warm, golden sand on the gentle slope of a small sand dune far back from the water. It was sunny, and there were only a few puffy white clouds against the backdrop of a deep blue sky. The spot they had picked for their picnic was somewhat sheltered by higher neighboring dunes. It was a perfect day, and the soft breeze whispered gently through the beach grass as the little family ate and laughed, and Emmett enjoyed a desperately needed, much deserved rest. After lunch, they all lay down on the blanket and went to sleep in the warm sun. About an hour later, Esther woke up and realized that fair-skinned Donnie had probably been out in the sun too long. She looked over at where he had been asleep on the blanket. He wasn't there. Frantically, she shook Emmett.

"Emmett, wake up. Donnie is gone!"

"Hunh, huh, what?"

"Donnie's gone!"

"What do you mean, gone?"

"Wake up! Gone means gone, you idiot. Oh. I'm sorry I called you an idiot, but I'm just so upset."

Emmett jumped to his feet. "Oh my God, weren't you watching him?"

"I fell asleep."

The pair began desperately running from place to place along the beach, each of them going in a different direction, looking behind every log and sand dune. Finally, while backtracking, they met.

"Oh, Emmett, I hope he didn't get to the water and get swept out to sea. There are so many footprints in the sand, I can't tell which way he went."

Emmett looked haggard as he said, "Well, I guess we'd better contact the police and the coast guard."

Esther bowed her head and said, "Oh God, please keep Donnie safe and help us find him. In Jesus name we pray, amen."

Emmett had also bowed his head, and said, "Amen."

The pair slowly walked back to where they had left their belongings. Esther began sobbing, tears streaming down her face, as she and Emmett reluctantly picked up the picnic basket, blanket and Donnie's little shoes. The full realization of this staggering event had been slowly building in their minds, and they each felt a tight, dull ache in their throat and stomach as they were preparing to leave without Donnie.

Esther, carrying the blanket, got to the car first. Suddenly, she screamed. The back door of the car was ajar, and through the open window she could see Donnie asleep on the seat.

Esther shouted, "Thank God! He's here in the car."

Emmett's voice broke with emotion as he said, "Yes, thank God."

They let Donnie remain asleep on the back seat, and started the drive home. Neither of them said anything for many miles. They were enjoying the happiness and relief they were feeling, and the memories of this fine day.

Finally, Emmett spoke. "Boy, I sure feel rested. I guess I needed this time off almost as badly as you did".

Esther smiled at how well her small deception had worked in convincing Emmett to rest. She thought to herself, As bad as I did? Indeed! Then she said out loud, "Yes, me too."

With the events of the previous day still fresh in his mind, Emmett took Esther, Donnie, Ma and Dad to church on Sunday. The Pastor was standing at the front door greeting people as they arrived.

"Well, Emmett and Esther, I haven't seen you for so long that I thought you had died. Welcome!"

Esther said, "In a sense, we had indeed died. We've been buried in work just to survive, but we're back among the living, at least for now." Then she added, "We plan to be here as often as we can from now on."

The pastor smiled. "I'm glad you've made that decision. Did something happen in your lives that brought you back to church?"

"Yes, but it's a long story. Remind me sometime and I'll tell you about it."

Emmett, who had been silent until now, shook the pastor's hand and said, "Pastor."

"Emmett. My, what calluses you have. You must be working hard."

"You don't know the half of it," Esther remarked.

Emmett looked embarrassed. "Oh, now Esther, it hasn't been that bad."

"No, I guess not, if you call 16 and 17 hour days, seven days a week 'not bad'," Esther retorted.

As the Pastor turned to go into the church he remarked, "Remember, even the Lord rested on the seventh day".

When the Pastor had walked out of earshot, Emmett whispered to Esther, "Yeah, but I'm not God. I can't produce food and housing by just waving my hands. I take seriously my responsibility to provide for my family."

"I know, but even you need to rest once in a while," Esther whispered.

At home after church, Emmett came out to lunch in his work clothes. Before anyone could ask, he said, "I feel well rested. My muscles are crying out for work 'as a voice in the wilderness'," referring to a passage that the Pastor had quoted in his sermon about John the Baptist. "Besides, I can finish putting on the roofing if I get to it right after lunch. Then I'll have a dry place to work when it rains."

This was a wise decision; the next day a torrential downpour hit the area. Logging was completely shut down because the logging roads in the woods turned into deep mud and were impassable. The rain continued for a week; it was still the rainy season in Western Oregon . Logging was sporadic for the next month. Most of the work at the logging company during this time was maintenance and repairs of its equipment. Emmett was occasionally asked to help, but since he wasn't a millwright he couldn't do much of the work. He was able to work on the house all day almost every day during this time.

In late-June, Emmett returned much earlier than usual one evening from working on the house. With a big grin on his face he said, "I've got a surprise for you". He took the entire family to the new house in the Model T.

Emmett said, "Let's go inside."

When they had all entered the front door, Emmett proudly said, "It's finished," as he flipped a switch in the living room, immediately bathing it in bright, yellow-white light from a ceiling light fixture.

Esther, Ma and Dad all exclaimed in unison, "oh-ooh-ahh!" The dim, yellow light from Kerosene lamps in the old farmhouse was nothing like this. The kitchen sink, bathroom sink and bathtub all had hot and cold water faucets with electrically pumped water.

Tears came into Esther's eyes as she thought about the superhuman effort that Emmett had put into providing this home, and she said, "Oh honey, you did it!"

Ma said jokingly, "This is so nice that we may have to move in with you."

Dad said, "Yeah."

Emmett looked a little flustered as he contemplated the four of them and Donnie living in this small two-bedroom house.

Ma noticed his anxiety and said, "Don't worry, Son, we're only kidding," and they all laughed as they enjoyed this special moment together.

The next two years, living in the new house was comfortably routine. When the winter rain subsided, Emmett had nearly steady employment until the following December. Esther worked year-around at the Post office. During the winters, Emmett worked part-time as a carpenter with his uncle George to repay him for the assistance he had given Emmett in building the house.

This was a peaceful, unhurried time with no indication of the serious difficulties that would soon befall the family.

CHAPTER 5

HARD TIMES

After the second year in the new house, when the winter rains had once again given way to infrequent spring showers, the logging roads were again passable most of the time, and Emmett again had steady work driving a log truck for Fisk as usual. However, this fateful day was not going to be entirely usual for Emmett.

The previous day had been warm, and cold air descending from the mountains into the Willamette Valley during the night had formed a light misty fog. A warm, early morning sun had lifted the fog from the mountaintops and valley, but fluffy white shrouds of it still nestled between the heavily forested ridges that extended like arms onto the flat valley floor.

Emmett was rumbling down a dirt road in a heavily loaded log truck. As he was driving across a rickety, high wooden trestle over a deep ravine and glancing out over the splendid mountain scenery, a sudden cracking sound startled him. A piece of the trestle had pulled lose under the heavy load and plummeted 100 feet to the bottom of the ravine. He felt a lump in his stomach and a cold chill down his spine as he was reminded how dangerous this job was. Bill Morse was killed last month when his log truck lost its brakes and crashed after racing unchecked down this same road. Last year, Fred Platt was badly injured when his truck crashed after it slid in some mud.

"I've got to find a less dangerous job that pays regularly," Emmett said to himself as he continued along the dirt road toward Charlie Fisk's sawmill.

At the mill, a saw was ripping through a log, and the noise was deafening. You had to shout to be heard. Emmett closed the open truck window to muffle the noise and drove into the unloading area. An unloader winch lifted the logs off the truck and placed then on a ramp. There the logs were released to roll down the ramp into the millpond with a huge splash that sent a wave rippling across the entire width of the pond. A man in a small boat used a long pike to maneuver the logs stored in the pond to a pickup point as they were needed. There a conveyor lifted them up onto a carriage that fed them into the saw. Each board sawed off a log fell onto a conveyor called the "Green Chain". One man operated the log carriage control, and another man pulled the newly sawn boards off the Green Chain and stacked them onto a cart.

Emmett had done most of the jobs in the mill operation at one time or another, filling in when needed. He felt a chill as he thought about the risks he and the other men were taking.

The truck was unloaded and it was nearly the end of the day. Charlie Fisk, came over and shouted to be heard over the din. "Hey, Emmett, would you help Bob load those empty 50-gallon drums onto the back of the flatbed truck over there?"

"Okay, Charlie, and by the way, would you pay me the two weeks back pay you owe me?"

"I would if I could, but most of the lumber yards have been slow to pay me and I don't have it yet. There's a depression on, you know."

"Well, I've got a family to feed and I'll have to get paid soon," Emmett shouted back in disgust as he started toward the 50-gallon drums.

Bob had begun loading the drums onto the truck. He was starting to lift one when he winced in pain and exclaimed, "Oh, my back!"

"Go rest your back, I'll load the rest of these", Emmett said as he picked up a drum and started toward the truck.

The bottom of the drum was covered with slippery clay mud from the ground where it had been sitting. Emmett's hand slipped off the muddy bottom, and the rim of the falling drum slammed down on top of his left boot. He grimaced from the pain, but picked up the drum again and carried it to the truck. When he'd loaded all of the drums on the flatbed, he limped back to the log truck and drove it home.

As he limped into the house, Esther greeted him with questions. "What happened?"

"Aw, I hurt my foot. Dropped a barrel on it today".

"Did you get paid?"

"Naw."

Esther looked thoughtful as she said, "Thank God for our cow, chickens and vegetable garden, and for my clerking job at the post office. It doesn't pay much after we've paid the babysitter, but we'd be worse off without it."

"Oh, I suppose", Emmett said grudgingly. "I've got to get into a line of work where I can make more money so you don't have to work outside of home."

"I don't mind working, Emmett, but I sure hate to leave Donnie with a babysitter all the time," she said, remembering how Donnie often stood at the front window crying as he watched her leave for work.

The next morning when Emmett got out of bed, his foot was swollen, black, and blue. He could barely tolerate putting any weight on it. Esther took one look at it, and exclaimed, "Emmett Green, you're going to the doctor!"

"Naw, it's just bruised a little," he said, putting on his best "brave face".

After breakfast, Emmett got up and hobbled out to the truck.

Esther followed him, saying, "At least let a doctor take a look at it."

"Naw, we can't afford a doctor for just a little nick like this," Emmett said out of the window as he put the truck into gear.

That evening, when Esther arrived home from work, she saw the log truck parked in the driveway. She felt her heart skip a beat. Oh Lord, I wonder what happened, she thought as she quickly walked to the house. Emmett almost never got home from work before she did. Going inside, she saw Emmett sitting in a chair with his injured foot encased in a white Plaster of Paris cast, and propped up on a box.

"What happened?" She asked.

"The damned thing swelled up so bad I had to take my boot off, so I went to the doctor."

"I'm glad you finally came to your senses. You seem to think the only reason to see a doctor is to pronounce you dead!"

"The doctor told me that I've broken one of the top bones in my foot, and I'll have to stay off it for a while," Emmett said, ignoring her sarcasm.

"Oh, honey, I'm so sorry!"

"What are we going to do?" Emmett asked. "I'll probably lose my job with Fisk, and I don't know where I can get another. There are bread lines and soup kitchens, but I'll be dammed if I'll take charity. People right here in this area have starved to death in spite of charities because there are just too many mouths to feed."

Esther bent down and hugged him. "I love you so much," she said, tears welling up in her eyes as she felt the depth of his pain and anxiety. "We sure won't starve with the large garden you planted and our cow giving two gallons of milk every day. We've scrimped and saved everything we could, so we even have a little money saved. Besides, we both come from pioneer families, and we've gotten through hard times before."

That evening, Emmett hobbled on crutches over to his parents' neighboring farm to milk the cows. He and Esther kept their cow there in exchange for milking his parents' herd of 5 cows each evening. His father had already put the cows into their milking stanchions, and they were contentedly munching hay from a long trough in front of the stanchions.

When his father saw Emmett's condition, he said, "My God, son, I'll do the milking until you recover."

"Naw. I hurt my foot, but my hands are OK. I'll do the milking," Emmett said as he sat down on a stool beside one of the cows and began milking her.

Emmett's father placed a stool near another cow and also started milking. The sweet smell and quiet "swoosh, swoosh" sound of milk squirting into foam floating on the milk in the buckets was almost hypnotically relaxing. It was an ideal background for quiet, serious conversation.

"Dad, I've got to get into a different line of work. My job with Fisk is dangerous, and it doesn't pay regularly. Now that I'm hurt, I may even get fired."

"Well, I don't know what to tell you, Son."

Emmett's dad thought about how Emmett had had to quit school after the eighth grade to work and help support the family. There were ten men waiting in line for every job Emmett could do: logging, truck driving, millwork and farming.

"Maybe you should learn a skilled trade."

The two men continued milking, each lost in his own thoughts listening to the quiet "swoosh, swoosh" of the milk.

As Emmett was arriving home that evening, a car pulled into the driveway, and Mr. Fisk got out.

"Take my car back to the mill and I'll meet you there," Fisk said to the driver.

Emmett hobbled over to Fisk and asked "What brings you out here this late?"

Fisk motioned toward the parked log truck and said, "I'm sorry Emmett, but you can't drive the truck with your foot in a cast, and I can't afford to have it idle. I've hired another driver, and he starts tomorrow morning."

Then he handed Emmett an envelope, saying, "Here's part of what I owe you. I don't know when I'll be able to pay you the rest."

Emmett opened the envelope and dejectedly stared down at the few dollars inside as Fisk quickly got into the truck and drove away. There's that damned knot in my stomach again, Emmett thought as he realized that he was again unemployed and now, at least temporarily, disabled.

Pedal pressure required to operate a passenger car is much lower than that for a logging truck, and a car doesn't require 10 gear changes or double clutching, so the next day Emmett was able to drive his 1924 Model T into town to get chicken feed. "At least I can put meat and eggs on the table by keeping chickens," he said to himself as he arrived at the feed store. When he entered store, he noticed an old man staring out the window at the Model T.

The old man said, "Damn, I sure wish I had kept my Model T sedan instead of getting a Model A coupe. I just can't get used to having to shift gears while using the clutch, and I never can find the damned gear I want. Even with the rumble seat, the coupe isn't big enough."

The Model T was simpler to operate, with just one brake pedal and two other pedals to get two speeds forward as well as reverse, and there wasn't any gearshift to worry about.

Emmett laughed, and jokingly said, "I'll trade you straight across".

The old man replied, "Okay, let's do it!"

Emmett smelled liquor on the man's breath. Not wanting to take unfair advantage of a drunk, Emmett said more seriously, "Oh, you don't mean that. Your Model A is only 4 years old, and my T is 13 years old".

The old man became angry and said, "You agreed to make the trade, so I expect you to honor your word!"

Emmett glanced around the feed store and was embarrassed to see several onlookers witnessing him trying to back out of the deal. Some of the men who knew him muttered "Go ahead and make the deal, Emmett".

Emmett knew that the old man might think better of it when he sobered up the next day, but he said, "OK, I'll do it."

The feed store owner produced a tablet of paper, and one of the onlookers, who had a bit of legal knowledge, wrote out two bills of sale with spaces to be signed by not only the two participants in the deal, but also witnesses. After both participants had signed the papers, several of the onlookers signed as witnesses.

When Emmett returned home in the Model A, Esther saw it though the kitchen window. As soon as he came in the door, Esther said, "Emmett Green, what did you do? You know we can't afford a car that new."

"Aw Esther, I just couldn't resist when the salesman sweet-talked me, and the payments are only $40.00 per month".

Esther reddened as she thought Emmett had lost his mind, and she stammered "B-b-but, we don't have any income except my low paying Post office job right now, and... ."

Emmett knew he'd better quit teasing before Esther popped a blood vessel, so he interrupted her and explained what had happened at the feed store.

"Oh Emmett, you shouldn't have taken advantage of the old drunk that way."

"Well, I wouldn't have, but the old guy got belligerent and insisted, and all the guys in the feed store thought I should honor the verbal agreement I made when I thought he was joking. What a stroke of luck. I guess God has finally decided to smile on us."

"Hmm, well then, you did OK." Esther replied. "But God's going to have to smile on us a lot more than this to get us out of our present difficulties."

"You've made a good point, Esther. God sure helped us out when we thought Donnie was lost." Then Emmett bowed his head and said, "Our Father who art in heaven, please help us get out of this mess."

CHAPTER 6

THE PARTY CONDUIT

The next day, when Emmett arrived home after the evening milking, Esther had dinner ready. After he sat down at the table, she brought some stew from the stove and began dipping it into his bowl.

Esther hesitantly said, "I got an -- invitation -- in the mail today. My grandma and grandpa want us -- to attend their 50th wedding anniversary party in Corvallis."

"Aw, Esther, you know I don't like parties and crowds of people."

"Oh now! I know you're the rugged outdoor type and would become a hermit if I'd let you, but please, I really want us both to go."

Emmett, realizing how important this was to her, gave in. "Oh, Okay, if you insist."

At the party, there was the usual cheerful, light conversation. One of Esther's uncles was cranking an ice cream freezer. There were tables loaded with home made pies and cookies, bowls of different kinds of punch, and an urn of hot coffee. On a central table was a large, home-made cake iced with red roses and green leaves on a white background. Centered on the icing were two arcs of large, pastel-yellow script, "Happy 50th," "George and Rachel."

Suddenly, the ice cream freezer cranking stopped. The uncle, who had been cranking, stood up and announced in a loud voice, "Grab a dish and gather around. The ice cream is ready."

As they filed past the tables, each person was given a napkin, a slice of cake or pie and a choice of cookies on a paper plate, a generous scoop of ice cream in a small bowl, a cup of punch or coffee, a spoon and a fork. This was a lot to handle, so each guest was anxious to find an empty chair as soon as possible. Emmett had large, strong hands, so he normally would have been able to carry the multiple items. However, now he was embarrassed; hobbling around holding onto a crutch with each hand, he couldn't carry anything. He hated being so helpless. To avoid the crowd, he chose a group of chairs near a far corner of the room where no one else was sitting. Esther brought him some cake, ice cream, punch, utensils and a napkin, then got some for herself and sat down on a chair beside him. A tall, dark complexioned man came over and sat down on the other side of Esther. They each placed their cup of punch and paper plate full of goodies between their feet on the floor, and began rapidly eating their bowl of melting ice cream. When they had finished their ice cream, the pace slowed down a bit. They placed their empty ice cream bowls on the floor, retrieved their paper plates and forks, and started eating their cake.

Now that there was no longer any hurry to eat melting ice cream, the dark complexioned man looked at Esther with intelligent, deep-set eyes and said, "Hello, Esther."

Emmett instantly felt a twinge of jealousy because this stranger was paying so much attention to his wife.

Sensing Emmett's feelings, Esther quickly said, with sweeping gestures of introduction, "This is my Uncle Chet. And Chet, this is my dear husband, Emmett."

"Glad to meet you," Chet said in a friendly voice. Then, after he had placed his plate of cake on the floor, he reached across to shake Emmett's hand. Surprised by this sudden change from possible rival to friendly relative who now wanted to shake his hand, Emmett dithered as he decided what to do with his paper plate.

"Likewise," Emmett said, after he finally placed his plate on the floor and reached out to shake Chet's hand. In his confusion, Emmett still had his fork in his right hand and accidentally jabbed Chet's hand with it.

"Sorry," Emmett said, turning red with embarrassment while shifting the fork to his other hand and finally grasping Chet's hand.

Chet had an easy social grace that came from a great deal of experience in managing and dealing with people. Seeing Emmett's social awkwardness, Chet immediately put him at ease by chuckling and saying, "No problem, I often jab my hand harder than that with my fork when I miss my meat at dinner. I've heard that you are interested in finding a good job."

"Yes, I sure am."

"I'm hiring men right now for a crew to demonstrate Hot Sticks that I've invented."

Emmett looked puzzled, and somewhat doubtful.

Seeing Emmett's expression Chet said, "Hot Sticks are special tools on the end of long, insulated handles for working on high voltage power lines without interrupting power to the customers. This is a new technology and it's really catching on. I have patents on these tools, and you would be getting in on the ground floor. Power companies are starting to use my Hot Sticks because they are much safer than the rubber gloves, and they can be used on much higher voltages. Rubber gloves can only be used up to 6000-volts. Even a small pinhole in a rubber glove can mean instant death."

Emmett said, "Only six thousand volts! My God, how high are the voltages you work on?"

"Up to 220,000-volts, but most often only up to 60,000-volts."

"ONLY 60,000-volts! Sorry, not interested," Emmett said in a voice tightened by horror.

"You could be a grunt and work on the ground. Then you'd just pass materials and equipment up the pole to a lineman using a hand line rope. You wouldn't have to work with high voltage. Starting pay for a grunt is 56 cents an hour, and it's steady work."

Emmett looked thoughtful. "Hmm, 56 cents an hour. Steady work? On the ground?"

"Yes, 40 hours a week, and overtime."

"What's overtime?" Emmett asked, never having been paid for the many hours of extra time he'd put in on other jobs to meet schedule requirements.

"When you work more than 40 hours in a week, you are paid 1-1/2 times the normal rate. You'd be given special training, and you'd be paid for it."

"Wow, 1-1/2 time pay would be more than 80 cents an hour! I could never make that kind of money in the kinds of jobs I've been doing. Also, special training with pay! Where do I sign up?"

Chet chuckled and said, "Just be ready to leave for Spokane, Washington, on the 28th of the month after next. Your injured foot should be healed by then. I will pick you up at 8:00 AM sharp."

Later that evening on the drive home, Emmett turned to Esther and asked "Are you sure this move is OK with you? I might be gone several months before I can send for you and Donnie. If we move to Spokane, we'll have to sell or rent our little house."

Esther said, "Of course. It sounds like a good opportunity to get out of the dangerous work you've been doing, and get ahead financially."

"Okay, Esther, and I hope it'll work out well enough that we can send Donnie to college someday. I want him to have an easier life than I've had."

CHAPTER 7

THE ROAD TO FORTUNE AND DANGER

Esther had just placed the last of Emmett's underwear into a large suitcase filled with all the necessities of travel when the horn of Chet's 1930 Chevrolet honked. "Good grief, he's here already," Esther said.

"Actually, he's late. It's nearly 8:30", Emmett said as he grabbed the large suitcase Esther had been packing, and another suitcase filled with work clothes. As Emmett approached the car, he was surprised to see several large suitcases tied onto the car top luggage rack, and four men in the car.

Chet said apologetically, "Sorry we're late. Harry and Bob weren't ready; Vern and I had to wait for them. Just throw your stuff up on top and I'll help you tie it on." Emmett added his suitcases to the pile on the luggage rack and said, "Wow, this car is sure overloaded. I hope it doesn't break down."

"Yeah. We'll have to drive hard to get into Spokane by dinner time after getting off to such a late start," Chet said, casting an accusing glance at Harry and Bob.

Emmett kissed Esther good-by and got into the car. The men quickly learned each other's names; they would become well acquainted before the trip was over. A sense of adventure filled the air as they talked excitedly about the new work, their hopes and their dreams. The conversation dropped off after a couple of hours as the car headed up the scenic Columbia River Highway beyond Portland, past beautiful Bridal Veil Falls and Multnomah Falls. Just beyond Bonneville Dam, they crossed "The Bridge of The Gods" into Washington State. The highway was smooth and paved, but had many curves as it wound its way along the side of the gorge carved out by the great Missoula Floods and the Columbia River in past eons. After traveling a few more miles east, the scenery along the highway changed from green trees and bushes to sagebrush and brown, dried up cheat grass typical of arid land at that time of the year.

Bob said, "My God, what happened to this place." He had never been east of the Cascade Mountains so he didn't realize how dry the land was there.

Chet said, "Clouds lose most of their moisture as rain when they are forced up and over the Cascade Mountains. There's not much moisture left in them by the time they get to this side of the mountains. That's why it's so green on the west side, and so dry here."

The car roared on mile after mile over reasonably good paved roads until they reached Eastern Washington. There, they took some shortcuts on gravel roads. They were on one of the roads near Lind, Washington, when a loud knocking sound suddenly came from the car's engine. Then the knocking stopped and engine began losing power. It made a "flub, flub" sound as a cylinder misfired on each revolution. The car slowed down and finally stopped altogether.

"Oh shit! It's quitting on us," Chet said as he steered the car off to the side of the road. "Do any of you know how to fix the damn thing?"

Vern, who was in the front seat, and had been quiet up until now, said "Yeah, I was working as a mechanic until the garage owner couldn't pay me. It sounded like you threw a connecting rod. But I'll need tools and parts to fix it, and a container to save the crankcase oil."

Chet said, "I've got a wooden toolbox full of tools in the trunk, and there's a car parts dealer only a few miles from here in Lind. There's also a waterproof oilcloth in the trunk. We can line the toolbox with a piece of oilcloth to drain the oil into."

An uncharacteristic grin erupted on Vern's face as he said, "Then we're in business. It'll take more than the few remaining hours of daylight to put in a new rod, and anyway, the parts dealer would be closed before any of us could walk to Lind, so we'll have to spend the night here. I'll take the crankcase pan off the engine so I can determine what parts we'll need, then one of us will have to go into town early tomorrow morning".

Vern jacked the car up, rolled a large rock under the front of the chassis for safety in case the jack slipped, crawled under the car, drained the oil and started removing the pan. As Vern worked on the car, Chet pulled the toolbox containing the oil from under the car, then supervised with suggestions that proved beyond a doubt that he didn't know anything about working on a car. This disgusted Vern, who was working hard in a cramped, uncomfortable space, but he managed to refrain from making any sarcastic remarks about the amateurish, distracting suggestions with which he was being bombarded. Emmett, Bob and Harry frolicked around and wrestled as young men often do when there is nothing else to do.

Harry said, "Let's wrestle to see which of us has to hike into town to get the parts!"

"Okay", the others echoed enthusiastically. A short melee followed, ending with Emmett standing over the two other men who he had thrown to the ground.

Emmett chuckled. "I guess you two will have to wrestle each other to see which one of you will go."

"Aw, I'll go", Harry generously offered, knowing full well that he couldn't beat Bob. "Besides, I'm too tired to wrestle anymore."

Under the car Vern shouted, "Son of a bitch," as his wrench slipped with a clank and he skinned his knuckles. A little while later, he excitedly said, "Good news. Someone forgot to install the safety tie wires through the bearing cap screw heads. The screws worked loose, so the bearing cap was damaged and came off."

"How is that good news?" Chet asked.

"Because all we have to do is get new bearing inserts and bearing cap, and install them. I should be able to finish the job by tomorrow evening. If the connecting rod had broken, I would've had to remove the cylinder head so that I could pull the piston and broken rod out of the top of the engine. That would have taken an extra day." Vern crawled out and immediately began penciling a list of the needed parts and materials to be carried by the "runner" who would be going into town for the parts.

The night was miserable for the men as they sat cramped together in the car trying to sleep. Harry kept falling over against Emmett. Vern, who was considerably older, was snoring loudly in the front seat, and kept farting in his sleep. No one dared wake him up since he'd need all his strength the next day to repair the car.

Finally, Emmett said, "That's it, I'm sleeping outside on the ground." He opened the car door and put one foot on the ground. Suddenly, there was a rattling noise that sounded like a pair of maracas. Emmett yanked his foot back into the car and slammed the door.

"Rattlesnake," Chet said nonchalantly. "A big one, from the sound of his rattles. They're common here. You'll want to buy a good pair of leather knee high lineman's boots to protect against snake bite."

Early the next morning, the men cautiously got out of the car. The rattlesnake had slithered away during the night, and Harry had begun his hike to Lind a little after daybreak. The men were hungry since they hadn't eaten since breakfast the previous day. The morning wore on, and about noon Harry came back up the road carrying a large bag.

"Where the hell have you been? It's only about five miles to Lind from here," Chet asked.

"I stopped to do a little shopping," Harry said. Then, seeing the redness of Chet's face and the veins standing out in his forehead, Harry said, "to get some food," as he pulled a couple of hamburgers out of the bag and held them up for Chet to see. He had brought burgers for all of the men, and Chet's anger immediately subsided as he and the others each devoured a burger.

After he'd finished his burger, Vern crawled back under the car dragging the tools and new parts with him. Hours passed and, except for various clinking and clanking sounds coming from under the car, all was quiet. The other men, who hadn't slept well during the night, sat slumped over in the car seats, or on the ground in the shade of the car.

It was nearly dark when Vern finally emerged from under the car and said, "I'm finished. Pour in the oil, and try stating the engine."

Chet turned the key, and pressed the starter, but nothing happened. "What kind of a mechanic are you?" Chet angrily asked Vern.

Vern angrily retorted, "A tired one. It's your damned battery. Don't you ever do any preventive maintenance on this wreck?"

"Oh", Chet said more calmly, realizing that much of this trouble was his own fault. "What are we going to do?" he said, with a little desperation showing in his voice. "I've got a lot that depends on us getting to Spokane in time to train a crew to demonstrate my new hot sticks."

The anger and tension that had built up in Vern from all the suggestions, that he'd endured earlier, erupted. "Aw crap, for an inventor you sure don't know much about cars," Vern said, as he jacked the car up and removed the big rock that had been placed under the front end. After lowering the car and removing the Jack, he carefully placed the jack and tools in the trunk of the car and closed it.

"What are you going to do?" Chet asked.

Without answering the question, Vern instructed Chet to get into the car, turn on the key, and put it into high gear. Then, continuing as one who has the authority of knowledge, Vern instructed Chet to the press the clutch pedal down, and told the other men to push the car as fast as they could. Vern ran alongside and, when the car was going fast enough, he told Chet to let the clutch out. The car sputtered to life, but jumped and jerked because it was in the wrong gear for the low speed it was traveling. All the men cheered loudly since they believed the end of their ordeal was near.

"Push in the clutch, you damned fool. Can't you hear the engine struggling?" Vern shouted. Chet, angered by Vern's chiding, depressed the clutch, shifted into a lower gear, and accelerated leaving Vern and the other men behind in the dust. The cheering gave way to looks of bewilderment as Chet sped away.

Harry said, "Hell, Vern, you went too far in criticizing the boss."

"Well, he's an arrogant son of a bitch, and I lost my temper. I wish I hadn't. It's getting cooler and darker, and the rattlesnakes will soon be coming out to hunt for food."

A moment later, a pair of headlights appeared over a little rise in the road ahead. It was Chet returning to pick them up.

"Just taking a little test drive," Chet said, grinning out the open window. "And reminding you who's boss. By the way, Vern, good work." Chet turned the car around, the men piled in, and they sped off into the night toward Lind.

By now, all of the men were hungry again, but when they got to Lind the restaurants were closed. A couple of the men's stomachs rumbled with hunger, and they all groaned as they passed the last darkened restaurant.

Chet said, "Spokane's not far. We should be there in less than two hours. I know a hotel there that has a coffee shop that's open all night."

When they rolled into Spokane, everyone but Chet and Emmett were asleep, and Vern was snoring loudly. Chet, who was driving, said the restaurant was just a few blocks away and asked Emmett to wake everyone up.

"Wake up, we're here!" Emmett yelled. The sleeping men were startled awake, except for Vern who had to be shaken awake. Seeing the hotel ahead the men cheered wildly. When the cheering subsided Chet announced, "We'll eat here and stay at the hotel tonight, provided you don't holler anymore." The men gave one more enthusiastic, but muffled, cheer.

After they had sandwiches at the coffee shop, Chet handed room keys to the men. There were only two rooms available, so several men had to stay in each room. At least there were two beds and a folding cot available for each room. The men drew straws to see who had to stay in the room with Vern and his snoring.

CHAPTER 8

LEARNING HOW TO LIVE ON LIGHTNING

At 7 AM, Chet woke the men in his room, then pounded on the door of the other room until someone responded. After getting dressed, the men sleepily filed down to the hotel restaurant, still tired from the ordeal of the past two days of travel. They all dove into coffee, juice, large plates of scrambled eggs, bacon, ham, sausage, fruit, toast, honey and jam that were set on the table, and ate like starving dogs. The waitress was a heavy set, rough looking woman.

"My God, Chet, don't you ever feed your men?" She asked.

"Yeah, Rosie, but they're trying to put on weight so they'll be as hefty as you," Chet said jokingly, swatting her gently on the butt. She made a motion like she was going to hit Chet with the back of her hand, but she broke into a lilting laugh. Her laugh was contagious, and all the men laughed too, setting a good tone for the day.

A short time later, Chet drove the men to a building near the hotel. They piled out of the car under a sign in front that said, "Washington Water Power". In one corner of the sign was a small logo with a little red stick-figure man made of lightning bolts, and the words "Ready Kilowatt at your service". Inside the building Chet directed the men to a meeting room where they joined eight others, Spokane men, that he had hired. Chet stood in the front of the room and said, "Men, you are the crews I have hired to open a new frontier in maintaining high voltage power lines. This will require a lot of training, and we will start today with movies that will acquaint you with the procedures, dangers and safety considerations in this work."

Several of the men appeared to be going to sleep as Chet pulled the screen into position and started the projector. The movie started with the usual kind of title frame and symphonic background music typical of 16mm educational films in the mid 1930's. In the stuffy, warm darkness of the room, several more men appeared to be dropping off to sleep. Suddenly, a loud scream came from the speakers in the front of the room. On the screen was the image of a man near the top of a pole. There was a large flash and he keeled over backwards, unconscious and hanging limply in his safety belt. His hands and arms were smoking. All of the men in the room were now wide-awake.

The narrator in the movie said, "This is an example of what can happen if you let your guard down, even for a moment, when you are working with high-voltage power lines. Remember, men, electricity is lightning in a wire, and it can be just as deadly as being struck by lightning."

Harry leaned over and whispered to Emmett, "Good God, do we really want to work with this stuff?"

"Remember the high pay," Emmett whispered, "They don't give 80 cents an hour to linemen and 56 cents an hour to grunts for nothing. It's the only chance a guy like me has to get ahead in these hard times."

The movie continued with a description of climbing hooks. "These are metal braces that have a stirrup-like metal support under the boot with a flat metal upright bar that is strapped onto the inside of the lower leg. A sharp spur, sometimes called a 'gaff,' projects downward and outward near the bottom of the upright." A lineman was shown stabbing one metal spur into the pole, taking a step upward, then stabbing the other spur into the other side of the pole and taking another step upward, and so on like climbing a ladder.

Emmett said, "Wow, that looks easy."

Chet overheard his comment and, with a knowing smile, said, "We'll see."

After the movie, Chet opened the blinds and again stood facing the men. "As you can see, working with wired lightning is dangerous, and that's why it pays so well. The average life of a lineman after he enters this kind of work is about 13 years. Of course, if you're careful, you can live a long and productive life even though you're making your living on lightning. If you want to stay alive, you'll have to pay close attention to the training you get here, and always be alert when you are working on hot wires. If any of you don't have the stomach for this, please leave now so I can get replacements."

Several of the local men got up and left the room.

"Anyone else?" Chet asked. "Okay, then, we'll watch more training movies and discuss them. Tonight, you out-of-town men can return to the hotel. I've booked rooms for you to use during the training course. All of you, meet me here tomorrow at 8 AM to start your field training."

The next morning, the men gathered under the "Ready Kilowatt" sign. Chet came out of the building, followed by several Spokane replacement men that had survived the training movies shown to them earlier that morning. All of the men followed Chet to the rear of the building. As they came around the building, they saw a large vacant lot with a dozen or so 75-foot vertical poles sticking up out of the ground. The tops of two of the poles had cross arms that had been fitted with insulators. Wires had been strung between them.

Chet said, "This is the pole yard. Here you will learn and practice the skills you will need to work for me. He gave each man a safety belt and a pair of climbing hooks, saying, "Although some of you will be grunts, and will normally work on the ground, you are required to know how to climb so you can rescue a lineman if he suffers an electrical shock and is unconscious on the pole. Quickly rescuing him and giving him artificial respiration might save his life."

Each man strapped on his hooks, went to the base of a pole, lifted one foot and stabbed the spur downward into one side of the pole as had been shown in one of the movies. One man missed the pole, stabbed his leg with the spur, and let out a loud yell together with numerous expletives. Most of the other men got a spur into the pole, but when they tried to step up they yelled and swore, and immediately lowered their weight back onto the foot that was on the ground. Chet laughed so hard that tears rolled down his cheeks.

When he regained his composure, he said, "What a bunch of sissies." Then, directing his comment to the man who had injured his leg, Chet said, "Sorry you hurt yourself. Go to the first aid office and get that tended to." He then turned to Emmett and said, referring to the remark that he had made during the movie, "Not so easy, huh?"

Turning back to the group, Chet continued, "Now men, I see that none of you are wearing lineman's boots. This was just a little demonstration to show you that you need them. Without boots, the hooks put concentrated pressure on your legs just below your knees, and as you just found out, that can be painful. Knee-high boots will protect your legs from the concentrated pressure. They will also protect your legs from snakebite, and they have heels that are fastened with wooden pegs rather than metal nails to help insulate you from the ground if you come into contact with a lower voltage line. Of course, coming into contact with a high voltage line will cook you in spite of the boots."

Chet glanced around the group and noted with satisfaction that they were all paying attention. Then he continued, saying, "Now, always, ALWAYS keep this in mind, 120,000 volts will jump out at least five inches, and 240,000-volts will jump out at least 10 inches and grab you with a lightning bolt arc. Under some conditions, it can jump out even farther. Once the electric arc is established, it will stretch out five or 10 feet, so there's no getting away from it. The moral to this story is: get lineman's boots and stay at least 10-feet away from high-voltage lines."

Chet was pleased to see that the men had paid particular attention to the part about the lightning bolt grabbing them. "Another thing I want you to bear in mind is that there is a corona, or field, that surrounds high-voltage lines. This in itself is not dangerous as long as you don't get any closer to the line than 10 feet. However, there is a danger that a new man climbing a high-voltage transmission tower for the first time will be startled by getting bit by harmless static charges that sometimes build up on his body, or parts of the tower. Surprised, he might let go and fall. The fall won't kill you, but the sudden stop at the end of the fall probably will, so no matter what happens don't EVER let go when you are high up on a pole or tower.

Now I want you all to go downtown and purchase your boots. If you don't have enough money, I'll advance you some against your first paycheck. Meet me back here after lunch at 1 PM."

After getting their boots, Emmett, Harry, Vern and Bob went to the hotel restaurant for lunch. Rosie, the hefty waitress, came to their table. Harry, who was in a jovial mood, slapped Rosie on the butt and said, "Hi hefty."

Rosy turned and administered a hard slap to the side of Harry's head, knocking him off of his chair. "Why did you do that?" Harry asked as he picked himself up off the floor. "You didn't do that when Chet slapped your butt."

"Because I've known Chet for 10 years, and he always leaves a big tip. If I let you peons get away with it, everyone will be doing it. Now gimme your orders if you want anything to eat!"

After lunch, all the men gathered back at the pole yard sporting their new boots.

Chet said "Now you're starting to look like linemen. I'm going to give you a little demonstration of how well you can climb with hooks." Then, gesturing toward a man who had just arrived, he said, "This is Ernie. He's an experienced lineman who will be teaching you a lot of what you need to know about line work and climbing poles."

Ernie put on a pair of hooks, went to the nearest pole, leaped onto it and bounded up to the top, digging in one spur, then the other in rapid succession and taking large steps. Then he climbed down even faster.

One of the men said, "Holy crap!"

Several others echoed the sentiment saying, "Yeah."

Ernie faced the men as he nonchalantly said, "With practice, you'll be able to do this in just a couple of weeks."

The men looked at this wiry, older man with new respect and awe.

Ernie said, "There are a lot more things you need to learn: how to serve a rope or cable to make a permanent loop on the end; how to splice a power line and bind it to an insulator; what to do and what not to do in this work to stay alive; and so on."

The days passed quickly. The men learned something new every hour or so, then practiced it until they knew how to do it perfectly. Emmett was eager to learn, and progressed faster than many of the other men.

Harry said, "Boy, Emmett, what a teacher's pet!"

"Well, I've got a family depending on me and I'm pleased as hell to have this job. I don't want to be stuck in some low paying, hard-scrabble job the rest of my life."

Harry looked thoughtful and didn't make any more comments. In fact, after Emmett's remark, Harry seemed to make a little more effort himself.

The last week of class, Chet gathered the men around a truck that had been driven into the pole yard. Inside the truck were a number of 10-foot hot sticks. Six tall stands were set up in the yard. There was an insulator about 14-feet off the ground on top of each stand. A shiny, new copper wire had been strung between all the insulators.

Chet said, "Now you are going to learn how to use Hot Sticks to replace a defective insulator. The insulator stands have been set up on the ground to make it easier while you are first learning to use the hot sticks. At the end of the week you will climb the poles that have cross-arms and practice changing their insulators using the sticks. Throughout the week, the men who had signed up as linemen practiced with the hot sticks. Most of the grunts just watched, since they would only be working on the ground and passing the tools up to the linemen using a hand line. Emmett, on the other hand, practiced along with the linemen trainees in case he ever decided to become a lineman himself.

The final day of class arrived all too soon. In the morning, Chet gathered all the men into a group. Then he said, "Men, today you will all take the final exam to test your proficiency. Some of you will pass and some may not. Those of you who pass, report to me at the end of the day for your work assignment. Any of you who don't pass, go to the cashier's office on Monday and pick up your final paycheck."

Emmett experienced a sick feeling in the pit of his stomach as he visualized what it would be like to fail; he would have to return to Philomath and struggle to make a living in an on-and-off, unreliable, lower-paying job. Many of the other men's faces showed that they were also worried.

The first test was pole climbing, and the men strapped on their hooks and safety belts. Harry was the first man to demonstrate his pole climbing ability. He climbed the pole at a moderate rate, using his hands to slip his safety belt a little way up the pole after each step. He only had a spur kick out a couple of times, forcing him to catch himself by grabbing the pole. His safety belt around the pole would have kept him from completely falling off, but without grabbing the pole he would have slid downward. Sliding down a pole was a thoroughly unpleasant experience since slivers from the pole invariably penetrated clothing and lodged in skin when this happened. When Harry reached the ground, he was breathing hard from the exertion. Ernie wrote Harry's grade in a notebook, and told him to go on to the next test, wire splicing. Harry looked relieved, since this meant he had passed the pole-climbing test.

Vern was next to take the climbing test. Being an older man in less than prime physical condition, Vern had a lot more trouble climbing. He got two-thirds of the way up the pole and stopped. He was breathing hard and wheezing.

"I just couldn't go any farther," he said after slowly climbing down the pole.

Emmett said, "Damn it, I'm sure sorry, Vern."

Then Chet took charge of the pole-climbing exam. He said, "You're next, Emmett."

Emmett was now 27 years old, and 6-foot 3-inches of solid muscle. He had worked at logging and at various other hard physical jobs from his early teens, so he was in excellent physical condition. Excited and happy for the chance to get a steady, high paying job for the first time in his young life, he felt a rush of fear and adrenaline, mixed with joyful gratitude for this opportunity. He walked briskly to the pole, leapt onto it, and literally ran to the top and back down.

Chet said, "My God, Emmett! I knew you would be good at this, but that was a phenomenal performance for a greenhorn. I was going to make you a grunt but, if you're interested and pass the other tests, I'm going to offer you a position as a lineman."

In the excitement of the moment, Emmett said, "Interested! I would almost kill for a chance like that." After that, Emmett took all the other skill tests, including the hot stick proficiency test, and passed with high marks. At the end of the day, Chet took him aside and said, "Emmett, report to line crew foreman, Fred Woodmyer at the dispatch yard on Monday morning at 7 AM. We'll give you further training on the job at full pay as a lineman." Emmett wanted to throw his arms into the air and shout

"Yahoo!" but his stoic personality prevented such an outburst. Instead, he just grinned from ear to ear and said, "Thanks, Chet. What about Vern?"

"I'm going to let him maintain and manage the tools, and he can serve as a grunt in a large crew where he can put his mechanical abilities to work, and where someone else will be there to climb and rescue a lineman in the event of an emergency."

That night, after the excitement had worn off, Emmett remembered how dangerous the job as a full-fledged lineman would be. He lay awake for hours imagining how it might feel to get electrocuted like the "smoking man" in the training movie, and he worried about how Donnie and Esther would get along without him.

CHAPTER 9

THE REAL THING

Monday morning, when Emmett, Bob, Harry, and Vern arrived at the dispatch yard it was bustling with activity. They had ridden on city buses to get there, and they had missed a transfer so they were late. Men were running here and there like ants, grabbing materials and equipment and loading them into trucks. Emmett asked several men where he could find Fred Woodmyer. Their response was always the same, "Dunno." They were evidently too busy to even think about it. Suddenly, all the trucks had been loaded, and they started to pull out. In desperation, Emmett waved his hands over his head, and stepped in front of the first truck.

The driver slammed on the brakes, bringing the truck sliding and screeching to a halt. His face contorted with rage, the driver leaned out of the window and yelled, "You idiot, get the hell out of the way."

"Not until someone tells me where I can find Fred Woodmyer."

The driver said, "He's sitting here beside me."

A slender, ruddy-faced, redheaded 35-year-old man sitting beside the driver chuckled with a funny "hwhoo hwhoo" sound and said, "You must be Emmett Green. Chet said you were enthusiastic, and now I believe it! I assume the three with you are the other new men Chet sent me."

Emmett said, "That's right."

"Okay. We'd almost given up on you. You can explain why you were so late after we get to the job site. All of you climb into the back."

The back of the truck was a cavernous, dark green canvas enclosure supported by a wooden frame. Ernie and two other men were sitting on bench seats along each side of the cavern. There was a large entrance into the cavern at the rear of the truck. A canvas cover was tied up in a tight roll at the top of the entrance.

During cold or rainy weather, the cover could be unrolled and tied in place.

Inside the cavern there was a strong odor characteristic of most line trucks: an intermingling of sweat, dust, hemp rope, electrical insulation, leather and rubber. Padded supports high up in the cavern projected outward from horizontal boards running the full length on each side of the canvas support frame. Three sets of hot-sticks had been carefully tied to the padded supports. Lower down were boards with hooks that supported numerous skeins of rope. Across the front end of the cavern were more horizontal frame members. These had hooks from which were hanging assorted tools, pulleys, block and tackle sets, come-alongs (cable pulling devices) and numerous other items. Below these, on the floor in the front of the cavern, was a box with a hinged cover and the stenciled words, "RUBBER GLOVES AND GUTS". The floor between the benches was littered with tools, ropes, pulleys and some of the men's lunch boxes.

Emmett, and the three other newcomers, climbed into the back of the enclosure and sat down on the benches. Ernie shouted "Hang on," and rapped twice on a frame member signaling the driver that they were ready to go. The truck lurched sharply forward, and they were on their way. The men engaged in small talk as the truck rumbled down the highway.

Suddenly, Harry, stared at the stenciled words on the covered box, and said, "Good God, are they planning to have us do some butchering?"

Ernie asked, "What makes you think that?"

"That box has rubber gloves and a place to put guts."

Ernie laughed, but then he became serious and said, "The rubber gloves are for handling live wires at voltages up to 6000-volts, and guts are rubber coverings that are placed over the wires so you don't accidentally get into contact with them and become the 'smoking man'. These work very well with one exception. If they get even a tiny pinhole in them, the electricity can arc through it and kill you. This is why they are carefully kept in a covered box to protect them from punctures."

Emmett asked, "How do we know they haven't gotten punctured during previous usage?"

"Two ways: First, no one got killed that day. Second, the equipment maintenance grunt is responsible for testing them at the end of each day using a special instrument. I highly recommend that you treat the gloves and guts with respect because your life depends on it."

The new men looked at each other, their faces reflecting the seriousness of what they had just heard. Emmett felt exhilarated, but at the same time, he felt that old familiar knot in the pit of his stomach as he pondered the risks he would be facing. Dead silence fell over the group like a thick, dark blanket as the truck roared onward toward the first assignment in the dangerous work they'd signed up for.

Ten minutes later, the truck slowed and lurched to a stop beside a power pole. A wire was strung between an insulator on its cross arm, and an insulator on the cross arm of a pole further down the road.

Fred got out of the truck's passenger seat and walked around to the back. "Okay, all of you new men, pile out." Emmett, Vern, Harry and Bob jumped out of the back of the truck.

Fred asked, "Vern, did you test the rubber gloves?"

"Yes."

Then Fred said, "Emmett, put on your climbing equipment, and snap a hand line onto your tool belt."

Ernie, the experienced lineman, had also exited the truck and was carrying a pair of climbing hooks, red rubber gloves, a hand line and a safety belt. Without being told, he obviously knew what came next. Emmett put on the gear as instructed and climbed the pole. Looking down he yelled to Fred, "Okay, now what?"

Fred yelled, "The wire attached to the insulator is a hot 6000-volt line. The tie wire that holds the line onto the insulator is loose, and I want you to tighten it."

"OK, Vern, send up some rubber gloves," Emmett yelled down to the grunt.

Vern attached the red rubber gloves to the hand line using a special clip that resembled a giant clothespin. Fred then asked all the men to step back. Emmett pulled the gloves up with the hand line and put them on. Pulling a pair of pliers from his belt, Emmett accidentally dropped them because he was nervous and it was awkward handling the pliers with rubber gloves. The pliers hit the ground with a heavy thud.

Fred said, "Now that's why you never stand too close to the pole. If that had hit one of you on the head, it probably would've killed you."

The new men on the ground moved even farther away from the pole, and Vern sent up another pair of pliers on the hand line. Emmett took them, reached over and gripped the tie wire to tighten it. He suddenly felt a tremendous, jolting electrical shock that caused him to throw the pliers. They landed about 50 feet away from the base of the pole.

Emmett shouted, "Hunnh. What the hell!"

"Come on down, Emmett, you've finished the job I sent you up there to do," Fred yelled.

"But I didn't do anything."

"Come on down, and I'll explain."

When Emmett reached the ground, Fred said, "This was a training exercise. The wire is only attached to the spark plug of a small gasoline engine, located down the road in a box by the next pole. You can barely hear it running if you listen carefully. Then he said, "Vern, how thoroughly did you inspect those gloves?"

"Well, uh, I thought I did it okay."

"One of the gloves has a pinhole purposely placed in it to test how well you inspected them. You should have detected the hole if you were using the test instruments properly. I want you to report to headquarters tomorrow for special training on this procedure." Then, looking at Emmett, Fred said, "Now Emmett, you should have inspected the gloves visually before using them. Look at them now and see if you can find the hole."

Emmett remembered that the shock had come from his right index finger, and looking at the glove he saw a tiny hole. "Damn", he said. Then Fred passed the glove around to all of the other men so they could look at it.

Fred said, "Now all of you, listen carefully. Notice that this pair of gloves is red. All red gloves are training gloves and must never, and I mean NEVER be used on live wires. Training gloves like this must never be put in the box with the good rubber gloves and guts. Ernie has charge of the training gloves for this crew, but you must all be alert to make sure that they don't accidentally get into the glove and gut box. They shouldn't ever be on the truck after a new man's first day. Now get back into the truck and I'm going to take you to a place where you can get acquainted with a 120,000-volt line that we have to work live today using hot-sticks."

When the truck stopped again, it was near a steel tower located a short distance away down a steep incline. Exiting the truck, the men saw the top of the tower at eye level about 300 feet from where they were standing. The high voltage power lines were supported from three insulators, strings of dark brown ceramic dishes, sometimes called "Bells". An insulator was suspended from the center, and one was suspended from each end, of a cross beam at the top of the tower. The lines were making an eerie, sizzling, crackling sound. The men got out of the truck and stared at the source of the sound.

Fred said, "The sound you hear is due to high voltage corona and leakage of electrical current. Leakage current passes through moisture and dirt on the surface of the insulators, or through cracks in one or more of the dishes. It causes power loss, radio static and noise. When a string is cracked we have to replace it. By the way, it's corona that causes an arc to jump out and electrocute you if you get too close to the wire." Then he cheerfully said, "Okay men, it's time for lunch."

When the new men finally managed to pull their attention away from the ominous, noisy wires, they each looked around nervously at the others, then looked for a comfortable place to sit down and eat lunch.

Harry started chuckling and whispered to Emmett. "Vern carries his false teeth in his lunch box".

As Vern installed his teeth in preparation for his lunch, some of the other men chuckled.

"Haven't you fools ever seen false teeth before?" Vern asked angrily.

After lunch, Fred led the men down the incline to the base of the steel tower. Pointing at the top of the tower, he said, "One of the insulator strings up there is leaking current. We're going to replace it today." Then, turning to Emmett, he said, "I want you and Ernie to work together on the tower, and Harry to act as your grunt. The rest of you men come with me. We've got another problem on the next tower."

"When do we start this work?" Emmett asked.

"Right now."

"Don't you want to turn off the power first?"

"No, that's the whole point of the new hot sticks. Turning off the power on this line would deprive 100,000 people of power. Hospital elevators, respirators, traffic lights, burglar alarms and other essential equipment would suddenly stop operating." Fred replied.

Emmett, Ernie and Harry walked over to a pickup truck, which had just arrived. Emmett and Ernie pulled a crated insulator string out of the back. Looking at Harry, Ernie said, "Go get the tools we'll need to uncrate and install this string." Harry went to the line truck to get the tools, while Emmett and Ernie carried the heavy crate to the base of the tower. A short time later, Harry staggered down the slope to the tower weighted down with tools and equipment. He returned to the truck to get Hot Sticks, while Emmett and Ernie attached a hand line and safety lanyard to each of their tool belts and started climbing the tower. They could not clip their safety lanyards to the tower until they reached the top.

Climbing a tower is nothing like climbing a pole. A safety belt can't be used during the climb since the cross braces on the tower frame prevent the belt from being slipped upward as it is when a pole is climbed. It's like climbing a giant set of Monkey Bars. There is no thick pole blocking the climber's view, so there is a spectacular view of the countryside. However, there is also a sense of exposure and vulnerability since the largest parts of a tower are thin angle-iron frame members only three inches wide. In training class, it had been pointed out that a fall of only 10 feet could kill you, so falling from a tower isn't really much worse. It seemed logical in the classroom but now, at this dizzying height, it didn't seem as convincing.

As the men climbed higher on the tower, and got closer to the sizzling and crackling of the high voltage wires, Emmett started feeling nervous and a little shaky. However, the hard work of the climb was more strenuous than climbing ten flights of stairs. Emmett was used to extreme physical activity, and the exercise helped dispel some of his nervous tension.

Ernie said, "Now Emmett, don't forget to stay at least 10-feet away from those wires, or the lightning could jump out and kill you."

"Do you think I'm crazy? Don't worry, I'm not going anywhere near them."

"And one more thing, don't forget what Chet told you about the static charge on the tower biting you a little. Don't be surprised and let go -- the ground looks like it would be pretty hard to land on at the end of a 100-foot fall."

"Thanks for reminding me," Emmett said, his voice tight with tension. His attention was already sharply focused on the dangers that lay ahead.

As they neared the top of the tower, Emmett felt a strange, prickling sensation all over his body. Emmett said, "It feels like something's crawling on me under my clothes."

Ernie chuckled, and said, "Oh yeah, I forgot to mention that corona also sometimes causes that prickling sensation, even when you're not getting bit by the tower."

Emmett took hold of a cross member on the tower and felt a brief shock, about like the ones he had experienced after walking across plush carpets on dry winter days and touching metal.

"Oh, I just got bit! Thanks for reminding me, Ernie, or I might have let go. I have to admit that I'm scared as hell of this stuff, and I'm about to jump out of my skin."

"That's perfectly normal. It's good to respect this stuff; that'll help keep you alive. As long as you stay at least ten feet away from the wires, you'll be safe."

"Ernie, I didn't know this job was going to be so uncomfortable."

"Most of the time it isn't. It's only this extremely high voltage stuff that has so much corona. Much of the time we work on lines that are at 11,000-volts or less, so the lightning can't jump so far, make your skin prickle, or charge up metal parts enough to shock you."

When the two men reached the top of the tower, they attached their safety lanyards. Ernie noted that several dishes in the center insulator string were cracked. The two men attached their hand line pulleys to cross members inside the tower frame on one side. Both ends of each hand line dangled to the ground from its pulley.

Ernie yelled, "Okay, Harry, send up two hot sticks with wire grip attachments, a gin pole setup, a 3/4-inch hot stick socket attachment, a cotter key puller, and five tool clamps." Harry attached the tools to the hand lines and pulled them up.

Ernie carefully installed the gin pole setup. After that he clamped the far end of a hot stick onto the 120,000-volt wire with a twisting motion. Using the stick together with the gin pole setup, he pulled the lower end of the defective insulator string into a position where Emmett could easily work on it, while maintaining a respectful 10 foot distance from the sizzling, crackling wire.

"Okay, Emmett, remove the clamping shoe that holds the wire onto the end of the insulator string."

Emmett took the remaining hot stick from its tool clamp and installed the socket wrench attachment on the far end. His pulse was racing and he was sweating, not so much from physical exertion as from emotional stress in this high-risk situation. However, he was determined to be successful in this work, so he forced himself to do what was necessary. At this moment, Emmett fully appreciated the bravery of men that do this kind of work.

He removed the four bolts holding the wire-clamping shoe. Then, with the block and tackle/gin pole setup, Ernie lowered the wire and tied the block and tackle rope onto the tower. The wire was now far below and held off to one side of the insulator by the hot stick.

Emmett climbed on top of the crossbeam, yelled "Headache!" to warn anyone on the ground that the insulator string was about to drop, and yanked the cotter pin out of the insulator-string support eye. Moments later, the defective insulator string crashed to ground, shattering many of the dishes and producing a beautiful momentary firework-like eruption of glittering glazed ceramic shards as they flew in all directions in the bright sunlight.

Fred shouted, "My God, Emmett, after this, lower defective insulator strings to the ground on the hand line. They can often be repaired by just replacing defective bells."

Emmett reddened as he said, "Sorry, Fred, I didn't know that."

Ernie said, "Emmett, you should have lowered the string on a hand line. Shattering it into flying fragments like that could have injured someone on the ground. Besides, some of the dish units in the string might have been tested and re-used."

"Okay, I'm sorry Ernie. Next time I'll do it that way."

Then Ernie yelled to Harry, "Okay, send up the new string."

Harry donned some leather work-gloves and attached the new insulator string to the hand line. The string was heavy, and it took a lot of effort to pull it up. Beads of sweat appeared on Harry's forehead as the insulator reached the 85-foot level on the tower. Suddenly, the insulator hung up on a tower cross member.

Harry said "I — I don't know if I can hold it much longer — this damn thing is really heavy."

Emmett sprang into action. In the excitement of the moment, he unclipped his safety lanyard and moved over to one side of the tower structure. Then, forgetting how high up he was, he quickly climbed down to the stuck insulator. He reached over with one hand and pulled the hand line sideways to free the insulator. Then, while holding onto the tower with one hand and using all of his considerable strength, he gripped the hand line with the other hand, pulled the string up and rested it on a cross member. In his excitement, he hadn't realized that he was getting closer than 10-feet from the 110,000-volt wire.

Ernie yelled "Careful, greenhorn. You're about to get yourself killed!"

Emmett shuddered and backed a foot farther away from the wire as he realized his mistake.

"Okay, thanks, Ernie, I'll be more careful from now on."

"Never get so excited that you forget where you are even for a second -- that'll get you killed. Slow and steady is best."

Balancing the insulator string on the cross member, Emmett yelled down to Harry, "Okay, Grandma, you can rest now." Harry's face turned red. He angrily took up the slack in the hand line and rapidly hauled the insulator up to the top of the tower.

Emmett began crawling on top of the crossbeam, but now that the excitement of the earlier crisis had passed he felt shaky and more aware of how high up he was. At the same time, he was mesmerized by the panorama that spread out before him. He could see distant purple mountains, nearby rolling hills and golden wheat-fields, buzzards circling in an azure sky, far off farmhouses and cars on the highway that looked like toys. The words "slow and steady" kept reverberating through Emmett's mind as he thought about his earlier carelessness.

He was distracted by all of these thoughts and his foot slipped off the metal frame of the crossbeam. Emmett plummeted downward and suddenly found himself dangling from the crossbeam by one hand, 100 feet above the ground.

The thought flashed through Emmett's mind that he had unfastened his safety lanyard earlier to help haul up the insulator string, and he hadn't reattached it. A cold rush of terror shot through his mind and body. Every fiber of his being was now focused on survival. His strength was amplified by a surge of adrenaline. He grabbed the crossbeam frame with his other hand, got a toehold with one foot, and slowly climbed back onto the cross beam.

Now, he felt even more shaky than he had earlier, and visions of what it would have been like had he been killed flashed through his mind: Esther unable to afford a baby sitter on her low pay, her and Donnie standing on a street corner with a tin cup begging for spare change from strangers.... Relieved that he was still alive, Emmett clipped his lanyard onto the crossbeam.

"My God, Ernie, that fall would have killed me."

"Naw, the fall wouldn't have hurt you a bit." Then, after a short pause, Ernie said, "But the sudden stop at the bottom sure would have."

Emmett chuckled nervously, trying to cover the anxiety he was feeling. He guided the insulator string into place as Ernie used the hand line to lift it up under the crossbeam. Harry helped by pulling on the hand line from below.

Emmett installed the cotter pin holding the insulator string onto the support stud, then he and Ernie moved 10 feet away from the insulator. Ernie used the gin pole/block and tackle system and the hot stick to pull the wire up to the lower end of the insulator string. Emmett then used a hot stick to install the clamping shoe, fastening the wire to the insulator.

Ernie said, "That's it, we're finished."

As they reached the ground, Fred announced that it was time to head back to the dispatch yard if they were going to get there by quitting time. Emmett gave a sigh of relief. He'd had plenty of excitement for one day.

The next day, the crew headed out to another repair job. They had just arrived, and had gotten most of the equipment and materials out of the truck, when the short-wave radio in the truck blared, "Dispatcher to truck #7".

Fred hurried to the truck and said, "Truck #7."

Then the men heard the dispatcher say, "There's a 24,000-volt line down near Southwood Ranch. We need you to get there and repair it as soon as possible. A large part of the Colfax district is without power. You'll have to stop at substation 3201 and open the air switch to kill line 14 A."

The air switch had to be opened. Otherwise, it would be too dangerous since the live end of the broken wire was most likely on the ground, writhing and arcing, and the pole could be on fire.

Fred said "Okay. Truck #7 out." Then he emerged from the truck looking grim. "Okay men, pack it up on the double."

The men scurried around picking up equipment and materials and throwing them into the back of the truck.

CHAPTER 10

DOWNED LINE!

The truck lumbered to a stop at substation 3201, and the men piled out. A steady electrical hum was coming from the large transformers inside a chain-link fence. Barbed wire sloped outward along the top of the fence. There were large white signs, at several locations on the fence, with bold red letters saying,

"DANGER!
HIGH VOLTAGE!
KEEP OUT."

Fred strode quickly to a gate in the fence and unlocked it. He searched through the substation and found a pole labeled "14 A". A large padlocked handle, that operated a gang air switch on top of the pole, was located on the pole about 4-1/2 feet from the ground. Opening the switch would disconnect all three phases of the downed line. Fred unlocked the handle. Then, turning to Emmett and the other new crewmembers, he said, "When I open the switch, don't look at it or it might fry your eyes."

The men thought he was joking, and they chuckled. Fred pulled up on the handle, and the blades of the switch began to move. With a sharp yank, he opened the blades all the way, producing gaps of about four feet between the stationery parts of the switch and the ends of the three blades. A wriggling, writhing snake of blinding blue-white light filled one of the gaps, accompanied by a loud "bawling" sound. The sound was like the humming of the transformers, but a hundred times louder intermingled with roaring, sputtering and snapping like a giant arc welder.

"Shit!" Fred said, as he slammed the blade back into its closed position, instantly extinguishing the arc. The little group of men around him were looking goggle eyed and blinking after looking at the dazzling light. Fred said, "I told you not to look! Your eyes are sure going to burn tonight. The arc on one of the phases didn't break on the first try because of the heavy fault current on the shorted line. I'll try again and hope that the switch opens when the arc current sputtering around at the fault is at a lower point."

Fred again yanked up on the handle, and this time the arc broke. He said, "Thank God it broke! Otherwise, I would've had to get someone at the main substation to open the oil switch and cut off power to the 110,000 volt bus that feeds the transformer for this section. That would have interrupted power to the entire district."

When Fred turned to face the men, they had their hands over their eyes like the "see no evil" monkey. Fred chuckled. "Hwoo, hwoo, I see you've learned something."

The men quickly got into the back of the truck as Fred padlocked the switch handle and the gate. When the truck arrived at the downed line, a grass fire was progressing away over a nearby hill, and a power pole close to the truck was on fire. Ernie piled out of the truck first. He grabbed a small hand-held fire extinguisher, rushed over to the base of the pole, aimed the extinguisher's nozzle, and pumped the handle. This propelled a pulsating stream of Pyrene extinguishing fluid into the base of the flames. Emmett grabbed a larger Pyrene fire extinguisher, pumped it up and squeezed the release handle, directing the stream of fluid into the flames further up the pole. Fluid striking the burning pole made a hissing sound, accompanied by white clouds of steam that stood out in stark contrast against the orange flames and blackened wood. The fire was extinguished in less than a minute.

Emmett saw that the grass fire had progressed over the hill and was still moving away from the pole. The pungent odor of burned grass and wood filled the air, and a broken wire dangled down the pole. Originally, the wire had been longer, but the electrical arc had melted the end off when the wire hit the ground. The arc had stretched several feet, from the ground up to the wire as the wire got shorter, and had set the pole on fire. There was a solidified puddle of glasslike material near the base of the pole. This had resulted from the arc when it melted not only the wire but also sand and other materials in the soil.

Turning to Emmett, Fred said, "Now is your chance to use some of what you've learned. Climb this pole and get ready to splice a new section of wire between the break and the old wire at the insulator."

"Why can't we just splice the old wire together at the break between poles and save all that wire?" Emmett asked.

"Well, a lot of the old wire has been melted away, so it's too short. Besides, unless you've sprouted wings, you'd have a tough time reaching up 50 feet to bring the old ends together."

All the men laughed, and Emmett reddened as he realized that he had asked a foolish question.

Emmett strapped on his tool belt and hooks, strode confidently over to the pole, and stabbed a spur into it about a foot above the ground. When he put his weight on it, the spur "kicked out" tearing out a large chunk of charred wood. Emmett dropped to the ground and bumped his head on the pole, leaving blotches of charcoal black on his forehead and the end of his nose. Laughter again erupted. Emmett hated to be laughed at. He reddened, scowled angrily as he unclipped his safety belt, and looked menacingly around at each man in the crew. Suddenly, dead silence descended on the group.

Fred broke the silence to deflect Emmett's anger before the situation worsened. He said, "I guess we'd better see how deeply this pole was burned. Emmett, get a digging bar off the truck and chip off charcoal until you hit good wood."

Emmett determined that the charcoal was only about 3/4" deep, so Fred sent Harry over to the truck to get a pair of tree climbing hooks. These hooks had extra long spurs to penetrate the soft bark on trees (or charcoal on poles) and dig into the stronger wood underneath. Emmett put on the hooks and his safety belt, and climbed to the top of the pole without any further trouble. Fred assigned a task to each crew member, and the line was soon repaired and ready to carry power.

When Emmett got back to the ground, he had charcoal black all over his gloves, safety belt, shirtsleeves and pant legs. Turning to Fred, he said, "Now I see why you gave the newest lineman the 'honor' of climbing this pole."

"Hwoo hwoo. You're a fast learner, Emmett."

It was noon, and one of the men asked Fred if they could eat lunch.

"No. Not until this job is done."

"But we have finished."

"No, the job isn't finished until power is restored to all those people that have been without for 6 hours. We have to return to the substation."

"Oh".

A half-hour later, they arrived back at the substation. As the men got out of the back of the truck, Fred went inside the substation to close the air switch. When he returned, he said, "Now we can eat lunch."

Ernie and Emmett were the last to get their lunch buckets. As they approached, the group was already sitting on the ground in a half circle facing one lunch bucket that was sitting on the ground in the shade near the truck.

Emmett overheard Harry whisper to Ernie, "Vern always leaves his false teeth in his lunch bucket until lunchtime. He's out taking a leak. Oh, here he comes. Watch this."

Vern sat down and opened his lunch box. Suddenly, his face contorted in horror, and threw his lunch box up in the air. Without getting up, he used his hands and feet to rapidly scoot backward several feet in a crab-like fashion as if to escape some monster in his lunchbox. A pair of chattering, clacking, windup novelty teeth rolled out of his lunchbox when it hit the ground,.

"OK, which one of you idiots did this and where'd you put my real teeth?" Vern said, glaring around at the circle of men who were all laughing hysterically. Vern was so angry that the veins stood out on his forehead. No one confessed.

One of the men said, "Isn't that your teeth in your lunchbox?"

Vern picked up his lunchbox, which was lying on its side. Sure enough, there were his teeth peeking out from under a sandwich. "If I ever find out who did this, you'd better be a light sleeper," he said in an ominous tone.

As the men finished their lunches, Fred used the short-wave radio in the truck to check with the dispatcher. The crew was directed to go back to the job that had originally been scheduled for that morning: routine replacement of a leaky insulator on a 6,000-volt branch service line.

When they arrived, Fred asked Emmett to climb the pole and replace the defective insulator. Vern, who had spent the past evening taking a crash course on testing rubber gloves and guts, had carefully tested all of the items that were in the storage box. He proudly retrieved a pair of rubber gloves and a set of guts from the box and said to Emmett, "These babies are free of defects, I guarantee it." Emmett took the rubber gloves from Vern and turned them over several times as he visually inspected them.

Vern said, "What's the matter, don't you trust me?"

"Once burned, twice cautious!"

Vern's face reddened as he remembered the painful lesson Emmett had recently learned when Vern hadn't properly tested red the training gloves.

"Hwoo, Hwoo", Fred chuckled. "You catch on quickly, Emmett. I think we'll be able to keep you alive after all."

Emmett climbed the pole and deftly changed the insulator on the live line. It was quitting time, and he'd survived another day. He was beginning to understand why men in this dangerous line of work develop a close camaraderie, a brotherhood.

CHAPTER 11

THE BIG DAY

For several months, Emmett continued working in the crew doing every conceivable kind of line work. He was becoming well known for his trademark of virtually running up an down poles. This made him the object of ridicule by some of the men who felt that this ambitious young upstart was making them look bad. When they criticized Emmett, he said, "I'm just so damn glad to have this steady, high paying job that I can't help it", and then he would give them a wry grin that bruised their egos. Sometimes, his critics would have liked to punch him in the nose, but they didn't relish the pain his 6'3" of solid muscle would have inflicted on them. Besides, Emmett was generally well liked in spite of his over-ambitious nature.

One evening, when the men returned to the dispatch yard, Chet was standing in the shade of one of the buildings. Fred led the men over to Chet, and another of Chet's crews joined them.

Chet addressed the combined group, saying, "It's time to demonstrate my hot sticks for interested power companies. Tomorrow, we will do some hot stick work on a live 60,000-volt line, and power company executives from all over the world will be there to watch you. Don't let the presence of these bosses distract you, and don't grandstand. I don't want anyone to get hurt or killed, so just do your work normally and be careful. This will complete your job with me. If you do well, and I sell lots of hot sticks, there'll be a nice bonus in it for each of you."

The men cheered, but Emmett looked perplexed, and turning to Fred, he said, "Hell, I thought this job was going to be permanent. I was going to move my wife and kid here."

Fred chuckled. "Hwoo, Hwoo, Don't worry, I've been offered a job as a crew foreman with Washington Water Power, and I'd be a fool if I didn't take you with me. I've already spoken to the regional superintendent, and he's agreed to hire you at journeyman lineman's wages, 95 cents an hour plus benefits and overtime!"

Emmett had never had a job with anything called "benefits", so he asked, "What are benefits?"

"You get free life insurance and a week of vacation per year."

"Wow, I'll be rich! I'll take the job."

"Okay, but I want you to know that, although we will be based in Spokane, we'll be out of town traveling to different locations in the state most of the time, staying in hotels, eating in restaurants, and we'll only get back here on weekends."

"That sounds expensive, but at that wage I'll be able to afford it."

"No. You don't have to pay for travel expenses. The company will transport us to and from the jobs, and will pay for meals and hotels when we are on the road."

Emmett said, "Wow! I'll make more money in a year than I've made in my entire lifetime."

That night, in his hotel room, Emmett missed Esther and Donnie with a deep, intense longing as he had so many nights in hotel rooms since starting this work. He missed the quiet, warm surroundings of his own home. He desperately hoped that the work would go well tomorrow, and that Chet would receive orders for many sets of hot sticks. Emmett believed that the bonus would make it possible for him to move Esther and Donnie to Spokane, or at least to afford a bus trip to Philomath for a weeklong visit. He lay awake for more than an hour worrying about all the things that could go wrong, such as making the hot sticks look clumsy or ineffective, and he wondered about the amount of the bonus check he would get if the demonstration was successful.

The next morning, the dispatch yard was the usual hustle-bustle of activity as Chet's crews loaded two trucks with equipment and then climbed aboard. A dozen or so large, black Buick touring cars that contained five or six passengers each were parked behind the second truck. The trucks pulled out, followed by the cars, and the big day had begun.

Fred's crew rode in the back of the second truck. Each man talked about the plans he had for spending the bonus he hoped he would earn that day. One said he was going to spend it on a trip to Hawaii; another wanted to buy a boat and motor and go fishing for a month; and another man said he was going on a month–long gambling, drinking and prostitute binge. Emmett said he planned to move his wife and kid to Spokane, put a down payment on a home and buy a new car.

The man who wanted to go on the binge said, "My God, Emmett, that sure doesn't sound like any fun."

Emmett said, "Aw, you just don't know what fun is."

The truck came to a stop near a 60,000-volt power line pole. The excitement of the big day was evident on the men's faces and in the way they moved as they jumped out of the truck. Emmett's pulse quickened as he thought about the bonus and what it would mean to him and his family. He hoped with all of his might that Chet's sales would go well.

Fred gathered his men around him and said, "We're going to use hot sticks to change out two insulator strings on this pole. You've probably noticed the other crew with their truck parked near the next pole. They're going to change two insulators on that pole while you are working on this one. The line is live, and the work will have to be coordinated so we don't whip the line around and drop it, or pull it onto each other. I'll be talking to the other foreman on the truck radio to coordinate each step of the operation. Wait for my 'go-ahead' before performing each step in this change-out. Ernie and Emmett, you work together as you usually do when we work with hot sticks."

Emmett walked over to the pole, strapped on his tool belt and hooks, clipped his safety belt around the pole and began to climb. He forced himself to climb at a moderate rate so he wouldn't look like he was showing off for the large group of dignitaries that were gathered in a location about 50 feet away from the pole.

Chet gave each of the dignitaries a white baseball cap that had a little red lightning man logo on the front. Then he insisted that they move across the road, another 50 feet away from the pole, "to maximize their safety".

Emmett thought to himself, That's a clever way of saying, without actually admitting it, that one of us might screw up.

When Emmett reached the top, Ernie climbed the pole and stopped just below Emmett on the opposite side. When Ernie's safety belt was just below the location where Emmett's spurs were dug in, Ernie stopped and Emmett stepped down and stabbed his spurs in just below Ernie's belt so Ernie could move up to Emmett's level. This belt procedure required careful cooperation between the two men. From then on, if they had to move up or down the pole, they had to move in tandem until they performed the reverse belt procedure.

Ernie and Emmett were now ready for action. They moved to the proper work position, then pulled the necessary hot sticks, attachments, clamps, hangers, and an assortment of other tools up on their hand lines, and waited for Fred's instructions. He was in the truck talking on the radio. Finally, he emerged and shouted, "Clamp the standoff stick to the center line." Ernie complied.

A few minutes later Fred got into the truck, then emerged and shouted, "Hold the line with the standoff stick, and remove the hold-down bail from the insulator."

Time after time, Fred got into the truck, then emerged and shouted instructions. The men on both poles proceeded to perform all the insulator replacement operations together in perfect synchronism, and one of the VIP spectators said, "My God, this is almost like watching a ballet!"

When the work was completed Emmett and Ernie quickly came down the pole. Chet gathered the executives together near the truck and Emmett heard him ask, "Well, what do you think?"

All the executives tried to talk at once, and Chet said, "Gentlemen, gentlemen, calm down. I'll give each one of you a chance to speak, but one at a time, please."

Emmett heard the executive from WWP (Washington Water Power Co.) say, "These hot sticks are a marvelous invention. For the first time, they will make it possible to work on live high voltage lines without interrupting the power." The other executives agreed. Then the WWP man said, "Your price of $300 per set is awfully high, but the hot sticks will save us much more than that by reducing the revenue that is lost when lines have to be shut down for repairs. We want to order a dozen sets of sticks with all the attachments."

When their turn to speak came, all the other executives also placed orders. The smallest order placed was for a half dozen sets. Chet, who had been writing down the orders as fast as he could, stopped writing and faced the group, saying "I will fill your orders as fast as I can, but this is a larger market than I anticipated. The rate at which I can produce the sets now is somewhat limited, so I will require at least partial payment in advance so I can gear up for a faster production rate."

This resulted in another hubbub, with everyone speaking at once; many offered complete payment in advance for early delivery. Some of the executives had checkbooks and were authorized to immediately pay Chet the entire amount. They wrote checks and handed them to Chet as fast as he could record them in his order book. When the last pre-payment check had been recorded, Chet said "Those who could not pay today must get a check to me this week, or your company will miss out on the present production cycle." The executives who had not yet paid assured Chet that he would have their company's check by the end of the week.

The big day was so successful that it surprised even the most optimistic experts who had for several years been following Chet's efforts to develop and sell the hot stick tools he had patented. Emmett and the other crewmen were ecstatic as they anticipated the bonuses they would receive. Some of Emmett's fellow crewmen stopped to celebrate at a bar on the way to the hotel and got drunk.

CHAPTER 12

NO MORE HARD TIMES

When Emmett returned to the hotel at the end of the big day, he sat down and carefully wrote a letter to Esther. In part, it said,

"Dear Esther,
Things have gone really well here, and our hard times are over, at least for now. I'm getting a big bonus and a high-paying job as a journeyman lineman. I want to move you and Donnie to Spokane right away. Please sell our Philomath house. It breaks my heart to have to let it go, but the opportunity here is much better than anything I could get there. I've really hit pay dirt here, thanks to your uncle Chet and the opportunity he gave me. ..."

The rest of Emmett's letter described how much he had been missing her and Donnie, and how much he ached to see them. He had wanted them to be with him during all those months in Spokane, but he had thought it unwise to move them to Spokane before his new line of work proved successful; he had felt that he couldn't even afford a round-trip to Philomath until things panned out.

A few days later Esther was at work sorting mail at the Philomath Post Office when she realized that one of the letters in her hand was addressed to her from Emmett. She put the letter into the pocket of her apron and continued working. George, the postmaster, was devoted to his job and had warned her not to use any work time for personal activities. He was a small man with the nervousness, quick movements, and personality of a bantam rooster. He made up for what he lacked in size with a nasty, hair-trigger temper.

During her lunch break, Esther retrieved her brown-bag lunch and sat down at a table in the back room of the Post office. At last, she could read the letter from Emmett. She opened it, and after reading a few lines she let out a loud shriek. Mabel came running in from the front counter looking worried. She asked,

"What's wrong?" Then she saw the letter Esther was holding. "Is it bad news? Has Emmett been injured? Has he been killed?"

Speechless, and with tears in her eyes, Esther handed the letter to Mabel.

Mabel read it and said, "Oh, this is very good news."

George came into the back room to see what all the commotion was about. Mabel handed him the letter and, as he read it, he blandly said, "Umm, that's nice." He handed the letter to Esther and headed out front muttering, "Someone has to keep this place running. Neither rain nor sleet nor dark of night shall keep them from their appointed rounds."

As she dabbed her eyes with a handkerchief, Esther said, "Oh Mabel, I've dreamed of this day for so long. I can hardly believe that our family will finally be together again."

"I'm so happy for you Esther, but we sure hate to lose you. You've been a good worker."

When Esther arrived home, her four-year-old son, Donnie, was waiting for her. As soon as he caught sight of her coming in the door, he ran to her and wrapped his arms around her leg. Millie, Esther's seventeen-year old half-sister, was living with them and babysitting Donnie while Emmett was away.

Seeing the happy expression on Esther's face Millie said, "My, don't you look cheerful. George must not have had any tantrums today."

"No, he didn't even throw any stacks of letters across the room for me to pick up," Esther said, referring to George's occasional angry reaction when things didn't go well. "But that isn't the main reason I'm so happy." She pulled Emmett's letter out of her purse and handed it to Millie. After reading a few lines, Millie grabbed Esther by the shoulders and they both jumped up and down, squealing like a couple of little girls.

That evening, Esther and Millie sat down at the kitchen table with pencil and paper to work on an ad to be placed in the local newspaper to sell the house.

"Millie, Emmett wants me to sell the house, but the economic depression is so bad right now that I don't think anyone will have enough money for a down payment. I'd better offer it for rent as well as for sale."

"Won't Emmett be upset if you don't sell it?"

"No. He has relied on me quite often for business decisions. Besides, I'm smarter than he is." Esther threw her head back, looking down her nose at Millie in mock haughtiness. They both laughed at this small joke.

When they had recovered from their giddiness, Esther said, "Seriously, Emmett and I share in all things and trust each other completely."

Millie got a pensive look on her face, then said, "Oh Esther, you have such a wonderful marriage."

Several days later, when Esther arrived home from work, Donnie greeted her as usual. Then Esther noticed two strangers with Millie in the living room.

Millie introduced the strangers. Gesturing with a dramatic sweep of her hand, she said, "Esther, this is Mr. and Mrs. Newt. They would like to rent the house."

Mr. Newt said, "We would really like to rent this house." Then he sighed and said, "But we can't afford to pay the security deposit or the first and last month's rent in advance."

Esther said, "Oh, I'm sorry. We really must sell the house if we can. But I will add your name to the list of people wanting to rent it."

Mr. Newt looked dejected as he stood up and said, "I understand," and they left.

After the Newts had gone, Millie looked puzzled and asked, "What list of renters?"

Esther chuckled. "The one I just started. We can't afford to rent to someone who doesn't have any money, but I didn't want to hurt Mr. Newt's feelings."

During the next few weeks several other people came to see the house. Some wanted to buy it, but didn't have enough money for a down payment. Others wanted to rent, but didn't have enough money to meet the required advance payments.

Finally a newlywed couple who were each employed came to see the house. They were well dressed; he in gray dress pants, a white shirt and tie, and she in a neat, black and white conservative dress. They seemed educated and well organized. Most importantly, they had enough money to pay the first and last month's rent, and the security deposit, in advance. Esther had just arrived home from work, and Millie was sitting with the couple in the living room.

"This is Mr. and Mrs. Wilson," Millie said with her usual dramatic introductory gesture. "They are both working, and can meet the required advance payment," she said with an officiousness that implied she felt she had become quite an expert at interviewing prospective renters.

Esther looked the couple over carefully, then she flashed a friendly smile and said, "Okay, but we will need a month to finish packing and sell our chickens."

The land around the house had a large garden space, and a number of tall oak trees. There was a chicken house in the shade of the trees near the back of the land. Strutting among the trees were a dozen large, plump Plymouth Rock chickens. Their dappled gray and white feathers made them hard to see in the shade of the trees.

Mr. Wilson said, "Don't worry about selling the chickens. We'll buy them from you".

"Okay, but I want all the eggs they produce until we move out, and I want to keep one hen. She has quit laying, and we'll have her for dinner tomorrow."

Mr. Wilson said, "It's a deal," and shook hands with Esther.

Esther had some rental agreement forms that she had purchased at a stationery store. She filled in the blanks on two of them, specifying the terms: rent, security deposit and move in date. Then she added a hand-written provision for the sale of the chickens. She and the Wilsons signed the duplicate copies. Mr. Wilson gave her a check, and she gave him a signed copy of the agreement.

After the Wilsons left, Esther, Millie and Donnie went out to the oak trees. Esther was carrying a bucket containing some chicken feed, and Millie was carrying a long thin pole with a wire hook attached to one end. Esther scattered some chicken feed on the ground, and the free-range, half-wild chickens warily approached it.

Esther said, "There she is, Millie, the one that walks with a limp. Now be careful and don't spook her or we'll be here all night!"

Millie tried to sneak up behind the old chicken and snare her leg with the hook. But Millie was too impatient and tried to snare the chicken before getting close enough. The old bird ran off squawking and flapping its wings as it darted through the trees. Millie was in the hot pursuit, swinging the chicken hook wildly as she ran. Donnie stood clapping his hands and giggling at the sight of his babysitter chasing the squawking chicken. Millie was gaining and was almost close enough when the old bird darted to the left. Millie tried to follow, but her feet flew out from under her and she crashed to the ground. She immediately jumped up muttering something about "damned chicken." With her lips drawn into a tight line, hair flying and wild eyes squinting with determination, Millie brushed oak twigs and dead leaves from her hair and clothing, and again took up the chase. Esther tried to run in front of the chicken to head it off so Millie could get close enough to hook a leg, but the crafty old bird abruptly changed direction again. Donnie, seeing how it was done, also started trying to head the chicken off, giggling and clamping his hands. Finally, after several more attempts, Millie hooked one leg and pulled the flapping, squawking chicken close enough to grab both of its legs.

Donnie was delighted with this game. Jumping up and down, he said, "Let the chicken go. Let's do it again!". Esther and Millie, who by now were exhausted, each looked at Donnie with one corner of her mouth pulled back in disgust.

Donnie looked disappointed and asked, "No more game?"

Esther said, "No, the chicken's old and tired, and it's time for her to take a nap."

Millie took Donnie into the house, while Esther got an axe in preparation for the chicken's "nap".

The next evening, they were just sitting down to a chicken and dumpling dinner, when they heard a car drive up on the gravel driveway. Esther looked out the window just as Emmett got out of the car. She exclaimed, "Oh, Emmett's here!" and ran out to meet him. Emmett wrapped his arms around Esther and embraced her in a long, affectionate kiss.

Millie, who had just come out of the house, said "Hey, come up for air!"

Emmett and Esther finally ended the long kiss, but then started kissing all over each other's faces in short, affectionate pecks.

Esther said, "Oh Emmett, I didn't expect you until tomorrow".

"I got a ride with Harry in his new car. Sharing the cost of the gasoline was cheaper than taking the bus."

Harry smiled at the couple as he got Emmett's two suitcases out of the back seat and said, "Hey, if you two lovers are finished sucking on each other's faces, I'd like to get going."

Millie said, "Maybe I should squirt a hose on them."

As he got into his car, Harry said, "That sounds like a good idea." Then, he backed out of the driveway and left.

Donnie finally ventured out of the house and stood looking puzzled at the behavior of his mother and this tall man who looked vaguely familiar. Emmett was dressed in a much more stylish, sporty outfit than when he'd been a log truck driver, and he was wearing a bill cap pulled down to shade his eyes. he took a step toward his son with his arms outstretched, but Donnie took refuge behind Millie and peeked surreptitiously around her at Emmett.

Esther said, "Give him time, Emmett, he doesn't recognize you yet." Then, directing her gaze at Donnie, she said, "This is Daddy."

Emmett removed his cap, and Donnie's eyes lit up. He said, "Daddy!" as he suddenly recognized this man who had built him a toy sailboat, and had given him brightly wrapped Christmas presents so many months ago. He ran to Emmett who swept him up into his arms and kissed him. Donnie shrunk back and said, "Daddy's stickery." Emmett hadn't shaved since morning, and his coarse stubble felt like a briar patch to Donnie's delicate, fair skin. Donnie squirmed to get down, and ran to Millie as soon as his feet touched the ground.

Emmett picked up one suitcase, and Esther carried the other as they went into the house.

The house was filled with the delicious aroma of chicken stew, and was warm and inviting.

Emmett said, "What's that wonderful smell?"

"Chicken and dumplings," Esther replied.

"Oh boy, a home cooked meal at last!" A warm glow filled Emmett's heart with joyful gratitude as he was at last able to enjoy being safely home again surrounded by his beloved family. His long, dangerous ordeal was on hold, at least for now.

The family sat around the kitchen table enjoying the stew and visiting for a few minutes, then Emmett asked, "Esther, did you sell the house?"

Millie thought, Oh oh, here it comes. I hope Esther was right about Emmett's reaction to this.

Esther said, "No one had enough money to cover the down payment and closing costs, so I rented it to a prosperous looking young couple."

"Good. I thought that might be what we'd have to do."

Millie thought, Whew, thank God Esther was right about Emmett's attitude.

The rest of the mealtime conversation was just jovial small talk, with Esther telling about catching the chicken, and about the various people that had looked at the home. Finally, mimicking Vern's facial expressions and lunchbox drama, Emmett related the incident involving the clacking windup teeth. They all roared with laughter until tears rolled down their cheeks. This released some of the tensions that had built up during the many months of danger, separation and worry. Donnie, not understanding the laughter, looked perplexed. This caused the adults to laugh even harder. Their arms and legs felt weak and completely relaxed when the last of the laughter had subsided. Any remaining tension had completely faded away like a spring thunderstorm moving off into the distance.

Emmett and Esther spent the next two weeks sorting and packing household items and clothes into boxes. Esther told Emmett that the young Wilsons didn't have much furniture, and that they would be happy if some items were temporarily left in the house. Leaving large items such as the icebox, wringer-style Maytag washing machine, Speed Queen laundry tubs, davenport and overstuffed chair for a few months would postpone the need, for Emmett and Esther to purchase a Spokane house and hire a moving van, until after they got settled. Large boxes could be shipped by standard freight. A few smaller boxes, containing immediately needed items, could be moved to Spokane in the rumble seat of the Model A coupe.

Esther said, "I hate to leave our appliances and furniture. We've only had most of them for a little while, and I've really been enjoying them."

"Don't worry, Esther, we'll get a furnished apartment in Spokane. We'll move our large items there after we purchase a house."

Emmett made a number of trips hauling boxes of bedding and other essential items to the freight terminal in the Model A coupe. The rumble seat and passenger seat in the little car were stuffed with boxes, some of which intruded into the driver's space and made it difficult to shift gears and drive. Emmett hadn't had the car in Spokane to hunt for an apartment, so the boxes were labeled with Fred Woodmyer's address. Fred had agreed to store the boxes in his garage until Emmett and his family arrived and moved into an apartment.

On moving day, Donnie was outside happily building a bridge, for his toy car, with a flat slab of wood across an eight-inch wide gutter drain ditch. Esther came to get him, and he gladly went with her not realizing that he'd never see his bridge again.

Esther said, "Take your toy car with you."

Donnie said, "I'll leave it here to play with when we get home."

Not wanting to upset Donnie, Esther said, "You'd better take it. I think you'll want to have it to play with at the place we are going." He tightly grasped the toy in one hand as Esther led him to the car. The first of the family's many coming adventures was underway.

CHAPTER 13

ROAD TO A NEW LIFE

Donnie climbed onto the seat of the model A coupe, while Emmett placed a few last-minute items in the rumble seat compartment. He had removed the rumble seat cushions and stored them in his father's barn. Emmett and Esther got into the car, sandwiching Donnie between them. As Emmett put the car in gear, Donnie said, "We go now?"

Smiling at Emmett, Esther said, "Yes, and this time we go together."

"Thank God for that," Emmett said, smiling back at her.

Donnie's dog, Trixie, wasn't in the spot where she usually stood watching them leave in the car. Donnie asked, "Where's Trixie?"

Esther said, "Trixie's visiting my brother, Verl, in Corvallis for a while. He'll be nice to her, and she'll on vacation having fun."

That satisfied Donnie, and he settled down. When they reached the end of the driveway, Emmett stopped the car and said, "Well, Esther, this is it. Take a last look at our little house."

They turned around in the seat so they could look out the back window. Esther was suddenly struck by the realization that they would probably never live here again. Images of happy times in the house flashed through her mind like a movie: birthday parties, laughing and working together in the yard and garden, happy visits from friends and relatives, Christmas and decorating the tree together, Thanksgiving dinners, and other special occasions. She suddenly ached inside, feeling as though she might be leaving all the happy times behind forever. Tears welled up in her eyes. She tried to conceal them from Emmett, but he saw them and his expression quickly softened into gentle concern.

"Esther, what's wrong?"

"Oh, it's nothing. I'm just remembering all the happy times we had here."

"If Mommy is happy, why is she crying?" Donnie asked looking puzzled. That changed the mood. Emmett and Esther looked at each other and smiled as Emmett put the car into gear and drove onto the highway.

It was dark and Donnie was asleep by the time they neared Spokane. There were scrub pines along both sides of the highway. Emmett slowed the car and drove off the highway onto the dirt road that ran through a sparse stand of trees.

"Where are you going?" Esther asked.

"I don't want to spend money on a hotel, so we'll sleep here among the trees tonight."

"Well, all right, whatever you think is best."

Emmett stopped the car and they spread some blankets out to make a bed on top of a nearby patch of Cheat Grass. They were blissfully unaware of the diabolic way Cheat Grass attaches its seeds to clothing and blankets. When Esther placed Donnie in the middle of the makeshift bed, he woke up and said, "This isn't a bed. I want my bed".

With feigned enthusiasm, Esther said, "This is like a picnic. We'll sleep outside tonight. It'll be fun like a picnic."

"Mommy, where are the plates? Where is the food? I'm hungry."

Esther gave Donnie some crackers, then further explained their sleeping arrangements to him while Emmett walked out into the darkness to relieve himself. When he returned, Esther took Donnie with her and they did the same. Then the family settled down for the night.

About an hour later, when they were all fast asleep, an awful roaring shook the earth under them. Suddenly, they were bathed in a bright white light from above. The roaring got louder and louder until it was almost unbearable.

Esther awakened and said, "My God, it must be the end of the world!"

An instant later, a huge twin-engine airliner hurtled overhead at an altitude of about 100 feet. They had made their bed just off the West end of the Spokane Municipal Airport runway. Emmett and Esther scrambled out of bed, placed a limp, sleeping Donnie in the car seat and quickly threw the blankets into the rumble seat compartment. Emmett didn't take time to turn the car around. He backed out to the highway as fast as he could.

They drove on into Spokane in complete silence. Emmett knew he had made a foolish mistake, and Esther didn't know what to say without sounding critical. After a while, Esther could no longer contain herself. The humor of the situation had been building up in her, and she started to giggle. She placed a hand over her mouth in an attempt to stifle her laughter, but air escaped out both sides of her mouth making funny hissing and buzzing sounds. Emmett, relieved that Esther saw humor in the situation and wasn't mad at him for his bonehead mistake, started to chuckle. This opened the way for Esther to finally release her pent-up laughter, and they both laughed so hard that Donnie started to wake up. They managed to stifle their laughter, but they silently giggled behind tightly closed lips. This made their heads to bob back and forth like two chickens pecking at a wall.

After they arrived in Spokane, Emmett drove around for an hour looking for a good place to sleep. It was after midnight, and they were so tired they could hardly keep their eyes open. Finally, they came to Liberty Park. A paved road meandered into the park and there were marked parking spots along one side. The park was well kept, with a manicured lawn on each side of the road. Esther said, "This is perfect." Emmett parked the car, retrieved their blankets from the rumble seat and they bedded down on the grass near the car.

At about 6:30 AM Emmett was awakened by a gentle tapping on one arm. He opened his eyes to see a large policeman standing over him tapping his arm with a nightstick. In a voice resonating with authority, the policeman said, "I'm sorry, but you can't sleep here."

"Oh, we didn't know that," Emmett said.

"Sleeping here is a violation of city ordinances and I should give you a citation, but I can see from your license plate that you are from out of town. I'll let you off with a warning this time."

Esther had awakened. She said, "Thank you officer. By the way, do you know of any reasonably priced apartments for rent?"

"No ma'am, I recommend you get a copy of the Spokesman Review. It has the best want ads section."

Emmett loaded their bedding into the rumble seat, then drove around until they found a restaurant called "Ma's Kitchen". It was a small place, with stools at a counter on one side of an aisle, and a row of booths along the other. As they walked to a booth for breakfast, Esther picked up a copy of the Spokesman Review that someone had left on one of the tables. While waiting for a waitress, Esther glanced through the "For Rent" section. She said, "Oh, here's a furnished apartment for $13 a month in the Dunsmuir Apartment Building."

After breakfast, Emmett drove to the address listed in the paper and the family marched up to the front door. The building was red brick, and old, but looked reasonably well built and maintained. It was in a neighborhood that had other apartment buildings and a number of old homes that had been elegant in their day, but were now in a state of decay and disrepair. Esther showed Donnie how to press the doorbell button. An elderly lady opened the door and led them to a ground floor apartment that was for rent. It was small, had a threadbare carpet, and smelled slightly musty, but it looked clean and reasonably well maintained. The windows looked directly out on a public sidewalk that ran along one side of the building, but they all had roller shades for privacy. It was no Waldorf Astoria, but it was a considerable step up from the family's sleeping accommodations the previous night.

Esther looked at Emmett. "Okay?"

"Okay, Esther."

Esther, whose negotiating skill had been honed by growing up in a large, impoverished family told the old lady, "If you'll knock a dollar off the rent, we'll take it." Emmett was embarrassed and reddened as he studied his shoes. In spite of his tall stature and great strength, he was shy and hated conflict that might make someone dislike him.

The old lady looked them over carefully. Then, deciding they looked more reliable than many of the previous tenants, she agreed to $12 per month.

Emmett and Esther spent the remainder of the day hauling boxes to the apartment from Fred Woodmyer's garage, where they had been shipped for temporary storage,. As they were carrying things from the Model A into the apartment, Esther noticed a few black persons walk past, and didn't think much about it. After all, this was a big city and, unlike Philomath which only had a population of a few hundred, it would have a mixture of black and white people.

By the time Donnie awoke the next morning, Emmett had left for work. After giving Donnie his breakfast, Esther sent him out to play. Later, he came in with a perplexed look on his face.

"Mommy, all the kids here have black skin. What happened to them? Is their blood black?"

Realizing that Donnie had never seen a black person before, Esther sat him down and explained that there are many different races of people in the world. Then she said, "Although people from different races look different and have some different customs, they are all basically the same as us."

A few days later, Esther realized the apartment was in a predominantly black section of the city.

Donnie asked, "Why won't the kids here play with me?"

"Because they don't know you yet", Esther said. Then she thought to herself, "and we are the minority in this neighborhood."

Donnie continued trying to make friends, but only one little boy was friendly with him. A week later, he told Esther that most of the kids still wouldn't play with him. She replied, "We'll only be living here for a little while until we can afford to get a bigger apartment."

When Emmett came home that night, he was beaming with excitement.

Esther, seeing his face, immediately knew that he had what he believed to be good news. "What happened?"

"The company is sending me out on construction of a new 60,000-volt line through the Palouse region of the state 50 miles south of here".

Esther said, "Sixty thousand volts! That's dangerous!"

"No, the line won't be energized until after it's completed. It'll be much safer than the hot stick work I've been doing on live 120,000-volt lines."

With tears in her eyes, Esther said, "Oh Emmett, 120,000-volt live lines! You've been doing such dangerous work. When you started this work, I thought you were only going to be a grunt and stay on the ground. I hadn't realized that you'd been doing such dangerous work when I read in your letter that you had become a journeyman lineman. Please quit this job immediately. I'll work to support us until you can find a safer job."

"Aw Esther, I have to take a little risk to make good money, and I'm being real careful, so I should live a lot longer than the 13-year average for a lineman."

"Thirteen years!" Esther said in a tight, high-pitched voice that reflected her horror. "Emmett..." she said, wanting to say more but was unable because of a tight lump in her throat.

"Aw Esther, I can take care of myself," Emmett said in a confident tone of voice that belied the internal turmoil that he was feeling because she was so upset. "Besides, construction work is much safer."

After a few minutes, Esther regained some of her composure. "Emmett Green, I'm really mad at you for getting into such a dangerous line of work," she said in a disgusted tone of voice.

"But how else can a guy like me get ahead with only an eighth grade education, especially during this damn depression?"

"Well, at least the construction work won't be so dangerous," Esther said somewhat more calmly.

"Oh, Esther, I almost forgot to tell you; I have more good news."

" I hope it's better than that last load you just dumped on me."

"We've gotten unionized and our wages are going up immediately."

"Finally, some actual good news. Now we can afford to move to a larger apartment."

With a sparkle in his eye and a big grin on his face, Emmett looked past Esther as if he were having a nice daydream. "Yeah, and now we can spare enough money for a down payment on a new car."

Esther said, "Hmm, I'm jealous. It's a good thing you weren't talking about another woman when you got that look on your face, or I might've had to murder you in your sleep."

The next day, Saturday, Emmett left at about 9:30 AM. When he returned, he was driving a brand new 1937 Plymouth four-door sedan. He was obviously excited when he came into the apartment with a big grin on his face.

Esther said, "Oh, oh, what did you do?"

"I have a surprise to show you, come with me."

When Esther saw the car, she asked, "Oh my gosh, how much did you pay for it?"

"$795."

"Oh, Emmett, that car cost almost as much as a small house. You should have taken me along to negotiate the price."

A dark cloud of anger passed over Emmett's face as he first felt insulted then, when he remembered past demonstrations of Esther's negotiating skills, his anger subsided.

"You're right, Esther, but I wanted to surprise you. Besides, I'm really hauling in the dough right now so we shouldn't have to pinch every penny anymore."

"Okay, dear. I was definitely surprised. Can we still afford to buy a house?"

"Yes, right after we sell our Philomath house."

"Well, Emmett, I hope we can at least afford a larger apartment right away."

"Definitely."

CHAPTER 14

A BETTER LIFE?

After a month in the Dunsmuir apartment, Esther found a larger apartment and the family moved again.

The new apartment was on the second floor of a large, old home, owned by a middle-aged lady, Mrs. Pistorius. Besides being larger, the apartment had several other desirable features. A garage was included, which pleased Emmett, since he would have a secure place to park his baby, the new car, out of the weather. A kindergarten that Donnie would be attending was within walking distance, and this pleased Esther.

When they had moved the last item into the new apartment, Emmett said, "I want to go to Philomath next weekend to check on our renters and to pick up Trixie."

Esther said, "Oh, you just want to show off your new car to your dad and your brothers and sisters."

"Yeah," Emmett said, looking a little sheepish.

On Friday, Emmett drove his family to Philomath. He spent most of the weekend visiting his parents and siblings. On the way back to Spokane, he stopped briefly to see the renters and pick up the dog at Verl's house.

Trixie was a quiet, gentle, cinnamon colored, shorthair terrier mix that was good with children. Esther and Donnie loved her and, although he wouldn't admit it, so did Emmett. In his farm upbringing, animals were supposed to be used for work or for food and were not considered part of the family. Seeing Esther, Trixie, wagged her tail so hard that it shook her entire body. A joyful reunion of dog and family followed with everyone's hands being licked.

Donnie shared the back seat with Trixie on the return trip. As they arrived in Spokane late that night, Esther said, "Donnie, we have to keep Trixie a secret. We're not supposed to have a dog in the apartment."

"Okay, mommy."

Emmett dropped Esther, Donnie, and the dog off in front of the house.

Esther whispered, "Now, be very quiet, Donnie, we don't want to wake Mrs. Pistorius."

Esther's heart was pounding with fear, worrying that Mrs. Pistorius would wake up and catch them with the dog as they crept up the stairs. Suddenly, someone grabbed Esther from behind, and she flinched and let out a little yelp. It was Emmett returning from putting the car in the garage. Fortunately the dog was used to such antics between Emmett and Esther and didn't bark.

"Oh Emmett, you almost gave me a heart attack," Esther said in disgust as she unlocked the apartment door.

"I just wanted to see if you were awake," he said, a broad grin spreading across his face.

"You big tease. You're entirely too pleased with yourself, scaring me like that. You know very well how nervous I am about breaking the rules by having the dog in here."

Several weeks passed, and Esther was able to keep Trixie secret by sneaking her in and out of the apartment on an outside stairway, and walking her far away from the building to do her business. Esther knew that even though she was cautious, it was probably only a matter of time before Mrs. Pistorius would find out about the dog.

Winter had arrived, and a few inches of snow had fallen during the night. Esther had just started to prepare lunch for herself and Donnie when someone knocked on the apartment door. Opening the door she saw Mrs. Pistorius standing, framed by the dark wood doorway, hands on her hips and a grim expression on her face.

"I know you have a dog in here. I saw its footprints in the snow, and I heard its toe nails clicking on the kitchen linoleum. You'll have to get rid of it, or find somewhere else to live," Mrs. Pistorius said emphatically.

Esther meekly said, "Okay," and closed the door.

When Emmett got home from work, Esther told him what had happened, and that she thought Trixie would have to be kept inside the car in the garage. Emmett agreed, so Esther made a nest in a cardboard box and placed it on the car's back seat. The temperatures had been down into the 20s at night, so Esther placed two 1-quart jars of hot water under rags in the bottom of the nest to keep Trixie warm. The next morning, when Esther went to the garage to walk Trixie, she saw that the tip of one of the dog's ears was frostbitten.

Esther said, "Oh you poor little dog."

After that, Esther made two trips to the garage every night during the cold weather to check on the Trixie and to replace the hot water jars. Using safety pins, cardboard and rags, she arranged a warm cover over the top of the dog,s nest.

Several nights later, Emmett and Esther were in the living room relaxing and listening to the radio. Donnie started playing with the electric hotplate in the kitchen. He was fascinated with the open spring heating element that got bright red when he switched it on high. Being a curious 5-year old, he decided to stick a metal fork into the red-hot element to see what would happen. He leaned forward, holding a fork in one hand and bracing himself with the other hand on the metal case of the hotplate. The instant the fork touched the element, Donnie felt a tremendous electric shock. It knocked him down on his rear, and the fork went clattering across the kitchen.

Esther called out. "What are you doing, Donnie?"

"N-n-nothing," Donnie said, trying to quell the shakiness in his voice.

Esther suspected that he was getting into mischief so she said, "Come in here and listen to the radio with us."

Thus ended Donnie's first experiment with electricity.

The family dropped back into their usual routine for several months, Emmett working and coming home on weekends, Esther taking care of the household tasks, and Donnie attending kindergarten. Then, Esther found a furnished house for lease at a price within the limits of their improving financial means. The house was on Ivory Street one block from Grant primary school where Donnie would be attending first grade. An added bonus was that pets were allowed, so no more carrying jars of hot water out to the car on cold winter nights. Arrangements were made, and the following Saturday was moving day -- again.

Living in the house was wonderful compared to living in apartments. There was almost no lawn, only a narrow strip of weeds, but the house had plenty of room inside for everyone to spread out. It even had a piano in the living room on which Esther could plink out a few tunes that she had learned when she was a youngster using her grandmother's piano.

Donnie found some old weather-grayed boards and four toy wagon wheels left behind the garage by the previous tenant. He used Emmett's tools to build a little car he could ride on. A 1" X 6" board 6 feet long was used for the body, and Donnie cut a 5-foot long, 2" X 4" board into two equal lengths for the front and rear axels. Donnie drove a single nail through the body board into the center of the front axel so it would pivot for steering. An elderly neighbor, Mr. Spaulding, saw Donnie struggling to build the car, and he was interested to see the six year old attempting such a project.

After watching for a few minutes, Mr. Spaulding asked Donnie how he was going to mount the wheels on the ends of the 2" X 4" wood axels. Donnie said he was going to use nails. Smiling, Mr. Spaulding quickly went to his house and retrieved four spikes. By the time he returned, Donnie had nailed the wheels on. The nails were too small, and they had bent and pulled out when Donnie tried to put any weight on them. Handing Donnie the four spikes, Mr. Spaulding said, "Here, try these," and he held each end of the car up as Donnie hammered in the spikes to mount the wheels. Now finished with his project, Donnie thanked Mr. Spaulding who then went home saying, "That's the most fun I've had this week."

Donnie brought Esther outside and proudly showed her the car. When he sat on the car, the body board bent enough under his weight that the middle of the board dragged on the ground. Esther struggled to keep from laughing as she praised Donnie for his creation. She felt proud, but also a little sad to see her "baby's" developing interests and ambition; he was growing up. Donnie's attention span had already been stretched beyond its limit while building the car. After showing off his work, he became distracted by the little girl next door who came over to play, and he abandoned his career in automotive design forever.

Time passed quickly, and it was late spring again. Donnie finished the first grade, and the one-year lease on the house was nearing expiration.

One weekend, Emmett came home literally beaming and joyfully said, "I got another raise. Now we can buy a small house, if we can find one that's not too expensive".

Esther said, "Oh, that's wonderful news. It'll be nice to live in our own home again, and fix it up the way we want."

"Don't get too carried away, Esther. Remember, we have to save for Donnie's college education. I want him to have a good life, and not have to struggle like I have to make a living."

"I can help with that, Emmett. I've made a new friend, Edith, and she showed me how to tint black and white photographs so they appear to be in color. A photographic studio has seen some of my practice photos, and they've offered to pay me 75 cents for each photo I tint. I've gotten pretty fast at it, and the oil tinting colors are inexpensive, so I should be able to make good money."

"Aw Esther, you don't have to do that. I'm making enough money to support us".

"It's easy and I like doing it, so it's hardly like work. I can do it at home and it'll help us get ahead faster."

Emmett said, "Well if you really want to, it's okay with me."

CHAPTER 15

HOME OWNERS AGAIN

The following Monday, after she dropped Emmett off at the dispatch yard, Esther purchased a newspaper and started pouring over the "Houses for Sale" section. Suddenly, her face lit up with excitement. One small ad read, "By owner. Cozy two-bedroom home close to Grant primary school, 1718 E. 9th St, $1700. Phone: Hawthorne 9527".

Looking at Donnie, she said, "I think I've found a house that's within our price range. I'm going next door to use Reverend Hill's phone."

When Esther returned, her eyes sparkled and her face was flushed with excitement. "Donnie, put on a coat. We're going out to look at that house!"

Emmett got home late the following Friday evening.

Wearily he said, "The power line we're building extends a little further from here each day. Before long, I may only be able to get home once every two or three weeks. I'm tired, but we'd better look for a house this weekend anyway."

"I've got a little surprise for you," Esther said with a wry smile.

"Oh God, has the car broken down? Is the toilet broken? Is the sink drain plugged?" he asked with a little bit of panic in his voice.

"No. I've put earnest money down on a house, subject to your approval. I'm sorry I had to do it without you having a say in it, but I had to act fast to tie the deal down. Another couple wanted the house, but they didn't have enough for the earnest money. They were trying to get a loan, but hadn't been successful by the time I made our offer."

"Oh Esther, I'm glad you went ahead with the deal. Our marriage is an equal partnership, and I trust your judgment. This has been a tough week and I'm worn out, so I'm happy that I don't have to run all over town looking at houses," Emmett said with relief in his voice.

Esther looked relieved too; she hadn't been sure about how Emmett would react to her making such a big decision without first consulting him.

On Saturday they all went to look at the new house which was a just as advertised if the words, "very small" were substituted for the word, "cozy" in the ad. (Esther had learned that this is a standard translation in many real estate advertisements.) Emmett carefully looked the house over, and said, "You really did well, Esther. The place is awfully small, but it's in good shape, and it's a bargain for the price we are paying."

On Monday, Emmett arranged to take a week of vacation. Within the next few days, he had obtained a loan, made the down payment on the house, and completed the deal. The family once again began hauling their belongings to another location. This time, however, they were excited and happy because they were moving into their own home for the first time since leaving Philomath. At last, they could again have their own appliances and furniture. Donnie was also caught up in the excitement, and he was trying to lift boxes too big for him to manage. Esther and Emmett laughed as they watched him trying to lift a box bigger than he was.

"Here, carry this important box very carefully out to the car," Esther said, handing a small box to Donnie.

"Okay mom," Donnie said, beaming with pride that he was being entrusted with such an important task.

As six-year old Donnie disappeared through the doorway, Esther noticed a worried look on Emmett's face. She whispered "Don't worry, it's only a box of our old flatware."

After a several days and many car trips hauling boxes, the last box was finally carried into the new house. Later, a moving van arrived with the appliances and furniture from the Philomath house.

While Esther was unpacking boxes, Donnie was standing around looking bored. She said, "Donnie, you can go out into the yard and play if you want to."

"Yard?" Donnie asked. Not having had a yard during the past two years, he wasn't sure what he was supposed to do with it.

Emmett looked pleased and said "Thank God we again have a yard for him to play in". Their conversation was suddenly interrupted when a Bell Telephone company vehicle drove into the driveway.

"What's this?" Esther asked.

Emmett said. "I have a surprise for you. We are getting a telephone."

"Can we afford it?"

"Yeah, we sure can. Remember the pay raise I got?"

"Oh, yeah. I guess I just can't get used to having money for more than the bare essentials. By the way, I meant to tell you that the Wilsons have offered to buy our Philomath house."

"Wilsons?"

"Yes, in all the hubbub of buying this house and moving, I forgot to tell you. We got a letter from them offering to buy the place."

"My God, Esther, that's good news. When were you planning to tell me?"

"I just did."

"Okay."

"You always have to have the last word, don't you."

"Yes."

CHAPTER 16

INTO THE STORM

Life settled into a familiar routine in the new home for several months. Donnie attended second grade, Esther took care of household chores and tinted photographs with her friend, Edith, and Emmett came home every other weekend. Things were going so well that Esther began worrying that something bad was bound to happen.

It was November, and the weather around Spokane turned cold, cloudy and windy. One Saturday, after Emmett had come home for the weekend, the telephone's irritating clamor pierced the softness of the night at 2 AM. Esther awoke and shuffled into the kitchen to answer it. A short time later, she returned and shook Emmett awake.

"Emmett, wake up. Some idiot on the phone wants to talk to you."

Emmett, suspecting what it was about, got a sly smile on his face and said, "Man or woman?"

Failing to see the humor, Esther said, "Some idiot man. He must not know what time it is."

Emmett disappeared through the bedroom doorway, but soon reappeared with an air of excitement. Esther had gone back to sleep, so Emmett gently shook her awake.

"Not now, I'm too sleepy," Esther mumbled.

"No, not that. I have to leave in a half-hour. A truck will be here to pick me up."

Esther was startled wide-awake by this news. "What is it?" she asked.

"There has been a high wind and heavy snow. Electrical lines are down all over. There are wires down right here in town and lives are in danger. They want all of the crews to report for work immediately."

"Oh Emmett, you've only had a few hours of sleep."

Gleefully, Emmett said "But Esther, think of the overtime pay!"

Esther jumped out of bed, put on a housecoat. There wasn't enough time to build a fire in the cook-stove and prepare a hot breakfast, so she rushed into the kitchen and made Emmett a lunch he could eat later. Just as she finished, Emmett came to the kitchen shaved, dressed and ready to go. He took the lunch, kissed Esther goodbye, and went to the front window to wait. A few minutes later, when the truck pulled up in the street out front, Emmett noticed that the snowplow hadn't yet cleared 9th Street. Snow was halfway up to the truck's wheel hubs, and tire chains had been installed. As Emmett waded through the deep snow, he thought, No wonder they sent the truck for me. I hope that at least the main streets have been cleared, or passenger cars won't be able to go anywhere.

He climbed into the canvass covered back of the truck. There were seven other men, huddled on benches along each side, and he greeted them cheerfully.

"Hi guys. Oh boy I'll bet we're gonna get a lot of overtime at 1-1/2 pay this week end, and maybe even some time at double pay."

A few of the men reluctantly replied, grumpily muttering about having their weekend disrupted, and having to come out in the middle of the night.

Emmett jokingly said, "Aw, what a bunch of pansies."

A short time later, the truck drove up to a place on a snowplowed main street where a large tree had fallen and had broken a 6000-volt line. The line was still hot, and it was writhing around in the street like a snake, spitting blue-white flashes and red-yellow sparks along with a roaring and popping sound. A car was sitting beside the writhing wire, blocked from going forward by the downed tree, which was lying in the street blocking both lanes. The hot wire draped down on the left of the car from a pole on the right side behind the car, so the car couldn't back up without contacting the wire. Trapped inside the car was a terrified woman holding a baby. Emmett was the first one out of the truck. He grabbed a 10-foot long hotstick with a wire clamp attachment, and ran toward the end of the wire. Suddenly the car door opened and the woman, reassured by the presence of a man from the power company, started to step out.

Emmett shouted, "Stop!" The woman, startled, pulled her foot back into the car.

The woman said, "My baby has a high fever and I've got to get her to a hospital right away."

"Okay ma'am, but you will most likely be electrocuted if you step out onto the ground now. Please stay in the car where it's safe until we secure the wire." The woman slammed the car door shut.

Emmett's attention now focused on the sparking, spitting, exploding end of the wire which was melting and getting shorter by the minute, moving closer and closer to the car's gas tank. He attempted to clamp onto the wire, but it kept jumping and writhing. He brought the clamp-end of the hotstick down again and again, attempting to get it onto the wire, but the crafty wire had a mind of its own. Time after time it jumped away at the last instant. The electrical explosions propelling the wire were so violent that there was some danger that it would suddenly jump across the 10-foot distance and strike Emmett. By this time, the situation had gotten desperate; the sparking, melting end of the wire was dangerously close to the car's gas tank. After trying and missing several more times, Emmett finally managed to get the clamp onto the wire. He pulled the wire off the ground away from the car, and the sparking and explosions stopped.

The car door opened a crack, and the woman timorously asked, "Can I get out now?"

"No, the wire hasn't been secured yet," Emmett said, breathing hard from his exertions and excitement in getting the wire under control.

The other men had arrived carrying hot sticks and tools from the back of the truck. Fred started giving orders. "Okay Joe, grip the wire with a hotstick about 10-feet behind Emmett and help him move it up and over the car so we can get the woman and baby out of there. Harry, after the line has been secured, help her get into the cab of the truck where it's warm. The rest of you get any additional tools we'll need to splice this wire hot. The hospital is fed from this line between here and the air switch.

Their backup power system has failed, so we can't kill their power."

Harry called the dispatch office on the truck's short wave radio and requested an ambulance for the woman and her baby. The ambulance would be more reliable than her car since the driver would know which routes to the hospital were clear.

The men set about their assignments. Ernie climbed the pole just beyond the break. He clamped a traveler pulley onto the top of the cross arm near the insulator. Then he cut the dangling end of the dead power line off near the insulator and let it drop. A Grunt got a length of new wire and some additional tools. Then two grunts took up standby positions near Emmett and Joe, who were supporting the hot wire, and Harry positioned himself near Ernie's pole. Fred said, "Okay, you guys know what to do, so go ahead and splice the line."

By this time an ambulance had arrived, and it had departed carrying the woman and her baby. Two adjustable spotlights on the truck were trained on the primary work areas. One of these was on the top of Ernie's pole and the other was at the end of the old, hot wire being supported by Emmett and Joe.

Ernie pulled the end of the new wire up the pole and through the traveler pulley with an insulated hand line. One of the Grunts near Emmett and Joe cut the new section of wire at just the right length. Emmett and Joe donned rubber gloves and continued holding the old hot wire off the ground while they spliced it to the end of the new wire. Using the insulated hand line, Harry pulled the now hot new wire through the traveler pulley with the insulated hand line and took up the slack in the now live new wire until it was at normal height between the two poles. Ernie expertly clamped a jumper from the old wire onto the new wire with a "hot clamp" to pick up the load on the cold line. His accuracy and speed in placing and securing the hot clamp prevented most of the flash that would otherwise have occurred. He spliced the new wire to the old wire near the insulator, removed the jumper, and the line was back in service.

At about 4 AM, the crew was just finishing up when a call came in on the truck short-wave radio. Fred ran over to the truck just as the dispatcher was saying "Over." Fred pressed the send button on the microphone and said, "Okay, go ahead."

The dispatcher said, "There is a power outage on Ivory Street near Grant school. Respond as soon as you can. All other crews are out on jobs. We don't know what caused the outage, so you will have to trouble shoot it yourself."

The men climbed into the back of the truck and proceeded to the Grant School area. Slowly driving down Ivory Street, Fred soon spotted the problem. First they came to a pole where burned out fuses were hanging from their supports on the cross arm. As the truck continued down the street it came to a pole that had been broken off and was on the ground. There was a wrecked car with its front end sitting on top of the pole's stump. Inside the car was a young man who appeared to be unconscious or dead. The lines on the ground were not hot since the fuses had blown. Fred opened the car door with some difficulty, reached in and felt the man's wrist for a pulse.

"He's alive! Call for an ambulance," Fred shouted.

Harry called the dispatcher on the truck radio and requested an ambulance and the police.

Fred surveyed the damaged power line, and said, "We need to get a new pole here as soon as possible". Harry got back on the radio and requested the pole.

Moments later, a police car drove up, and two policemen got out. One photographed the accident scene with a large Graflex camera using flashbulbs, while the other took notes and made measurements. The accident had occurred at the bottom of an incline. A glistening layer of ice and snow, compacted by traffic during the night, covered the road. The car didn't have tire chains, and the driver evidently hadn't realized how slippery the road was. Just as the policemen were finishing their work at the accident scene, an ambulance and a wrecker arrived. After the victim had been taken away in the ambulance, and the car had been towed away, the line crewmen took turns rapidly digging out the old pole's stump.

The crew continued dealing with this and other various power emergencies all day Sunday and throughout the night. Monday at 4PM, Esther and Donnie were in the living room when a Washington Water Power car drove into the driveway. Esther was alarmed, but then became weak with relief to see Emmett get out of the car instead of a stranger coming to tell her that he had been injured or killed.

She said, "Daddy's home!" and she and Donnie hurried to the front door. When Emmett came into the room, his appearance was shocking. Instead of his normal rugged outdoorsman look, he had dark circles under his eyes, and his lips were dry and cracked. His skin was a pale blue gray color, and it was obvious that he was utterly exhausted.

"Oh Emmett, what happened?" Esther inquired.

Emmett said, "Aw, we had to handle a little trouble. I haven't eaten since they fed us a box lunch yesterday. Could you fix me something?"

"Yes, you poor dear. You rest while I make you a big breakfast", Esther said as she hurried into the kitchen. She prepared a hearty breakfast with eggs, sausage, pancakes, fruit, orange juice, coffee, a small steak and milk. She set the kitchen table with the good flatware and two candles. When she had lit the candles, she went into the living room - - and found Emmett fast asleep in the overstuffed chair.

"Oh Emmett, you poor guy," she sighed with quiet resignation as she turned to go put the food away. An hour later, he was still fast asleep. Esther decided not to wake him. She loosened his bootlaces, covered him with a blanket and told Donnie to "be very quiet while Daddy is asleep." About 1 AM, Emmett came into the bedroom.

Esther awoke and said, "Oh, I'll get up and fix you something to eat."

"Naw, I saw the food you made for me yesterday that was in the icebox. I built a fire in the cook stove and warmed up as much as I could eat. I sure appreciate that nice breakfast you'd made. Sorry I passed out on you."

"Oh, that was my fault. I shouldn't have gotten so fancy and taken so long to get it on the table, but I was just so glad to have you home safe... ."

Emmett said, "I'm gonna take a bath, then come to bed for the rest of the night. Go back to sleep. I'll have to get back to the dispatch yard by eight this morning, so I'll need you to warm up the rest of the food at seven o'clock for my breakfast."

Esther laughed. "Okay, I can handle that - - especially the sleeping part."

The next morning, it was snowing hard. Just as Emmett was finishing his breakfast, the phone rang. Esther answered it and said "Uh-huh, uh-huh, okay, I'll tell him," then hung up the phone.

"That was Fred Woodmyer. The company is sending a truck to pick you up in about half an hour. Roads are too bad to drive a passenger car on them this morning. There's a major 110,000-volt line down between here and Colfax. Fred said there are lines down all over this end of Washington, and you might be on the road for a week or more, so pack what you'll need."

Emmett gleefully said, "Oh boy, lots of overtime!" Then he solemnly said, "But I hate to be away from you and Donnie that long."

CHAPTER 17

SUFFERING IN THE COLD

Emmett had just finished packing when he heard the truck horn beep. He kissed Esther goodbye and asked her to explain the situation to Donnie when he got up.

"I will. And please be careful. We want you home alive and in one piece."

The canvas covered crew compartment in the back of the truck was filled with men, equipment and suitcases.

Seeing how crowded and disorganized it was in the usually orderly compartment, Emmett said, "My God, I'll have to sit on someone's lap." Then, as he squeezed past Harry with his suitcase, he said, "How about your lap." Harry smiled and shook his fist in a mock threat as he said, "Not on my lap." Emmett found a place to put his suitcase, then sat in a space on one of the benches just wide enough to squeeze himself into. The man closest to the truck cab slapped it three times, signaling the driver to start up.

The truck slowly bumped, slid and swerved for more than two hours to get to the damaged line. Normally, the trip would have only taken about 45 minutes. It was bitterly cold in the back of the truck, even though the canvas flap had been tied down over the entrance. The truck stopped and the flap was suddenly raised to reveal a raging snowstorm outside. Wind-driven snowflakes were shooting past the entrance in a horizontal, white blur. Fred, who had been riding in the truck cab, appeared at the entrance and said, "Okay men, up and at it. Colfax has been without power for six hours. We've got to get them up and running. Many people don't have heat, and the Iron Lung at the hospital is on emergency power."

As Emmett jumped down out of the back of the truck, he was struck by the bitter cold wind and blowing snow. Visibility was less than 100 feet in the blurry whiteness. Crystalline shards of snowflakes, driven hard by the wind, stung his face and eyes. He could barely see the power line as they approached it in the near white-out conditions. One of the 100-foot towers supporting the line had collapsed.

Emmett said, "My God we've got a big job here."

Fred said, "Yes, and we've got to work fast. Lives depend on it."

Fred and four of his crewmen staggered against the wind and snow to get to various parts of the downed tower. They each inspected a section, then congregated near its base.

"Well, how bad is it?" Fred asked.

Harry said, "The top of the tower is a little bent, but still salvageable."

Emmett said, "My side of the center section looked okay."

"Likewise on my side of the center section," Joe said.

Ernie said, "My side of the bottom section looked okay, except for one foot bracket. It got bent when the tower went over."

Fred said, "Same thing on my side of the bottom section. We'll be able to repair it well enough to hold temporarily until the weather clears. Harry and Ernie, go get some sledgehammers, long handle pry bars, wrenches, a backing rail and a torch. Joe and Emmett, go inspect the downed line to see how much ice formed on it before it went down. Don't worry about touching it. The air gang switches are open, and they will stay open until we finish the work. Another crew is coming to help, and they have placed grounding jumpers on the lines at a tower on each side of us so you don't have to worry about inductance and static charge."

Joe and Emmett staggered through the blizzard to the top of the downed tower, and then disappeared into the snowy whiteness as they branched out in opposite directions along the downed wires. Emmett felt that he was now completely isolated in a cold, white coffin of blinding, wind driven snow. It muffled outside sounds, and except for the sound of the wind and Emmett's own breathing, all else was silent. He thought, "My God, I've never felt so cold and alone."

New snow had filled in the impressions left by the fallen wires, so Emmett dug down in the snow with his gloved hands to find a wire. It wasn't there! He felt around under the snow, but still didn't find the wire. He'd wandered away from it, and had become disoriented. His footprints had rapidly filled with snow, making it impossible to follow them back to the tower. Suddenly his heart started pounding, and he felt an ache in the pit of his stomach and a tightening in his throat as he realized he could be lost in this blizzard.

Meanwhile, Harry and Ernie made several trips to the truck, parked 50 feet away from the downed tower, to get the needed tools. On what they thought was their last trip, Harry said, "Thank God we've finished carrying this stuff. My arms are about to fall off, and my hands are freezing."

Fred said, "Just one more trip, and you'll have it."

"Huh? What'd we forget?" Harry asked.

Fred said, "We'll need the backing rail to back up the bent angle iron tower legs when we hammer them back into shape."

Harry said, "Oh crap! That thing weighs at least 75 pounds."

Chuckling, Fred said, "Well, that's only 37-1/2 pounds each with two of you carrying it."

As Harry and Ernie turned to go, Harry grumbled, "Well, I'd better not drop it on my foot. My hands are so cold I can't feel my fingers."

"Well, put hand socks on under your leather gloves. I thought you'd have enough sense to do that without being told," Fred said as the two men walked toward the truck.

A moment later, the sound of a large vehicle slowly pulling up near the truck pierced the snow-clogged air. The sound was loud enough that Emmett heard it too. He headed toward the sound and stumbled on something solid under the snow. It was one of the downed wires. He quickly lifted it up and saw a thick layer of ice on it. Following the wire, he found his way back to fallen tower, and proceeded to its base. Joe was also just arriving.

As Joe and Emmett approached Fred, Joe said, "There's a heavy ice buildup on the wires I looked at."

Emmett said, "Likewise."

Fred said, "We'll have to knock it off before we can pull the wires up and splice them. Another crew has just arrived in a bus. You guys look cold. If you want to, you can get into the bus and warm up before we start repairing the tower. The other crew can start straightening the bent tower and knocking the ice off the wires."

Joe, Emmett and Fred headed for the bus. Just then, Harry and Ernie were approaching the base of the tower carrying the heavy backing rail between them.

"Where are you guys going?" Harry asked.

Fred said, "To the bus to get warm."

"Yahoo!" Harry and Ernie shouted in unison.

Then, Ernie said, "Even though I have on two pair of long underwear, two shirts and two pair of pants, this cold wind is penetrating right through them."

"What a couple of pansies," Emmett said, trying to suppress his own shivering. His hands ached with the cold from digging around in the snow searching for the wires.

The men gratefully got into the warm bus after the other crew got out. Fred stayed outside for a while explaining the situation to the other foreman. The intensity of the blizzard was diminishing and, although the visibility had increased to several hundred feet, the wind was still blowing.

As Fred got onto the bus, he said, "We have about 20 minutes to get warmed up, then we'll join the other crew and put this mess back together".

During the next twenty minutes, two groups of three men from the second crew busily tried to remove ice from the wires. In addition to the weight of the ice, the wires for this power line were heavy copper cables. Two men in each group held up a 10-foot length of the wire at a time, while a third man used a metal rod to beat off the ice. After 20 minutes, Fred got off the bus, surveyed the de-icing progress, and decided it was too slow.

Fred said, "We've got to get the power on in Colfax, so let's just cut out the section of line between the standing towers and replace it." The other foreman agreed, so Fred went to the truck radio and requested a four-wheel drive trailer truck with several reels of wire, and four new tower anchor foot brackets.

Men working on a tower leg had heated the bent section red-hot. They used a sledgehammer to straighten the bend against the heavy backing rail. Several other men were knocking ice off other parts of the tower. Emmett and Joe were busy using wrenches to remove bolts from the damaged anchor brackets. The coldness of the steel wrench handles penetrated their leather gloves and glove socks, and their hands ached.

The work continued for a time, then Fred said, "Okay men, as soon as you are finished with your present task, get back into the bus and warm up while we wait for the crane truck." Each man getting into the bus was chilled to the bone. Most of the men were shivering, and their teeth were chattering.

Even Emmett, who usually made fun of anyone who complained, said, "Damn, I've never been so cold."

A short time later, a truck pulled up behind the bus. On a 30-foot trailer behind the truck was a crane equipped with traction treads designed to move over snow and rough ground. There were four 30-foot sections of the crane's boom on the trailer, two on each side of the crane. The truck driver and the crane operator were already loosening the chains holding the boom sections in place.

Fred said to his crew, "Okay, enough loafing around. Meet me by the crane."

Fred's men grouped near the first two boom sections, and were joined by the second crew. Fred instructed them to lift the first section off the trailer. The men lined up along the section and lifted with all their strength. The section weighed over 1000 pounds and, even with all the men lifting, it required considerable effort. The same operation was repeated on all four sections of the boom until they were laid all out in the snow.

Fred led his men to the rear of the trailer where there were two heavy handles. He said, "Two of you grab each of these handles, lift up and pull out to extract the crane loading ramps."

Emmett and Joe grabbed the handle on one side, and Harry and Ernie grabbed the other. Grunting and straining, they were able to slowly pull the two heavy ramps rearward out of their compartments under the trailer bed. It required all the combined strength of two men to lift each ramp up and outward over the retaining lip. The ramps were on rollers, so they moved easily after they cleared the retaining lip.

"Now, get these off the trailer and install them under the ramps," Fred said, pointing to four ramp support braces.

After the braces were installed, Fred directed his attention to the crane operator. "Okay, Felix, do your stuff."

Felix climbed into the cab and drove the crane slowly down the ramps onto the snow. Then he went through the procedure to install the boom sections on the crane.

Meanwhile, Fred determined the reason for the tower's collapse. Digging the snow off the concrete base pads, he discovered that the bolts anchoring two of the tower's feet had broken off as brittle as glass. Just then, Emmett and Joe arrived for more job assignments.

Fred said, "See these stumps of broken bolts? The bolts must have been installed before ductile-to-brittle transition temperature was understood. Older steel becomes brittle when it gets too cold. Newer bolts are alloyed to prevent this. We'll have a devil of a time getting these stumps out. They're threaded into a steel anchor plate embedded in the concrete, and they are probably rusted in. They're too short to get a pipe wrench onto, so we'll have to weld extension studs onto them."

In Colfax the effects of being without power for so long were starting to have serious consequences. The emergency power generator at the hospital had failed. Orderlies were pumping the iron lung by hand to keep a paralyzed polio patient alive. Frozen foods In the grocery store were starting to thaw and would have to be moved outside. There had been two car crashes because the traffic light at a major intersection was not working. Many homes were without heat. People who had electric refrigerators, instead of iceboxes, had to place containers of compacted snow in them, or put the food outdoors where it would freeze. There was an almost continuous stream of irate telephone calls to the local power company office complaining about the long outage. Callers were unaware of the intense drama unfolding on their behalf just a few miles away. They only knew that they had been too long without power, and they weren't seeing anyone working to restore it.

Back at the job site, a welder had just finished welding studs onto the broken bolt stumps.

"Well, here goes," Emmett said as he clamped a 3 foot pipe wrench onto the first stud. With a mighty effort, he managed to turn it a little.

Teasingly, Fred said "Oh come on, Emmett, don't be such a little girl."

Emmett's face reddened at the thought of being considered anything less than a strong, masculine man. With a mighty effort, he put all of his strength into it and the weld suddenly snapped.

"My God Emmett, I said unscrew it, not break it. Take it easy," Fred said.

"Sorry, but you made me mad when you called me a little girl."

Fred chuckled. "Hwoo, hwoo, Remind me not to make you mad in the future."

After the broken weld had been repaired Emmett applied penetrating oil to the old bolt stumps, then carefully removed them.

A truck arrived carrying reels of wire and new foot brackets. Grunts from both crews started laying out three new sections of wire side-by-side on the ground between the two adjacent towers that were each about 400 feet from the fallen tower.

Fred shouted, "Bring up the crane."

The crane roared to life, then clanked and creaked into position and lowered its hook at the top of the downed tower. Ernie attached the crane's hook to the newly repaired tower and signaled the operator to begin lifting. Fred gave various hand signals to the crane operator to guide the tower up into position. The wind was blowing the crane-suspended tower back and forth, requiring several men to steady it and line it up with the foot brackets.

After the tower was bolted onto its foot brackets, Emmett and Ernie began climbing to the top. The sharp wind blew snow crystals into the men's faces and eyes, and some of it was sticking to the tower, piling up in a little ridge on top of each horizontal structural member. Emmett's hands were numb with cold as he gripped the icy steel during his climb. His feet were slipping on the snow-coated metal. He couldn't fasten his safety lanyard until he got to the top since cross bracing of the tower would prevent him from sliding it upward during the climb. Thirty feet from the ground, Emmett's right foot slipped completely off the tower as he was stepping upward, and he found himself dangling by his cold, numb hands from the cross brace. He thought, I can't feel my hands well enough to even tell how secure my grip is on this brace. My God, I wonder if I'm going to make it to the top without falling? Even though the temperature was a freezing 20 degrees, and his hands and feet were cold, Emmett was sweating profusely due to the nerve strain and physical stress of climbing the tower. He managed to get his foot back onto the cross brace and continue climbing. At the 80-foot level, he slipped again and nearly fell. He worried that even though the line was not hot, he might not live through the dangers of this day. Finally, he arrived at the 100-foot level and the tower's crossbeam just as Ernie detached the crane hook from it. The crane operator lowered the hook, and a grunt hooked it onto one of the new wire sections that had been laid out past the tower on the ground. The wire was then lifted into position.

Emmett climbed out to the end of the tower's crossbeam to fasten the new wire to the bottom of the insulator string. Normally, a hook-ladder would have been hung from the crossbeam so the lineman could stand on it to perform this operation. However, the icy wind 100 feet above the ground was much stronger than at ground level, and Emmett decided it would make a ladder too hard to handle.

Emmett's woolen long-underwear had soaked through with sweat making it less protective against the icy blast, and he began shivering. His eyes were burning from being bombarded by the shards of wind-driven snow, and he thought about how nice it would be to climb down right now and get into the warm bus. However, the vital work of restoring power to Colfax still had to be finished.

Emmett attached his safety lanyard to the slippery, snow covered cross beam and wrapped his legs around it. Inching forward to a good position, he leaned down and pulled the crane hook supporting the wire over to line the wire up with the clamp on the bottom of insulator string. Then he signaled the crane operator to lift slightly to bring the wire into the clamping groove. Leaning down even further, he bolted the clamping shoe in place, secured the wire, and released the crane hook. He pulled himself back up on top of the cross beam and sat upright with his legs dangling as he placed the wrench back in his tool belt. A sudden, powerful gust of wind rammed into him, knocking him off balance, and he plummeted toward the ground. A second later his safety lanyard yanked upward on his tool belt, making a sound like snapping a towel. Emmett was relieved and thankful for his safety lanyard, but a sharp pain shot through his body as his tool belt dug into his side. He was dangling helplessly on his lanyard 6 feet under the cross beam. The wind was blowing him around, causing him to swing and whirl wildly on the lanyard. He was in pain, getting dizzy, and starting to feel sick. Gripping his safety lanyard, he tried to pull himself back up to the crossbeam, but the snow-coated lanyard was too slippery.

Suddenly, Ernie appeared above Emmett and dropped a hand line to him after tying it to the crossbeam. Emmett grabbed the hand line and stopped whirling. Supported at his middle in a horizontal position by his safety lanyard, he used the hand line to pull himself upright. Then, getting one turn of the rope wrapped around his hand, he pulled himself up where he could grab the crossbeam with his other hand. He grimaced from the pain in his side and the effort it took to get both hands on the crossbeam. Finally, he got a leg over the top of the beam and pulled himself up.

Ernie said, "Emmett, you look awful. Are you in pain?" Emmett's face was ashen, and his eyes were slits half closed against the pain and wind driven snow. He was gritting his teeth, and his lips were so tightly pressed together that there was a band of white around his mouth.

Emmett said, "Yeah, my damn belt nearly cut me in two!"

"I'll bet you're glad it did."

"Yeah, it hurt like hell, but it kept me alive."

"Emmett, you go on down. I'll finish up here."

"No thanks, Ernie. I've got a job to do and I intend to finish it."

Finally, after finishing the work at the top of the tower, the two men began climbing down to the ground where the warm bus and a much-needed rest awaited. Emmett was chilled and exhausted from his painful ordeal and the physical work he'd done. His arms and legs felt like they were made of lead, and he had to stop every few minutes to rest during his descent. Ernie was also tiring and had to rest often. Both men knew that they would freeze unless they pushed hard to keep moving. Giving in to the urge to sleep would result in certain death. Finally, after 20 minutes that seemed like an eternity, they got to the ground, staggered onto the bus, and settled into the blessed warmth and comfort of padded seats.

The other linemen climbed the adjacent towers, cut away the ice-coated sections of old wire, and completed the repair work at this location.

Fred got on the truck radio and informed the dispatcher that the air switches could be closed. A few minutes later, the electricity came on in Colfax. The iron lung started with a whir, much to the relief of the exhausted orderlies who had been pumping it by hand for many hours.

Fred let the men stay on the bus to drink coffee and rest for half an hour. Then he stood up and said, "That's enough loafing around. We've got more work to do. Let's go."

Emmett, whose pain had diminished somewhat, said nothing. Some of the other chilled, exhausted men groaned at the thought, but they all accepted the responsibility of restoring power to the many customers who still had none. Every man in Fred's crew dragged himself out of the warm bus and climbed back into the cold crew compartment of the line truck to continue their struggle against the destructive power of the wind and snow.

CHAPTER 18

THE ACCIDENT AND THE AMAZON COOKS

The snowfall had dwindled to only a few sporadic flakes, and the wind had diminished to 20-MPH, but it was still below freezing. The truck rumbled along various back roads for an hour, then stopped near a downed 60,000-volt power line that had broken in two places. There were three poles between the breaks, and one pole just beyond each break. The distance along this five-pole section was about 1200 feet. After they had gotten out of the truck, the men surveyed the damage.

Fred said, "This wire is old, and fatigue caused it to break. We'll have to string new wire through this entire 5-pole section." Fred saw that the fuses located on the first pole had blown, so the line wasn't hot. He thought this would make the work easier and safer. Before the day was over, he would have a reason to reconsider this thought.

The men climbed all the poles, removed the old section of wire, and installed traveler pulleys on all of the cross arms. Emmett installed the pulley on the first pole. He had to lean out on his safety belt and twist his body to reach far out on the cross arm. Sharp pains shot through his side that had been injured on the tower earlier. He grimaced and gritted his teeth against the pain as he attached the pulley on the end of the cross arm. Because of its 1200-foot length, the new wire was to be pulled through the pulleys using the truck.

Emmett, Joe and Ernie threaded a strong, flexible, lightweight tow cable through all of the pulleys and attached it to the truck. Emmett had threaded the cable through the pulley on the first pole, and he had remained at the top of the pole to connect the new wire to the old wire after the tow cable finished pulling the new wire through all of the pulleys.

Vern and Harry had placed a payout reel of new #2 wire on the ground near Emmett's pole. Harry attached the end of the tow cable to the end of the new wire, and gave the signal for the truck at the other end of the tow cable to start pulling. At first, the wire came off the reel smoothly. However, after the cable-to-wire joint had passed through Emmett's traveler, the wire started traveling with a jerky, tightening and loosening motion. A snarl formed in the wire about 15 feet from the pulley, and Emmett could see that it would have to be straightened out before it would pass through the pulley.

Emmett shouted, "Whoa! Hold it!"

The truck driver couldn't hear Emmett's distant shout above the noise of the truck engine. Emmett watched helplessly as the snarl in the wire rapidly approached the pulley. As it got closer and closer, Emmett braced himself for the inevitable impact, and wondered if he would be thrown off the pole by the wild swaying that was about to happen. He wondered if the snow on the ground 40 feet below would cushion his fall enough to prevent broken bones. The snarl struck the pulley and the cable suddenly pulled taut with a buzzing roar as it vibrated like a giant double bass violin string.

There was a loud crack, then a splitting sound as the 5/8-inch bolt holding the cross arm on the pole was forced by the pull at the end of the cross arm to split the pole lengthwise. More than half of the pole split away from top to bottom and fell to the ground, leaving Emmett standing on the one climbing hook that had a spur stuck into the remaining upright snag. His 3-inch wide, 1/4" thick leather safety belt around the pole had pulled taught around the pole, then broke, leaving Emmett with the two ends of his safety belt dangling from the clips on each side of his tool belt. He hung onto the snag with all his strength as it swayed violently back and forth. Then, Emmett's remaining support spur kicked out and he slid down the snag with his arms wrapped around it to slow his descent. He felt searing pain as hundreds of slivers from the pole stabbed through his jacket and shirt.

When Emmett reached the ground, Fred asked, "My God Emmett, are you all right?"

"Yeah, I just picked up a couple of slivers," Emmett said, trying to maintain a brave face.

They went to the truck and got into the warm cab. Fred unclipped the first aid kit from its bracket in the truck cab. He took out a bottle of Mercurochrome as Emmett removed his jacket, woolen undershirt, and shirt. The skin on his chest, and inner surface of his arms, was black with slivers from the weathered pole. He also had a large bruise on his side just above his waist where the safety lanyard had stopped his fall from the tower earlier.

"We'd better get you to a hospital," Fred said, after seeing the extent of Emmett's injuries.

"Nah, it's just a scratch. I'll live. We've got to finish repairing this line," Emmett said, in his best tough guy voice.

"Well, okay, but at least let me pull out the largest slivers and swab some Mercurochrome on it."

"Yeah, OK," Emmett said.

Fred used a pair of tweezers to pull out at least 50 slivers ranging from matchstick to toothpick size. Then he dug out many of the smaller slivers.

After half an hour, Emmett said, "This is taking too long, and we've got a lot of work to do, so just leave the rest of the slivers. I'll go to a Doctor and have them taken care of when I get home."

Fred agreed, and painted Emmett's chest and arms with the red antiseptic. When he was done, he chuckled and said, "Remind me to put a quart of Mercurochrome in the first aid kit. Next time you do this, would you please avoid the slivers?"

In spite of the searing pain from the remaining slivers, Emmett maintained his tough-guy image by chuckling as he said, "If you're going to split poles when I'm on them, you'd better put in a gallon."

Fred gathered the men together at the truck and said, "We'll have to wait for another pole to be brought out here before we can finish this job, so let's take a break and eat lunch while we wait." The men climbed into the truck's canvas covered crew compartment and got their lunch boxes, while Fred used the truck radio to request a new pole.

After lunch, the men took turns digging out the old, split pole, leaving an 8-foot deep hole for the base of the new pole. Fred told Emmett to rest and recover from his injuries. The top layer of soil was frozen, and there were many fist-sized rocks and gravel in the deeper soil. The soil had been deposited during the last Ice Age by the Missoula floods that occurred several times between

13,000 and 15,000 years ago. Ice dams had blocked a narrow river passage through the Montana mountains. Each time this happened, the dam produced a great lake, near what is now Missoula, Montana, then broke releasing a wall of water up to 80-feet high that roared through the mountain valleys as the lake suddenly drained. These torrents passed through the panhandle of Idaho, and the Spokane Valley, at speeds up to 85 MPH finally exiting through the Eastern Washington and Oregon plains into the Columbia River Gorge and then into the Pacific Ocean. Soil and rocks ripped out of the mountains by the torrent's headlong rush were deposited everywhere in its path. Boulders, some weighing more than 35 tons, dot the landscape in eastern Washington and Oregon. These boulders were carried to their final locations as cargo embedded in islands of glacial ice floating on the raging flood like storm-tossed ships. Each chunk of ice deposited its cargo wherever it melted enough that it could no longer support its heavy load.

The men were just finishing digging the hole when a truck and trailer carrying the new pole arrived. They installed the new pole together with the old cross arm and insulators. The new section of line was installed and connected, blown fuses were restored and the line was again delivering power to irate customers who had little tolerance for having been without power since morning. By this time it was dark. The final work had been done in light from spotlights on the truck, and large hand-held electric lanterns directed onto the worksites by the grunts. Fred gathered the men together at the back of the truck. There in the chill night, and in the harsh light and deep shadows formed by the electric lanterns, he made a solemn announcement. "Men, you've worked hard and I think I'll let you rest a little while before we do the next job."

The cold, exhausted men groaned.

Fred chuckled. "Hwoo, hwoo, a little while -- like overnight."

Hearing this, the men gave a loud cheer.

The line truck hauled the men to an old farmhouse that had been converted to a boarding house. Two large, rough-talking, Amazon-like women in their early 60's ran the place. They were notorious for bickering and cursing in the kitchen as they prepared meals. They kept the place spotless, except for a male bulldog they called "Baby". The dog was loved by the old ladies as if it were their only child, and it was allowed to roam everywhere in the house.

At dinner, the dog stationed itself a short distance from the table and begged for food with a well practiced whimper. Steaks, potatoes, gravy and vegetables were served to the men family style in copious quantity. The men dug in enthusiastically, each taking a large steak.

Emmett sawed off a small piece of his steak and popped it into his mouth. It was immediately obvious that the steak must have once been part of an old boot. He managed to swallow the piece almost whole; chewing it was impossible. Overhearing the "gourmet" cooks loudly arguing and swearing in the kitchen, he decided that it would be best not to upset the two poor old ladies by refusing to eat his steak. He was pondering how to unobtrusively get rid of it.

Seeing that Emmett wasn't eating his steak, the dog realized there might be a real opportunity and he moved closer, whimpering directly at Emmett and pawing the air with one front foot. Thick drool began oozing out of the dog's mouth forming puddles on the floor. Strands of drool hung down from his chin. Whenever Baby moved, the hanging drool swayed back and forth under his chin like transparent strands of limp spaghetti. After seeing several of the men struggling with their steaks, most of the men placed their steaks untouched back onto the serving platter.

Emmett, angered by the quality of the steak, and the sickening spectacle of the drooling dog, decided to use the steak as a weapon and get rid of it at the same time. He threw it at the dog's face. The dog grabbed the meat in his jaws and tried to chew it. Failing that, he tried to swallow it in one piece, but choked on it. He ran into the kitchen choking and gagging, with half of the steak hanging out of his mouth. This caused a loud uproar in the kitchen as the cooks shouted and swore while extracting the meat from their choking, snarling Baby, who couldn't chew or swallow it, but didn't want to give it up.

After a few minutes, the commotion in the kitchen subsided and the cooks burst into the dining room. Surveying the scene, they saw that only a couple of the men had steaks on their plates. The rest of the men were sitting before meatless plates trying to look as innocent as possible. "Okay, which one of you bastards wasted good meat, and damn near killed Baby?"

Silence.

"Tell us or there will be no more food served here for any of you."

Silence.

"Okay, have it your way. There'll be no more food."

At that moment, Emmett wasn't certain how the other men felt, but he thought to himself, Thank God!

The next morning, Fred took the crew to a restaurant in a nearby town, and they all enjoyed a hearty breakfast. Emmett was considered somewhat of a hero for releasing them from the clutches of the Amazon cooks.

The crew completed a number of other line repair jobs, then returned to Spokane. When Emmett arrived home, Esther and Donnie were in the living room listening to the radio. Donnie was on the floor playing with some toy cars, and Esther was busy with needle and thread mending a shirt. They hadn't heard the truck, and it caught them by surprise when Emmett opened the front door. They both excitedly jumped to their feet and Donnie exclaimed, "Daddy!" as he ran to Emmett and wrapped his arms around one leg. Esther walked over and gave Emmett a big kiss.

"Oh Emmett, I'm so glad you were able to come home this soon. I thought you might be gone for several more weeks, and we've missed you terribly," Esther said as she gave him a hug. The hug made him wince because of his injuries.

When his parents finished hugging and kissing, Donnie was still clinging to one of his dad's legs. Emmett started limping toward the kitchen and asked, "What's this growth on my leg? I can hardly walk."

Donnie giggled and hugged the leg even harder. Then Emmett reached down, plucked the "growth" off of his leg, and hugged and kissed it. Pleased with all of this attention, Donnie laughed.

"Are you hungry?" Esther asked.

"Yeah. I haven't eaten anything since lunchtime", Emmett replied.

When she started for the kitchen, she suddenly noticed that Emmett's coat was frayed and even torn in a couple of places.

"What happened to your coat?" she asked.

"Here, I'll show you", Emmett replied.

He removed his coat, shirt, and undershirt to reveal his bruised side and sliver-laden chest and arms.

"Oh, Emmett! What happened?" Esther asked, with an expression and tone of voice that reflected the horror she was feeling.

Emmett told her the story of his fall from the tower, and how a pole had split and had nearly thrown him off.

When he had finished telling her about the dangers he'd faced, Esther got a determined look on her face and said, "That's it! I want you to get a safer job!"

Emmett said, "Okay. After what's happened the past couple of days, I've been considering that myself."

CHAPTER 19

A SAFER JOB?

For the next year, Emmett continued working in the power line crew. The work was almost as uncomfortable and dangerous in the hot, dry, dusty summer as it was in the winter. Summer temperatures in the arid sagebrush country of eastern Washington often exceed 110 degrees in the shade, and there isn't much shade at the top of a power pole.

Emmett was more experienced now, and more safety equipment and procedures had been developed, so narrow escapes happened less frequently. However, they still happened occasionally, so he signed up for a night class in an attempt to prepare himself for a safer job. The class met on Wednesday and Saturday evenings, and was taught from a 2-inch thick textbook entitled, "Audel's Handy Book of Practical Electricity", by Fred D. Graham. This book instructed the student on everything from the basic physics of electricity to details of electrical circuitry. Nearly all electrical machines available in 1936, such as transformers, power converters, generators, and motors were described. The title page of the book claimed that it was a "Ready Reference for Professional Electricians, Students and Electrical Workers", and that it included wiring diagrams. Especially impressive was the picture of Thomas Edison on the flyleaf.

When he first saw the book, Emmett verbalized his thoughts. "Aarrgh, how can I learn all this stuff with only an eighth grade education?" Then he thought, What have I got to lose? Taking a class taught from such an impressive book would surely be worth the expense and effort, and if I can pass the course it might help me get into a safer, well-paying job.

During the next 6 months, Emmett only missed one class. His crew had been called out to respond to an emergency. In keeping with his habit of working as hard as he could at anything he did, he studied intently every spare moment. Finally, the night of the dreaded final exam arrived. Emmett's heart was in his throat. His old nemesis, feeling inferior, was doing its best to paralyze his brain and cheat him out of the success for which he'd worked so hard. Nearly everyone else in the class had graduated from high school, and he felt that they were all smarter than him. He worried that their scores would push the grading curve up so high that he wouldn't even pass; he was dead wrong. Many of the other students were not as highly motivated as Emmett, and they hadn't studied enough. Emmett passed the course with a "B". Now, for the first time in his life, he had the advantage of accredited specialized education helping him stand out from the crowd.

After completing the course, Emmett watched the Washington Water Power Company's bulletin board hoping to spot postings of safer job opportunities for electrical work within the company. A year passed without any suitable postings. Just as he was beginning to get discouraged, Emmett's perserverence paid off. His pulse rate quickened as he read,

"Wanted: Substation operator. Prefer man with power line experience and knowledge of electrical machinery. Will be responsible for operation of the primary substation and generators serving the Bonder Mills and Mulligan Mining Company in Kellogg, Idaho. Good pay. Housing furnished."

Emmett thought, This looks perfect! His heart pounded with excitement as he removed the bulletin and hurried to the main office. Showing it to the receptionist, he said, "I want to apply for this job."

"Here, fill these out and give them back to me", she said handing him some forms.

As Emmett filled out the blanks on the forms, he saw that he was perfectly qualified for the position. He felt light headed and giddy with excitement when he got home that evening.

Esther asked, "what's the matter with you. I've never seen you like this. Have you been drinking?"

"No. I won't tell you because I'm not sure of it, and I don't want to jinx it. But if it works out, I'll be able to grant you a wish."

"A mink coat?"

"No."

"A big diamond bracelet?"

"No."

"A full time servant?"

Emmett looked perplexed. "It's better than any of those things. But I'm not going to tell you, so stop asking."

Esther flushed with excitement as she tried to consider what would be within their means, but better than any of the outlandish things she'd mentioned. "Emmett Green, you haven't been gambling have you?"

"No, now stop asking."

Two weeks later, the telephone rang at about 6:30 PM and Emmett answered. After a brief conversation he walked over to Esther with a pleased expression on his face and said, "Guess what. You've gotten your wish."

"What wish?" Esther asked, looking puzzled.

Emmett said, "I'm getting a less dangerous job. And the best part is this: in addition to decent pay, we will live free of charge in a nice 3-bedroom house supplied by the company. We can sell our present house and invest the money.

"What kind of job is it?"

"Substation operator, and it's completely safe."

"Then why do they pay such good wages?" Esther asked suspiciously.

Emmett chuckled. "Because I'm so highly skilled."

It was true that he now had more credentials for this job than did most men, but he had no idea of the dangers and poor working conditions that were the real reasons for the free rent and high pay. After all, what could go that wrong in a substation and generator building where everything was neat, orderly, and insulated?

Emmett purchased a used trailer and had a trailer hitch installed on his 1937 Plymouth. He engaged a realtor to sell the house, and arranged for a moving company to move household items too large to haul himself. The family packed as many of their belongings as possible into the car and trailer. After the movers had loaded the rest of the items into a van, the family locked the little house for the last time, left the keys with the realtor, and headed for Kellogg, Idaho, 70 miles east of Spokane. Items were packed nearly to the roof in the back seat of the car. The family dog, a recently acquired female Cocker Spaniel that had replaced Trixie after she died, was placed on top of the load in the back seat. She was unhappy about not being able to stand up in the small space, and whined loudly until Emmett opened the back window a little so she could stick her head out into the fresh air.

As they drove, Donnie, who was now 9 years old, laughed. "Look at that crazy dog. Her ears are flapping in the wind like wings and she thinks she's flying." His childish delight made Emmett and Esther laugh too, and they were filled with anticipation and hope.

Just as the last load was carried into the new house from the car and trailer, the movers arrived. They had been delayed by having to wait in line at a truck weighing station. While the movers carried items from the van into the house, Esther set about unpacking the boxes and putting things away. Emmett directed placement of the furniture, set up beds, moved the refrigerator into place, put up towel rods, curtain rods, and took care of other tasks to make the house livable. Donnie was completely absorbed in exploring every nook and cranny of the new house, its basement and its yard. Finally, the big move was over, and although many small tasks remained to be done, the house was reasonably ready. Exhausted, they all sank into bed.

For the next three days, Emmett attended a substation operator's orientation and training class in Spokane. Rather than spending money for an expensive hotel room, he got up at 5:30 each morning so he could have breakfast at home, pack a lunch and get to class by 8:00 AM. Each evening, he drove back to Kellogg in time for dinner.

Some of his classmates found out about the things Emmett was doing to save money, and razzed him on the way to their cars after class. "Hey, Green, you sure are a penny pincher." Emmett just laughed and quoted one of Ben Franklin's sayings, "A penny saved is a penny earned." Emmett's frugal nature had been forged in the furnace of poverty, which had made it necessary for him to work rather than attending high school.

At the end of the class, the men had to take a written qualification exam. Some of the men hadn't paid close enough attention in class, failed the exam, and had to repeat the class. If they failed a second time, they would be fired. Emmett was worried. Once again, he felt inferior due to his lack of formal education. But he had diligently taken notes during class sessions, and had studied hard at home. He was stunned when he got his exam results: 100%! He'd passed! The others who had passed wanted him to go with them to a local bar for some celebratory drinking, but he had to drive home on a winding, narrow mountain highway, and he wanted to get home as soon as possible to give Esther the good news. He had shared with her his fears of failing the course, so she had been worried too. When he got home, she was overjoyed to hear the good news, and they shared a celebratory drink -- lemonade.

The next day, Emmett entered the substation for the first time, accompanied by his partner operator, Harold Morton. A high fence topped with barbed wire surrounded a large area full of humming high voltage transformers, poles, air switches and other equipment required for handling power from the 100,000-volt power lines that descended from the surrounding mountains. The leakage and corona of these lines made a sizzling, rushing, snapping sound, just like the high voltage lines on the poles and towers Emmett had worked on when he was a lineman. Emmett thought, thank God I don't have to climb into that stuff and work on live lines anymore

Leading the way into a small building located on one side of the substation, Harold said, "This is the panel house."

Emmett was overwhelmed by 6-foot high, gray panels that ran the full length of the building and were completely covered with round meters, rectangular recorders drawing wiggly red lines on charts, red, green, yellow and blue pilot lights, red and green switch levers, and black pushbuttons.

Looking intently at Emmett, Harold said, "Men's lives depend on us performing the proper switching actions in response to emergencies."

Emmett was filled with apprehension as the full weight of his new responsibilities started to sink in. Seeing the worried look on Emmett's face, Harold knew that his words had accomplished the desired effect. This was the perfect time to introduce Emmett to the operating manual for the panel house.

Handing Emmett a 3-inch thick loose-leaf notebook crammed full of pages, Harold said, "Here, this describes the latest information on all the equipment and procedures. Learn it by tomorrow morning."

Emmett looked horrified.

Then Harold said, "Don't have a heart attack. I was just kidding. It took me a week to learn the basics, and several months to get comfortable with the rest of it."

Harold pointed to a small, black telephone on an oak desk as he said, "This phone is connected to the city's public telephone system." Then he pointed at a large, old fashioned, crank telephone on the wall opposite the door and said, "This is a special phone that piggybacks voice signals on high voltage power lines between substations for rapid communication. It's called the 'Highline Phone', and it's the only communication link between the main substation here, and many of the smaller substations in remote areas that don't have telephone lines."

That night, Emmett started reading the manual. On the first page it said, "At least one operator has to be at the substation, or on standby, 24 hours a day, seven days a week. The operator's regular duties of reading meters, replacing used-up recorder charts, writing reports, and maintaining equipment are to be performed during an 8-hour shift. This shall be followed by 4-hours on call during which time the operator may go home. Alarm bells will ring in both operator's houses if the instruments detect trouble at the substation. If an alarm bell rings, the operator who is on duty or on call shall, within 4 minutes, reset the alarm system at the substation and take corrective action." Emmett thought, my God, I'm sure going to be tied to this place on a short leash.

Summer lightning storms were intense and frequent that year in the mountains around Kellogg. One morning Emmett was working in the panel house and Harold Morton walked in accompanied by Stan Stephens, the area supervisor.

Emmett was surprised to see them. "What are you guys doing here? Harold, aren't you are on nights this week?"

Stan said, "There's a bad lightning storm headed our way. We're expecting trouble, so we're here to lend a hand. They say that the metal deposits in the mountains around here attract lightening, and this may be a rip-snorter."

Emmett chuckled. "Oh, you didn't think a greenhorn could handle it, huh?"

Stan looked worried. "We'll see."

A moment later, the highline telephone rang. Emmett answered it.

"This is Andy Harris. There's been a lightening strike here in Substation 9. Something has shorted out and a transformer is overheating. Kill the power to this station immediately or the transformer's gonna blow!"

Emmett told Harold and Stan, then ran out of the panel house followed by the two men. The clouds overhead were roiling, black and threatening, and a few large drops of rain were just beginning to pelt the substation, splashing upward from any hard surface they hit. Emmett arrived at a power pole labeled No. 9 and started to unlock the padlock on the operating handle of an air switch.

Harold, who was just coming up behind Emmett, said, "Wait. I think this is switch No. 6. Yes, see here, the nail has come out of the top of the metal number and let it turn upside down. Number 9 is over there."

They ran over to pole No. 9. Emmett removed the padlock and opened the air switch. They looked away as the switch was being opened. A light brighter than daylight illuminated the substation and there was a low, growling roar as a long blue-white arc jumped the 8-foot gap in the open switch. Before either of the other men could say anything, Emmett slammed the switch back closed, then again yanked it open. The arc still didn't break. Emmett slammed the switch closed again and said, "The load is too heavy to break with the air switch. I'll phone the central station in Spokane and get them to open the oil switch and kill power to this district for a few minutes so we can open the air switch."

Emmett ran to the panel house. A few minutes later, he yelled from the doorway, "Open the air switch. You've got three minutes before the district's feed power comes back on."

Harold opened the switch. By this time, the rain was starting to fall faster, drumming heavily on the roof as Harold and Stan ran back into the panel house. A few peals of distant thunder were beginning to echo off the surrounding mountains, and flashes of light danced through the clouds overhead. The storm was getting closer.

Emmett called Substation 9 on the highline phone. "Hello. We opened the air switch. Is everything OK? Good."

Emmett and the others sat down on chairs in the panel house waiting to perform any further switching or resetting of equipment that might be needed. Emmett was sitting beside the highline phone as Stan regaled the men with stories of his adventures as a substation operator years earlier. After a short time, Emmett went over to the panel and began reading meters and recording the data on a clipboard.

Suddenly, there was a loud explosion and the panel house filled with acrid smoke that burned the men's eyes and throats. The wall, where the highline telephone had been, was on fire. Lightning had struck the highline in the substation; it had blown the telephone off the wall and out through the door.

Emmett was startled. Finally, he found his voice. "My God, I'm glad I was over here and not on that chair beside the telephone!" The chair was smoldering.

Harold grabbed a Pyrene fire extinguisher, approved for electrical fires, and began extinguishing the flames.

Meanwhile, Esther had heard the loud boom from the lightning strike, and the alarm bells in the house were ringing. She ran to the window and saw thick smoke rolling out of the panel house doorway. Frantically, she ran to the telephone in the living room and called the fire department.

"Hello. There's been an explosion in the main Bonder Mills substation and it's on fire! My husband's in there. Please come right away."

"Ma'am, is your husband hurt? Shall we send an ambulance?"

"I-I don't know. Just a minute, I'll take another look."

Running back to the window, Esther saw all three men coming out of the panel house, coughing and choking from the smoke.

Relieved, she ran back to the phone and replied, "No. He appears to be okay, thank God."

A few minutes later, bright red and gold fire engines arrived with their sirens screaming. Occupants of nearby houses poured outside to see what had happened.

Esther ran over to the substation fence and frantically shouted Emmett's name. He had gone back into the panel house to inspect the damage and to help Stan and Harold reset equipment that controlled power that fed the mines. This power was required for vital equipment that pumped air into the mines, as well as for lights, elevators, and small electric trains that transported miners and ore for miles through many levels of tunnels. Hundreds of men working in the mines depended on this equipment.

In response to Esther's frantic shouts, Emmett emerged from the still smoking panel house looking embarrassed. "My God, woman, go home. I've got work to do."

"I just wanted to see if you were alright."

"Yeah, yeah. Now go home."

This show of bravado was for the benefit of the other men in the panel house, and the firemen extinguishing the remaining embers. Esther understood this. She had lived with Emmett long enough to know that one of his greatest fears was that other men would see his soft, compassionate side, instead of his tough-guy image.

When he came home for dinner that night, he apologized. "I'm sorry, honey, but I didn't want the other men to think that I'm tied to your apron strings. I have to show that I'm a man or the others will think I'm weak and can't be depended upon in a crisis."

"Oh Emmett, I was so hurt", she said, faking a little sob.

Emmett melted. "My God, I'm sorry. Hurting you is last thing I ever want to do."

Esther brightened up and gave him a big smile. "I was just teasing, you big faker. I know all about your soft side as well as your need to always look tough. Don't worry, I was overjoyed to see you were alright and I wasn't the least bit hurt."

Emmett wasn't on duty, but he returned to the panel house after dinner and stayed all night. The weather conditions were so severe that both operators would almost certainly be needed to handle emergencies.

All night, loud peals of thunder boomed and roared across the sky, and bright flashes from lightening strikes on the nearby hillsides penetrated drawn window shades, momentarily illuminating rooms. Time after time, alarm bells rang in the house where Esther and Donnie were trying to sleep.

Donnie came to Esther's bedroom door looking scared the first few times the alarm bells rang. "Mom, what happened? Is Dad OK?" Donnie was now old enough to understand the dangers his Dad faced.

As calmly as she could, she said, "Yes, son, he's working to keep the power on in the mines."

Finally, she told Donnie to crawl into bed with her. Now, feeling safe, he slept through the uproar for the rest of the night. Esther wasn't so lucky. Time after time, she went to the window and saw great, roaring electrical arcs as air switches were opened. Once, she witnessed a terrifying spectacle; lightning came in on one of the high voltage lines and exploded into arcs and sparks as it was shorted to ground through a lightning arrestor near the panel house. She was afraid that she might lose Emmett to this monster electrical storm. All around him, its lightning bolt offspring were dancing with careless abandon through the substation equipment.

Finally, as morning approached, the storm let up. Emmett came home looking haggard.

Esther greeted him at the door. "I see you are still alive. Harold's wife told me about your narrow escape when lightning came in on the telephone and hit the chair where you had been sitting."

"Yeah, I wasn't going to worry you with that. The panel house is so crowded with equipment that the only place left for the third chair is by the phone. A phone explosion is unusual. The highline system has excellent lightning arrestors, but this time the lightning struck inside the substation."

"I thought you told me this job would be safe."

"Aw, a little lightning couldn't get me."

"Do you want some breakfast?"

"Boy, I'll say. I could eat a horse."

"Will scrambled eggs, ham and toast do?"

"Yeah, it'll do if you don't have a horse."

"Then I imagine you'll want to go to bed. You must be dead tired."

"Naw, I'm on days this week, so I'll have to go right back after breakfast."

CHAPTER 20

NERVE CENTER AND HEART

Several days later, Emmett was getting ready to go to work when Donnie came to him and said, "Dad, during the storm, when the alarm bells were ringing, I started wondering about your work. Could you explain it to me?"

Emmett was pleased that Donnie was interested, and decided to show him the substation, panel house, and generator house. First, he took Donnie into the substation and explained the high voltage lines, the air switches, and the lightning arrestors that prevent damage most of the time. Then he took Donnie into the panel house and explained the meters, switches and chart recorders, which were the nerve center of the power system for the mines.

Donnie quickly got bored. "Dad, this doesn't look very hard. Is reading charts and operating switches all you have to do?"

As they left the panel house, Emmett felt a little barb of anger because Donnie had jumped to the conclusion that the work was simple and unimportant. Emmett decided to explain enough of the details that the kid could better appreciate the nature of what his dad did for a living.

As they walked toward the generator house, Emmett said, "I'll explain the generator house to you as we walk. It's too noisy to explain it when we are inside."

Donnie nodded his head.

Emmett then launched into the explanation. "Just as the panel house is the nerve center of the power system for the mines, the generator house is the heart of the system. When we go in, you'll see two five-foot tall, gray machines called 'generators'. They are powered by drive motors that run on electricity from 2400-volt AC feeder lines from the substation. The generators each produce a low-voltage, high-current DC output that is used to power equipment in the mines. Men's lives depend on a reliable, continuous power flow to critical equipment mines, so a large battery backup system provides temporary DC power for half an hour or so if an emergency shuts down a generator."

Donnie was staring into the distance as he visualized the massive equipment.

Emmett asked, "Is this more interesting to you, Son?"

"Gosh, yes, Dad."

Emmett smiled as he continued. "If a generator becomes overloaded, a protector circuit kicks the generator off line, it starts running down, and the backup automatically takes over to provide power until the batteries run down. When a generator kicks off for any reason, alarm bells ring in our house, and I'm expected to reset the alarm, find the problem and get the generator running within 4 minutes. If I'm on call at home, I have to run to panel house to determine the problem, clear it, then run to the generator House and reset the generator as fast as possible. If the alarm goes off at night while I'm taking a bath, I only have time to pull on my pants and slippers, and run shirtless to the panel House as fast as I can. That's why I try to avoid taking baths when I'm on call."

"What do you mean by 'reset', Dad?"

"To go through a procedure that makes the generator run normally again, Son. Then, Emmett explained some of the emergency procedures, as well as his routine daily tasks.

"Dad, that's an awful lot of stuff to keep track of."

Emmett smiled at his son and said, "This job isn't so simple, is it Son?"

Donnie looked up admiringly at his dad and said, "Wow, I'll say not. How do you know all this stuff?"

Emmett felt a little surge of pride as he said, "From courses I completed, from memorizing the operating manual, and from experience."

Then Emmett said, "Responding to emergencies and performing so many tedious, routine tasks in such a noisy environment is nerve racking, and a lot of men that have done this job became drunks."

"But Dad, you don't drink, do you?"

Emmett paused as he thought of his partner operator, Harold, who had been in the job for a number of years, and was well on his way to becoming an alcoholic.

Then Emmett chuckled as he said, "No, Son, and I don't intend to ever start."

When they entered the generator house, they were assaulted by an intense wall of sound: a high-pitched whine, and a low rumbling roar that shook the concrete floor under them. Ahead of them on both sides of a gray-painted central aisle were the sources of the noise: two mammoth, blue-gray generators. The cavernous generator house's roof was 30-feet above the floor, and was supported by exposed black steel beams. It was dingy and poorly lighted, typical of industrial buildings in the 1930s.

Donnie covered his ears. "My gosh, Dad, it sure is loud in here."

"Huh"?

Shouting, Donnie repeated the question.

"Huh?"

Donnie could see that it was no use trying to make himself heard over the din so he gave up, placed his hands over his ears, and stayed close to his dad. After a short time, as Emmett continued the tour, Donnie's arms got tired and he no longer could hold his hands over his ears.

Just then, a klaxon horn, which served as a bell on the telephone, blared with an explosive BRAAK! The sound was more than loud enough to be easily heard anywhere in the building over the din of the generators. Donnie jumped like a startled deer.

Emmett laughed and shouted into Donnie's ear. "Scared ya huh?" Donnie knew he couldn't shout loud enough to be heard, so he just pulled Emmett's hand toward the door, indicating that he wanted out. The telephone was located in a sound isolation booth beside the door, so Emmett let Donnie out and then answered the phone.

"Hello, this is Emmett Green."

"This is Sam Brayton. An ore train has derailed in the mine. It has shorted out the track power, and is probably causing an overload."

"Thanks for letting me know, Sam. I'll switch off the circuit that supplies your power while you get the train back on its track."

Just as Emmett was hanging up the phone, one of the generators kicked off line from the overload and started running down. Emmett quickly pulled the disconnect switch for the overloaded line, then went through the reset procedure. Even though it had only been off line a few minutes, it would take the massive generator 15-minutes to reach a speed at which its drive motor would again be synchronous with the AC input voltage and able to drive the generator's DC output at full load. The motor was nearly up to synchronous speed when there was a loud boom and rumbling outside that could be heard above the din in the generator house. Another lightning storm had arrived, and lightning had struck nearby.

Emmett looked startled, then relieved. "I'm sure glad that didn't strike any of the equipment while I was in here," he said to himself.

Suddenly, there was another boom. All the lights went out, except the battery powered emergency lights. Both generators began to run down.

CHAPTER 21

EMERGENCY! EMERGENCY!

Emmett surveyed the meters on the control panel, and determined that there wasn't any AC power coming into the generators from the substation. As he ran to the panel house, he saw Harold running toward the panel house from home, pulling up his suspenders. Lightning was striking in the surrounding hills. Two alarm bells were ringing in each man's house, and in the substation. This indicated an extreme emergency with both generators off line, which required the efforts of both men.

Arriving at the panel house first, Emmett found the recently repaired highline telephone ringing.

"Hello. This is Emmett Green."

"Emmett, this is Archie at substation #4. Kill the power to this station. We have to replace the primary transformer."

"Okay, Switch Number 4."

Emmett ran out into the substation yard just as Harold was arriving and said, "Harold, would you open air switch Number 4, then reset the generator feeder power? I have to restart the generators and get them back on line."

"Yeah, OK Emmett."

An unnatural quiet greeted Emmett when he opened the generator house door. He went to the control panel and waited. When the feeder power came on, Emmett sprang into action operating switches and dials that would bring the generators back up to synchronous speed. After 10-minutes, the generators were up to 1/3 of full speed. Emmett was reading meters and writing the information on a clipboard.

Suddenly, a brilliant flash of light outdoors lit up the interior of the generator house through the windows. The flash was simultaneously accompanied by a deafening boom. Smoke and showers of sparks shot out of both generator drive motors, as crackling blue arcs flashed from the motors to the floor and metal control panel, barely missing Emmett. Startled, he jumped away. The building lights went out, and both generators were running down. Lightning had hit the feeder line just outside the building. Emmett tried to get the generators back on line, but they wouldn't respond. A deep silence again slowly descended on the generator house.

Emmett went to the telephone, and called the mine emergency coordinator.

"Hello, this is Martin."

"This is Emmett Green. Lightning took out both generators and the mines are on battery back up power. There's no hope of getting the generators back on line for at least several hours, and the backup batteries will run out of power in less than an hour."

"Emmett, are you sure you can't get the generators started sooner?"

"Yes, the motors are damaged, and it could even take a day or so to repair them."

"Damn it, we'll have to evacuate all of the men from the mines immediately."

"Okay, Martin. Remember to have them turn off all non-essential lights and electrical equipment as they leave."

The gravity of the last two statements weighed heavily on Emmett's mind. Without the ventilation blowers, methane gas would start building up in the mine tunnels. There were hundreds of men on different levels of the mine as deep as two miles underground, and many of them would have to walk a mile or more to lifts that would take them to the surface. Using the transport trains on power from the backup batteries was prohibited; power had to be reserved for the ventilation blowers and the lifts.

After he inspected the generator drive motors, Emmett placed another call. "Hello. This is an emergency. Give me the Regional Power Superintendent." When the superintendent got on the phone, Emmett said, "Stan, this is Emmett. We have a serious problem. Lightning has blown out both generator drive motors, and the mines are now on battery backup power."

"Emmett, have you notified the mine emergency coordinator?"

"Yes."

"Is this a problem you and Harold can solve?"

"No, the motors appear to be too damaged. I think we need to get a repair crew here as soon as possible."

"Are you positive the motors are damaged, and it's not some other problem?"

"Yes, sparks and smoke shot out of both motors, and they won't reset.

"Alright, Emmett, I'll get someone out there as soon as I can, but it'll be after midnight. The Electrical Equipment Engineer is working on a job near Seattle."

"Okay, we'll look for the crew to arrive around midnight."

Emmett was noting meter readings on the backup battery output current and voltage in a logbook when the telephone klaxon horn shattered the silence. Emmett, surprised by the sudden loud noise that stabbed through the unusual quiet, reacted in a manner honed by years of working around dangerous high voltages. He jumped, threw both arms up in front of his face, as if to protect it from some unseen explosion, and let out a strange, primal utterance. "Huunnh!"

Harold, who was just entering the generator house, laughed. "My God, Emmett, your nerves are really shot to hell".

Emmett laughed too. "Yeah, I guess I'm a goner all right."

Harold reached into his pocket and produced a flask of whiskey. "Here, Emmett, have a little of this to calm your nerves."

"No thanks, I never touch the stuff."

Harold said, "Okay, suit yourself," then he took several gulps of firewater from the flask.

The klaxon let out another high intensity "Braaak," and Emmett answered the phone.

"Hello, this is Emmett."

"Hi Emmett. This is Sam. We've got the train back on the track, and we need you to switch our power back on."

"I can give you power from the backup batteries, but both generators are down and…"

"Yeah, the Emergency Coordinator called."

"Oh, you've heard already. Okay, remember not to use the train. You should have power for the lift in a couple of minutes. Good luck!"

Emmett went to the control panel and closed the disconnect switch to send power from the batteries to Sam's section of the mine.

Harold, having overheard Emmett's side of the conversation with Sam, looked surprised, and said, "What happened? The meters and charts in the panel house show that the generators are off line, and that you haven't reset them. I thought maybe you had gone to sleep over here."

"That last lightning strike blew the generator motors and I can't restart them. Sparks shot out of them, and there are beads of metal on the floor around them, so some of the wiring inside the motors must have melted. I called the superintendent and he's arranged for a repair crew to get here around midnight."

"Midnight! Well, there goes any chance of getting some sleep tonight. We'll have to be available to help. They always send the smallest crew possible."

At 12:30 a.m. a panel truck drove into the parking space beside the generator house. Emmett and Harold walked quickly out to the truck. A man, who appeared to be about 50 years old, got out carrying a roll of blueprints. Clean-shaven and well dressed, he was wearing gray slacks, a dark brown dress shirt and a solid color yellow tie. He had the appearance of a professional man, was balding, and his forehead looked twice as high as normal making him look especially intelligent.

Emmett asked, "When is the rest of the crew getting here?"

"My name is Harry Murdel, and I'm the Electrical Equipment Engineer. No one else is available, so I'll need your help to repair or replace the damaged units."

Harold looked at Emmett and said, "Uh huh, what'd I tell you?"

Harry took off his tie, retrieved a toolbox, some meters, and a roll of drawings from the truck. He handed the toolbox to Harold and the meters to Emmett, and they all went into the generator house. Harry spread the drawings and a list of specifications out on a table near the generators. Then, after disconnecting some of the external lead wires going into the generator motors, he began making measurements using one of the meters.

A short time later, he looked up at Harold and Emmett and said, "The motors are broken."

"Oh, are you sure? I suppose the sparks, smoke, and the beads of metal on the floor might have been a clue," Emmett said sarcastically.

Harry said, "It's a hell of a lot of work to repair or replace these units, so I had to make sure that we weren't going off half cocked."

Harry removed bolts that fastened the end on one of the motors. Then he retrieved a heavy beam, and a short cable that had hooks on both ends, from his panel truck. When he returned, he said, "One of you stand on each side of the motor and support this beam." He looped the cable over the beam and hooked it onto the motor's end lifting ring."

Taking a chisel and a large hammer out of his toolbox, Harry cautioned, "Be ready. This will release the end suddenly. It weighs 300 pounds, and I don't want any hurt backs."

Placing the chisel into the end joint, he gave it a couple of sharp whacks. The joint let go. Emmett and Harold staggered backward straining to support the end of the motor.

Harry said, "Set it over there," as he pointed to a vacant area on the floor".

Harry began examining the exposed armature and field coil windings. After a short time, he made a technical announcement.

"Oh crap! The field coils and armature are fried. This'll take specialized equipment and work that we can't handle here. You might as well get some sleep while I order new motors from the warehouse. They should be here by tomorrow afternoon. There won't be much chance to rest after that. I'll spend the rest of the night in my truck."

Emmett said, "Oh, you won't be comfortable in the truck. Come on over to my house. I have a davenport and some extra bedding you can use. You can use my phone to order the new motors."

"Thanks, Emmett. I wasn't looking forward to spending the night in my truck."

By this time, it was 4 AM. When they arrived at the house, Esther got up and put on a housecoat. She greeted the men cheerfully. "Are you hungry? How about some sandwiches? Can I get you something to drink? I've got some chocolate milk."

Harry expressed his approval with childlike glee. "Oh boy, chocolate milk!"

The men slept until about 11 AM. Esther had instructed Donnie, saying, "Be very, very quiet because Daddy and his friend worked all night, and they are still sleeping."

When Esther heard Harry moving around in the living room, she went into the bedroom to wake Emmett. He was already up and nearly finished dressing. When the two men emerged, they looked well rested.

Esther finished cooking breakfast, and called, "Come and get it!" The men quickly sat down at the table and devoured ham, eggs, bacon, toast, orange juice, coffee and Harry's favorite, chocolate milk. Donnie, who was always hungry, wandered into the dining room and joined the men for his second breakfast.

Emmett and Harry returned to the generator house, removed the hold-down bolts from the two generator motors and disconnected the remaining cables. Harold, who had been in the panel house reading meters and replacing recorder charts, walked into the generator house just as the last motor hold-down bolt was being removed.

Emmett jokingly said, "Boy, Harold, you sure timed that right. All the real work is done."

"Well, since you lazy bums decided to sleep all day, someone had to maintain the substation," Harold said cheerfully. (He failed to mention that he hadn't gotten to the substation until 10 AM.) Harold was a little too cheerful. He'd obviously been drinking.

The telephone klaxon blared and Harold answered. "Hello, this is Harold."

"Harold, this is the Mine Emergency Coordinator. Methane gas concentration is increasing in the #1 mine, and it'll soon reach a critical explosive concentration if we don't get power to the ventilation blowers."

"Oh my God! I'm sorry to hear that. The backup batteries have run down, and there's nothing we can do about it until we install the new generator motors. They won't be delivered until this afternoon. I'll let you know when we're closer to getting the power back on."

After hanging up the phone, Harold looked grave as he told Emmett and Harry what he had just heard. The men set about checking the control panel switchgear, doing everything they could think of to determine if it had been damaged; no damage was found.

At 3 PM a flatbed truck carrying two new motors and a small crane pulled into the parking area by the generator house. The crane operator got out of the truck, pulled loading ramps out of the back end, and drove the crane down the ramps. He hooked the crane cable onto one of the motors and hauled it to a large roll-up door in the rear of the generator house.

He opened the door and yelled, "Merry Christmas. I'm Santa Clause. Where do you want me to set this present?"

Harry said, "Set it back on the truck until we've remove the old motors."

"Damn. I wish you'd told me that a little earlier!"

Harry said, "You didn't ask me what I wanted for Christmas."

The crane operator returned the new motor to the truck, and used the crane to move the old motors outside. Then he unloaded the new motors. Harry and Harold helped him carefully set them in place, ready for connection to the generator shafts and input power cables.

Emmett, Harry and Harold sprang into action bolting the new motors down, and connecting them to the electrical supply lines. As they worked, they could hear the crane operator outside, loading the old motors and crane onto the truck, and driving away.

When they had completed the last electrical connection, they installed the shaft couplings. Harold ran to the substation to close switches that would restore power to the feeder line for the generator motors. The telephone klaxon pierced the silence in the generator house, and Emmett answered the phone.

"Hello, this is Emmett."

"This is the Mine Emergency Coordinator. The concentration of methane gas seeping into the mine has reached 95% of critical. It's only a matter of time until something sets it off. We desperately need those blowers. How soon will we have power?"

Emmett said, "We're about ready to start the generators. You should be getting power within the next hour."

As Emmett hung up the phone, Harry looked perplexed. "My God, Emmett, they sure ride you hard here. Don't they know we're going as fast as we can?"

"Harry, I don't blame them for being anxious. One of the tunnels is only about 100-feet under the surface, and it is directly under part of the city."

"Under the city? My God, let's hope nothing else goes wrong!"

Just then, Harold arrived running from the substation. Breathing hard, he said, "I closed the switches. You should have juice now."

Emmett rushed to the generator control panel, and with shaking hands, rapidly performed the reset procedure. Then he pressed the start button for the #1 generator. Nothing happened!

Harold confidently rushed over to the panel. "Oh here, let me do it, newby." He went through the same procedure. Nothing happened.

Harry quickly read a voltmeter on the panel and said, "There's no feeder power input. Harold, are you sure you switched on the correct line?"

"Yes, the output voltage meter for that line indicated 2400-volts after I closed the switch."

Harry continued checking the generator control equipment and new cable connections, while Emmett dashed outside to inspect the feeder line. He ran along the line, stopping to inspect each pole as he came to it. The top of the third pole was cracked and slightly scorched. Three badly burned fuse holders dangled from the cross arm, indicating that the fuses were blown. Harold got to the pole just as Emmett finished surveying the damage.

"Harold, lightning scored a direct hit on the line here. It must've arced through the fuse holders after the fuses blew. That's why the motors were so badly damaged."

"Damn it, Emmett, it'll take another half day to get power to the mines."

"Why?"

"It'll take that long for a line repair crew to get here."

Emmett said, "Why not replace the fuses ourselves?"

"I've never climbed a pole in my life."

"Well, I may be a newby as a substation operator, but I'm a journeyman lineman and I still have my climbing hooks, boots and safety belt. I can replace the fuses in less than an hour."

Harold's face reddened as he realized that the newby knew a lot more than he'd realized. He took a consolation swig of whiskey from his pocket flask, then said, "Okay Emmett, we have some fuse wire in the equipment room, and I know the fuse amperage rating we need."

"Good, I'll run home and get my equipment while you're getting the fuse wire. Open the switch in the substation so I won't have to work the line hot."

Emmett returned wearing his lineman's gear and carrying a skein of hemp rope to use as a hand line. Swinging from a "D" ring one side of his tool belt was a safety belt.

Harry arrived, and said, "I couldn't find anything wrong with the equipment or connections in the generator house."

Harold filled him in on the feeder line problem, and Emmett's plan to replace the fuses.

Harry and Harold watched in awe as Emmett scampered up the pole with practiced ease. Attaching one end of the hand line to his belt, Emmett dropped the other end to the ground. Then, surveying the fuse holders, he loudly expressed some frustration. "Crap!"

Harold and Harry looked up, worried that Emmett had discovered something that meant further delays, and asked in unison, "What's wrong?"

"Lightning welded the fuse wire clamping screws. These fuse holders are useless".

Harold and Harry each uttered some appropriate expletives. When they calmed down, Harold said, "I'll go call the line repair crew."

Looking down from the top of the pole, Emmett said, "Damn it, grunt, who's running this job? You give up too easy. Send up the fuse wire".

Harold reddened, as he once again found himself in the position of newby, rather than an all-knowing expert, and tied the fuse wire on the end of the hand line.

Emmett's experience had taught him to always ensure that a line isn't hot before touching it. He pulled a Wiggins voltage tester out of his pocket, and checked each of the three lines on the supply side of the melted fuse holders. He found that the 2400-volt power hadn't been switched off.

"Damn it, Harold, you didn't cut the power!" he shouted.

"Oh hell, Emmett, I forgot. I'll do it now."

Harold ran to the substation. Emmett knew that when his partner operator was drinking, which was most of the time, he couldn't be trusted in life and death situations.

When the power had finally been switched off, Emmett pulled up the hand line and removed the fuse wire Harold had tied on earlier. After cutting it into three equal lengths, he used Fargo clamps to fasten them onto the power lines, bypassing the gaps left by the damaged fuse holders. He'd built three makeshift fuses.

Scampering down the pole, Emmett smiled as he commanded Harold. "OK grunt, go close the switch and re-energize the line."

Harold felt a new respect for this newby substation operator, and obeyed the journeyman lineman's command.

Back in the generator house, the men again tried starting the #1 generator. Nothing appeared to be happening. Then, slowly, almost imperceptibly, the floor began to vibrate. Then a slight whir could be heard.

Emmett gave a tentative cheer, "Hooray?"

Harry cautioned him. "Too early for that. The generators aren't up to half speed yet."

Just then, the telephone klaxon burst into the stillness of the building, making Emmett and Harry jump. Harold didn't jump. He'd had enough alcohol that he was quite relaxed. Feeling somewhat redeemed from his recent newby-grunt status, by resisting the klaxon shock, he chuckled at the other men as he answered the telephone.

"Hello. This is Harold."

"Good God, Harold, when are you going to get power to us? The gas in the mine is at 98% of critical. It's only a matter of time until something sets it off. We'll have to evacuate part of the city."

"We're just starting the generators now. We should have power to you in about half an hour."

Hanging up the phone, Harold grimly turned to Emmett and Harry, and gave them the news.

Generator #1 was up to about 1/3 of full speed, and the men started through the procedure for starting generator #2. The huge machine was just beginning to turn over, when the input power for both machines suddenly failed and the generator house lights went out.

Harry couldn't help expressing his frustration. "Shit!"

The men ran to the fuse pole and saw that two of the three fuse wires had melted.

Harry turned to Harold and asked, "How did you figure the amperage rating for the fuse wire?"

Harold said, "I used the Amperage readings I recorded a couple of days ago when both generators were running."

Harry's eyes narrowed, his face reddened, and throbbing blood vessels were visible in his forehead. However, he realized that blowing his top would hamper progress, and he managed to maintain his composure. He explained that starting current for the generator drive motors is much higher than the running current after they are at synchronous operating speed.

Then, Harry said, "Harold, you'd better lay off the whiskey when you're working."

Harold, realizing his mistake, was once again red faced. Harry whipped out a small pocket slide rule and calculated the starting current for the generators. Harold went after fuse wire for the newly calculated current rating, while Emmett again strapped on his lineman's gear.

Twenty minutes later, Emmett climbed down the pole. "I think we're in business. Let's give it another try."

Harold ran to the substation and closed the switch to re-energize the generator power-supply line. Then he ran back and caught up with Emmett and Harry as they were entering the generator house. Just as they got inside, the phone klaxon horn went off. In the abnormal silence, the horn was earsplitting and all three men jumped and threw their arms up in the air. Harold had apparently recovered from his alcoholic haze.

Harry said, "I guess our nerve strain and lack of sleep is starting to show."

Harold answered the phone. "Hello. This is Harold."

"Hello, Harold. Gas in the mine has reached the critical explosive level, and the part of the city over the tunnel has been evacuated. When are we going to have power?"

"We had another problem, but we fixed it and we're starting up right now. We should know whether it's going to work within the next few minutes. I'll call you as soon as we know."

After he hung up the phone, Harold looked pale and haggard as he told Emmett and Harry what the Emergency coordinator had said. Then Harold said, "I sure hope we can get the generators started now. Damn it. This delay was my fault for not selecting the correct fuse wire."

The men all felt the gravity of the situation as they once again flew into the procedure for starting the generators. When the necessary switches and dials had been set, and the start button for generator #1 was pressed, there was no immediate response.

Emmett said, "Oh my God!"

Harry said, "Patience."

Then slowly, ever so slowly, there was a slight vibration of the floor under the men's feet. A slight whir and a low moan came from the generator, a portent of the anxiously anticipated deafening sound to come. The men were breathless with anxiety, intently watching the RPM meters, as they started generator #2 and impatiently waited for both generators to get past half speed. Upon reaching that speed, the starting current would be low enough that the makeshift fuses should hold.

It was dark now. Esther had given Donnie his dinner, and was worrying about Emmett who hadn't eaten since their late breakfast that morning. She decided to go ask Emmett if he could take time to eat. As she opened the generator house door, she heard loud whooping and cheering over the still moderate background noise of the generators, both of which were finally running safely at a little over half speed.

Not knowing about the events preceding her arrival, she said, "Oh calm down. I didn't bring any food, and I know you're not so starved for female companionship that you're cheering for me."

Emmett was quick to respond. "The boys were just pleased to see such a beautiful girl."

"Oh Emmett, you're really full of it tonight. Tell me what you were really cheering about. Were you guys listening to a ball game on the radio?"

Emmett related the events of the day, ending with "... and we finally have gotten these damn generators up past half speed."

Esther beamed as she realized that she would soon get her husband back. "Good, I'll go cook dinner. How about you, Harry, would you like to join us?"

"Boy, I sure would! A home cooked meal is an answer to a traveling bachelor's prayer."

Esther realized that Harold probably hadn't eaten lately either. "And how about you, Harold?"

"Naw. My wife will be expecting me for dinner."

Suddenly, the telephone klaxon let out a loud "Braaak". Hearing this sudden ear-splitting sound over the generators, which were not yet up to full speed, Esther and the men were startled.

Harold answered the phone. "Hello."

"This is Martin. Are the generators back on line?"

"Not yet, but the generators are past the halfway point, and they're running fine. We should have power to you in about fifteen minutes."

After listening to Martin for a few more minutes, Harold said "Sorry it took so long for us to get the power back on line. Goodbye."

After hanging up, Harold turned to Harry and Emmett. "I guess you know who that was. Emergency units are standing by with loudspeakers, waiting to give the all clear for people to return to the part of town that's over the mine tunnel. I'm supposed to call the Emergency Coordinator when the generators are back on line. I'll stay here and do the switching if you two want to go with Esther and eat dinner."

Emmett said, "Aw, that's OK, we can stay and help for a few more minutes while Esther goes home and gets dinner started. Besides, something else might go wrong, and we'd just have to drop everything and rush back over here."

Esther said, "Well, don't be too long unless you want crispy critters for dinner"

Harry asked, "What are crispy critters?"

Emmett laughed. "That's what you get when a good dinner has been turned into something resembling rocks, leather and mush by being badly overcooked."

The generators were nearly up to their normal, deafening whine and roar as Esther left to prepare dinner. The men began checking meters, and a few minutes later, the noise suddenly shifted, from some whine and mostly roar, to nearly all roar.

"That's it, they've synchronized!" Harry shouted.

"Thank God," Emmett shouted.

Harold shouted, "Amen."

Emmett and Harry set about switching the generator outputs to the mine's electrical loads, while Harold called the Emergency Response Coordinator.

"Hello. This is Harold Morton. We're back on line. You can start the blowers."

After Harold hung up, the men heard a loud rumbling roar. "My God, what was that? Did something blow?" Harold shouted.

Harry frantically scanned all the meters on the control panel, then shouted, "No, all the electrical circuits are normal. It must have been something outside."

Harold's eyes widened, his forehead wrinkled, his mouth flew open and his face blanched. "My God, do you suppose the mine blew up?" He immediately called the Emergency Coordinator.

"Hello, this is Harold Morton again."

"My God, Harold, don't tell me the generators have failed again."

"No, everything's all right electrically, but we heard a loud boom. What's the status at the mine?"

After listening for a moment, Harold hung up the telephone, and slowly turned to Emmett and Harry with a pained expression on his face.

Emmett shouted, "Tell us, tell us!"

After a long, dramatic pause, Harold suddenly burst out laughing as he shouted over the noise of the generators. "It was only thunder. You should have seen the look on your faces".

Harry looked relieved, and Emmett said, "whew!"

Harold was feeling guilty because of his earlier mistake with the fuse wire, and because of the joke he had just played on the

men. "I'll stay for a while to watch the equipment just in case…
Why don't you guys go to dinner?" he shouted.

Then Harold shouted a question to Emmett. "Are you still
planning to take your day off tomorrow?"

Emmett shouted a reply. "Yeah, if nothing else goes wrong.
I'll take the night shift tonight so you can get some sleep."

"OK. That sounds good to me."

When Emmett and Harry arrived for dinner, Esther had most of
it ready. "You guys go ahead and wash up. I'll have dinner on
the table in about 5 minutes." During her late teenage years,
Esther had worked as a restaurant cook, and she knew how to
quickly prepare lots of good food.

As summer passed and finally faded into fall, there were a few
more lightning storms. None of them was as bad as the two rip-
snorters that had caused so much trouble in early July.

CHAPTER 22

A DAY IN INFAMY

The next morning, after a few hours of sleep, Emmett drove their 1937 Plymouth to the house from a rented garage on the other side of the substation. Harry had spent the night sleeping on the couch again. He had to stay an extra day to make sure the new motors performed correctly, and he'd agreed to stand in for Emmett who was supposed to be on call on his day off, but was taking the family to Spokane for the day. When Emmett arrived at the house, Esther and Donnie were waiting on the front porch. Esther was carrying a picnic basket and a thermos jug.

Emmett looked puzzled. "What's the basket for?"

Esther said, "I thought we'd have a fried chicken picnic lunch at Liberty Park."

Emmett said, "But it'll be cold in the park this time of year."

"We can eat in the car while we watch the ducks in the pond, and toss them bits of bread. It'll be fun."

Emmett, recalling Esther's excellent fried chicken, said, "I'm all for that."

The family spent a pleasant day picnicking and shopping in Spokane. As they were walking past the front window of a radio repair shop, something on a display deck inside the window caught Donnie's attention. It was a box with a picture on the front cover showing a boy holding a soldering iron and building an electronic circuit. In a broad sweep across the top of the front cover were bold, black letters on a red background; "RCA Electronic Experimenter's Kit For Boys". In smaller, black letters on a red background at the bottom were the words, "Build amazing electronic projects: a one tube radio receiver, electronic relay, radio transmitter, and more." The front cover of the box had been removed and placed beside it to reveal the contents. The box contained items that looked strange and wonderful to Donnie: an EK-1000 vacuum tube, a microphone, an earphone, many colorfully banded cylindrical objects in transparent bags labeled "resistors" and "capacitors", and other fascinating things. Donnie stared at these in rapt wonder. He'd read about radio controlled model airplanes in "Model Airplane News" magazine, and he was interested in building one someday. No radio control equipment was available on the market, so the hobbyist had to build his own. Donnie knew he'd have to pass the Federal Communications Commission's electronics and Morse code tests and obtain an Amateur Radio License before he would be permitted to build and operate a radio control transmitter.

Emmett and Esther had walked 50 feet beyond the shop when they discovered that their son wasn't with them.

Esther yelled, "Come on, Donnie. We still have shopping to do."

No response.

Emmett yelled, "Come on."

No response.

Walking back to see what had frozen their child, they found that he was intently focused on the Electronic Kit.

Emmett said, "Hmm, $13.95." Teasingly, he added, "That's expensive for a kid's plaything. Wouldn't you rather have a nice suit of clothes?"

"No, Dad. This kit is really interesting, and I'd sure like to have one."

"Okay, Son, I'll think about it."

Actually, Emmett was pleased that Donnie was showing an interest in something that could lead to a profession. He realized the positive impact this gift could have on his son's life, if the kid's interest didn't flit off in some other direction before learning anything from the kit. While Esther and Donnie went into a department store, Emmett circled back to the radio repair shop and purchased the kit as a Christmas gift for Donnie.

On the way home that evening, Esther turned on the car radio to hear the daily news. President Franklin D. Roosevelt was giving a speech; "...yesterday, December 7th, 1941 -- a day that will live in infamy -- the United States of America was suddenly and deliberately attacked by naval and air forces of the Empire of Japan." Shocked, Emmett and Esther hardly heard the rest of the speech until the president said "...a state of war has existed between the United States and the Japanese Empire...."

Donnie didn't fully understand what the president had said, but he understood the worried looks on the faces of Mom and Dad as they looked at each other in stunned disbelief. He asked, "What's wrong?"

Esther carefully explained. "The Japanese attacked us, and now we have to go to war with them to defend our country."

Donnie, who was now nearly 11 years old, and had studied a little U.S. history in school, asked, "Why would they attack our strong country?"

Esther answered. "Their country is ruled by an emperor and a bunch of warlords that have an inflated idea of their own strength. They don't understand the strength of a free country where most men are willing to fight to the death to remain free, and they think we are weak because of the high value we place on life."

A week later, a registered letter arrived from the War Department that required Emmett's signature on a return receipt as proof that he'd received it. Quickly opening the letter, he read: "As an operator/line patrolman at the substation supplying power to the Bonder Mills and Mulligan mine, you are required, in addition to your other normal duties, to serve as a guard until further notice. As you know, the United States is at war with Japan. The Bonder Mills lead mine is considered a critical strategic facility, and it is feared that saboteurs may attempt to disrupt operations there. For this reason, you are required to carry a pistol or rifle at all times when you are outdoors near power structures, and keep one nearby when you are inside power buildings". The letter went on to say that since he was working in an essential industry, Emmett would not be drafted into the army.

"What is it?" Esther inquired.

"I've been excused from military service since I'm in a job considered essential to the war effort".

"Oh, That's nice, but from what I've seen you would be safer in battle than dealing with the lightning, high voltages and explosions here."

"Well, I'll be safer than most folks here because the government wants me to carry a gun to work."

"I didn't know you could shoot lightning!"

"Aw, Esther."

"Okay, so it was a bad joke. Why do they want you to carry a gun? This is a long way from the battlefields."

"Saboteurs."

Esther's eyes widened, and her brow furrowed. "Oh, Emmett!"

"Aw, don't worry. I don't think there is much danger in a town this small and this far inland."

The next morning, Emmett was scheduled to patrol the high voltage feeder line that brought power over the mountains to the substation. At breakfast, Emmett looked intently at Donnie.

Seeing his Dad suddenly focus directly on him, Donnie was a little bit spooked. "What'd I do, Dad?"

"Nothing, son," Emmett chuckled. "I was just thinking that you might like to go with me on line patrol today."

Donnie relaxed and looked relieved. "Oh". Then after some thought, he regained enough composure to ask a question. "What do you do on patrol?"

"Oh, I just hike along the power lines over the hills behind our house and look for problems like cracked or broken insulators, split or leaning H structures, trees growing up too close to the line and so on."

"What are H structures, Dad?"

"They support the high voltage lines. You know, the pairs of poles that look like a big letter H. There's a support beam high up between the poles, and three insulator strings hanging down supporting the wires."

Esther, overhearing the conversation, asked, "Emmett, do you think it's wise to take Donnie out where there might be saboteurs?"

"There's almost no chance of meeting one out on a power line. The substation right here would make a much juicier target, and Donnie can't hide under his bed for the duration of the war. Besides, like I said before, I don't think it's likely that a saboteur would strike here. There are a lot more important targets elsewhere, like shipyards and aircraft plants."

Donnie was pleased to get so much attention from his busy father. He had no idea what hardships he would encounter on the hike, or the adventure that was about to unfold.

CHAPTER 23

ON PATROL

At about 10 AM, Donnie and Emmett started up the hill behind their house. Emmett was carrying his rifle as required by the government. The sun was well up in the sky, and the morning chill was beginning to retreat from the warm, golden rays. Each time Emmett and Donnie reached the crest, of what had appeared to be a hilltop, another uphill stretch having only slightly lesser slope came into view in front of them.

Donnie was breathing hard, and he was getting concerned. "My gosh, Dad, how much further to the top? This hill is turning into a mountain."

Emmett chuckled. "Keep at it, son, we'll get there soon."

"Dad, I'm getting awfully tired."

"Aw, come on, getting tired won't hurt you. A little hard work is good for you."

Inwardly, Emmett was worried. He realized that unlike his own boyhood, doing chores on the farm and working with his father to log and cut wood, Donnie had never done any hard physical work and was soft and flabby. There were several miles of line to patrol, and Emmett was scheduled to be at the substation at 1:00 PM. The final crest of the hill was in sight, and Emmett knew the terrain ahead was more level. He decided to press on rather than wasting time taking Donnie back home. By the time they reached the top, Donnie was red faced, breathless and sweating profusely.

"Donnie, you look like you could use a drink", Emmett said, unfastening a canteen from his belt.

"Yeah, I, -- sure -- can," Donnie said, gasping so hard for breath that he was barely able to speak.

After a drink and a short rest, they pressed on. At about 11 AM they were trudging through an open field on a high flat-topped ridge. There were weeds up to Donnie's elbows.

Donnie started hollering. "Dad, Dad! My hands are burning like fire!"

"Aw, stop yelling. That won't hurt you. Hold your hands up over your head. The weeds around you are just stinging nettles."

"What are nettles?"

"They're weeds that have stuff on them that makes your skin burn a little when you touch them. Keep your hands out of them and they'll quit burning after a while."

They trudged onward, and Emmett inspected each H structure as he came to it. Donnie lagged behind, barely catching up by the time Emmett was ready to go on to the next structure.

Often, as they came to a structure, Donnie asked the same question. "How much further, Dad?"

Each time, the answer was the same. "Only a little bit farther."

Finally, after asking a dozen or so times, Donnie got the answer he had been anxious to hear. "Down a steep place, just beyond the little rise you see ahead, Mom will be waiting for us in the car."

Donnie gave a long sigh of relief. "Thank God. My feet are hurting, I'm tired, and I'm all sweaty."

They soon arrived at a narrow game trail etched into a steep hillside by the feet of thousands of deer that had passed that way over the centuries. The trail lead diagonally down the slope through an outcropping of marble sized gravel. At the bottom of the slope was a 15-foot drop-off with large, sharp, jagged rocks at the bottom.

Emmett cautioned Donnie. "Now, be careful, son. Stay centered on the path. One misstep and you will slide down the slope as if you are on ball bearings. See the drop-off with the rocks at the bottom?"

"Yeah, Dad. But I'm awfully tired and kind of shaky."

"Aw, you can do it son. Remember, you're descended from a long line of pioneers and woodsmen. You're a Green!"

Instead of paying close attention to where he was placing his feet, Donnie was thinking about how tired he was, and about Mom waiting in the car. Oh, how nice it will be to sit in the soft, comfortable car seat, and just be whisked away home. Donnie got too close to the downhill side of the path, and his foot instantly rolled out from under him on the ball bearing gravel. He went down, instinctively rolling over onto his stomach with his arms outstretched as he fell. When he hit the ground, he spread his legs out and dug his fingers and toes into the gravel trying to get a grip and stop sliding. About eight feet from the path, he managed to stop sliding. At that point, he was about half way down the slope from path to the drop-off. Whenever he breathed too deeply, or moved at all, he slipped a few more inches downward.

It didn't help Donnie's confidence to see the worried look on his Dad's face, and the wild look in his eyes. Emmett checked his rifle to make sure there was no bullet in the chamber. Then he tried to stretch out far enough to reach Donnie with the barrel of the rifle. The gun was too short.

"Hang on, son. Don't move. I've got to find something I can use to pull you up."

"Okay, Dad", Donnie replied, slipping a few inches further down the slope.

Emmett, sure-footed from his years of climbing poles and balancing on cross beams, ran up the path and soon returned with a long, dead tree branch.

"Son, this stick is all I could get. It's brittle, so don't bend it when you grab the end. Just hold it straight when I pull. Dig your toes in and try to push with your feet. We'll inch you up a little at a time."

Emmett lowered one end of the stick and Donnie grabbed it with one hand. With Emmett gingerly pulling, Donnie started moving up the slope inch by inch, digging in his toes and pushing with his free hand. He had moved about three feet up the slope, when the end of the stick suddenly broke off in his hand. Donnie slid about a foot back down the slope.

"Dad!"

"Don't panic, son, we'll get you out of this."

Emmett tried to sound confident, but he was terrified as he visualized his son's broken body lying on the rocks below. He laid down on the path with his left side toward Donnie. Bracing his right arm across the path under his chin, he lowered the remaining length of the stick with his left hand, barely reaching Donnie.

"Grab the stick, son".

"I'm afraid to move. I'll slide some more."

"Just grab the damn stick. It'll keep you from sliding. Otherwise, we'll have to stay here forever."

Visions of lying there on that slope in the rain, wind, and snow through the seasons flashed through Donnie's mind, and he could see that trying to grab the stick was the only reasonable choice.

"Okay, Dad."

Once again, Donnie grabbed the end of the stick and slowly inched his way up the slope. After what seemed like an eternity, Donnie's hand was only about a foot from his dad's powerful hand and safety. Just as both of them were feeling confident that the ordeal was about to end, the stick shattered near Emmett's hand. With the sudden release of the load on the stick, Emmett's hand recoiled and broke the remainder of the stick against the hillside.

Donnie slid about 2 feet back down the slope. He was still holding onto the broken end of the stick and dug it into the gravel to stop his descent. No remaining part of the stick was long enough to use in the rescue.

Emmett grabbed his rifle. Lying on his stomach, he quickly lowered the end of the barrel down toward Donnie.

Meanwhile Esther, who wasn't aware of the dangerous scenario playing out on the hillside above, arrived in the car. "Hmm, I thought I was late. I wonder where my men are? I hope nothing has happened to them," she mused.

Back on the ball bearing gravel slope, the dangerous scenario was still playing out.

"Grab the gun barrel, son."

"I'll slip if I move!"

"Now son, you've got to do it. We've already been through this."

Donnie made a desperate grab and slipped a little further down the slope. However, he managed to grasp 2 inches on the end of the gun barrel with one hand. Then he dug his part of the stick deeper into the gravel with his free hand to get better traction.

"Now be careful inching upward, son, don't try to move too fast. Slow and easy does it. You don't want to lose your grip on the gun. Get the other hand on the gun as soon as you're able."

Donnie, exhausted, once again inched his way up the slope, regaining some of the distance he had lost earlier. Then he quickly moved his free hand up and grabbed the gun barrel with it.

Now, grasping the gun with both hands, he was in a position to be securely pulled up the slope.

"That's the stuff, son! Now, don't get excited and lose your grip. We'll just do this slow and easy."

Emmett's calm voice reassured Donnie, and the boy confidently worked his way back up toward the path. Finally, Emmett was able to grab Donnie's hand and pull him up onto the path.

"Now, watch your step, son."

Donnie picked his way down the remainder of the path slowly, with extreme care, until he reached the bottom of the slope. Emmett had followed closely behind him, ready to grab him at any sign of trouble.

As Emmett dusted off Donnie's clothes, he said, "Son, don't mention our little adventure to your mother. We don't want to worry her."

"OK, Dad."

As Donnie and Emmett got close to the car, Esther could see the expressions on their faces. Her highly sensitive woman's intuition told her that something unusual had happened.

"All right, you guys, what happened?"

Donnie's face turned red. "N-nothing, Mom."

Emmett looked sheepish. "Nothing unusual, Esther. What're we having for lunch?"

"Don't try to change the subject, Emmett. I know something happened. Did a rattlesnake almost bite you? Were you attacked by a saboteur? Shot at by a hunter who thought you were a deer? C'mon, spill it!"

Donnie had turned a deeper shade of red, and could no longer hold back under his mother's intense interrogation. The words welled up and exploded out of his mouth in spite of his best efforts to stop them.

"I fell down a steep place and almost slid off a cliff onto some rocks! Sorry, Dad, I had to tell."

Emmett looked embarrassed now that Esther knew that he had allowed Donnie to get into danger. "Aw, Esther, it wasn't that bad. The drop was only about 15 feet."

"Only 15 feet! Emmett Green! That would have been like falling out of a second story window onto the rocks! Donnie could have been killed! You don't have the sense that God gave geese."

On the drive home, a heavy, dark silence descended between Esther and Emmett. The only thing audible was the car engine. Donnie felt uncomfortable since he was the one who had spilled the beans. He thought he might ease the tension by vindicating his dad. "Dad told me to be careful because the path was dangerous, but I wasn't careful enough and it wasn't Dad's fault. He could have pulled me right up, but the stick broke and…"

Emmett interrupted him. "Quit talking, Son, you're making it worse."

An uncomfortable silence continued to loom inside the car for the rest of the trip.

After an eternity, they completed the 4-mile trip home. Esther and Emmett immediately went into their bedroom and closed the door. Donnie heard agitated voices through the door, but they were muffled and he could only understand occasional words.

"…only eleven years old…could have been killed…"

"But Esther… …and when I was a boy… …make a man out of him…"

Finally, the door opened and two storm clouds blew out of the bedroom. Donnie, seeing the expressions on their faces, looked worried.

Emmett saw Donnie's expression. "Don't worry, Son, Mom's a little upset, but she'll get over it."

The air was heavy with a tomblike silence all through lunch. Donnie was worried. He had never seen his parents act like this. Then he remembered his dad's calming words, "she'll get over it," and felt a little better even though he had a nagging feeling that things might never be all right again.

CHAPTER 24

THE PUNISHMENT

By early evening, Donnie had lost himself in an exciting story in a "Big Little Book" about "Smilin' Jack", an airplane pilot and adventurer. Emmett arrived home from the substation, and he spoke quietly to Esther. The words were too quiet for Donnie to understand, but at least Mom and Dad were speaking to each other, so things seemed OK. Donnie settled back into his reading.

Suddenly, Donnie's reading was interrupted by Esther's voice. "Donnie, grab your coat. Daddy is taking us out to dinner."

Donnie responded enthusiastically. "Do you mean we're going to a restaurant?" He was surprised. His parents' frugality, forged by their earlier years of scrimping and saving just to get by, had developed into a habit. Even now that Emmett had a secure, well paying job, a restaurant meal was a rare occasion for the family.

As he was putting on his coat, Donnie was surprised to see Emmett hugging and kissing Esther. "I thought Mom was mad at you, Dad."

Esther said, "No, we just had a little disagreement." Then she chuckled as she added, "Daddy's been a bad boy and he has to be punished by taking us out to dinner."

Emmett shot back. "Just wait until I get you in the bedroom tonight. I'll show you how bad I can be."

Donnie was worried. He had thought the trouble was over but now, remembering the spanking he'd gotten in the bedroom last year, he was afraid that Mom was going to get spanked.

Seeing the worried expression on Donnie's face, Esther and Emmett both laughed. This relieved Donnie's anxiety as he realized that this had been some kind of joke.

After they arrived at the restaurant, and had a chance to look over the menu, the waitress came over to their table. Looking at Donnie she asked, "What would you like, little man?'

"I'd like two hamburgers with cheese, some macaroni and cheese, a large milkshake, a coke, some ice cream and some pie."

Emmett looked amused. "Whoa now, Son, I know we hiked a long way today, and we haven't eaten since lunch, but I'd be embarrassed to have people think that we haven't fed you anything for a month." Then, looking at the waitress he said, "make that just one hamburger with cheese and a large milkshake. If he's still hungry after that we'll order again. I'll have the Steak Dinner and my wife would like the Pot-roast Dinner."

While they were waiting for their food, Emmett looked earnestly at Esther, reached over and grasped her hand. "Honey, I'm sorry I caused you so much upset and worry today. How would you feel about me getting into a less dangerous job?"

"You mean like joining the Army and going into battle?"

"No. I saw an advertisement in the 'International Brotherhood Of Electrical Workers Newsletter' last night. It said that the shipyards in Portland, Oregon, desperately need experienced electricians to work on electrical systems in warships."

"Oh. Emmett! That would be wonderful. Most of our relatives live in that part of the country, and with gasoline rationing, we aren't able to travel far enough to visit them now. But how will we get enough gas to move that far?"

"Don't worry. I can go to the rationing board and request an increase in our gasoline allotment to cover the move. I'm sure they'll give it to me since I'll be fulfilling a vital defense need."

"I just hope this turns out better than the last time you thought you were getting a less dangerous job. It has been almost as dangerous as being a lineman. All of your electrical jobs so far have scared me to death."

CHAPTER 25

THE HUNT

Donnie, who was now called "Don" by his teachers and friends, was nearly half way through the first semester of the seventh grade, and he was doing well in science and mathematics. Emmett and Esther had decided to minimize the impact on Don's education by waiting until January so they could move during his school's two-week winter break. This would allow plenty of time to prepare for the move, and some time after the move to settle in and get Don into a Portland school before the winter break was over.

The move had to be made in one trip since it was more than 400 miles, and gasoline rationing was tight. Moving companies cost a lot of money. Emmett was not only extremely frugal, but also highly independent because of his upbringing on an isolated homestead in the mountains of Western Oregon. These were factors in his decision to make the move without the help of a moving company.

Travelers in northern Idaho during winter have a high risk of encountering snowstorms on mountain highways. This can cause severe problems for a passenger car pulling a heavily loaded trailer. Emmett, with his usual optimistic attitude of "aw, it'll be alright", bought a used trailer, and Esther started collecting cardboard boxes from grocery stores.

At breakfast one day in late October, Emmett looked lost in thought.

Esther noticed, and asked, "What are you thinking about?"

"The mountains around here are full of deer and I want to go hunting before we leave."

"But Emmett, you aren't as familiar with these mountains as you were with the ones in Oregon."

"That's OK. I'll get one of our friends to go with me."

"Who?"

"I don't know. I'll have to ask around."

"But Emmett, this job has tied you down so much that we don't have any friends outside of the company."

"That's true, but I think I can get Dan or Stan to go with me. Harold can't go since he'll have to run the substation while I'm gone."

Emmett telephoned Dan and Stan. His conversations with both men were almost identical.

"Hi, this is Emmett. I plan to go hunting on Monday, my day off, and I was wondering if you would like to go."

"Gosh, Emmett, it's awfully late in the season."

"Yes, I know, but there are a lot of deer left out there."

"I'm sure sorry. I'd like to go with you, but I have to work on Monday, and I don't have any vacation time left."

"Oh, I'm sorry to hear that. Well, maybe another time."

"Yeah, Emmett, maybe next year,"

"Okay, maybe next year. Goodbye."

Esther had overheard the conversations. "It sounds like the other guys can't go. What are you going to do?"

"I'll have to go alone."

"Oh Emmett, you aren't familiar with …"

Emmett cut her off. "You've already said that. I'll be all right. Remember, I spent my boyhood and youth hunting to put meat on the table for the family."

"Yes, but that was in familiar mountains where you grew up, and your father and older brothers went with you until you knew all the landmarks. What if you are injured? There won't be anyone to help you."

Emmett was irritated, thinking that Esther didn't have confidence in him as an experienced Mountain Man. "I'm going, and that's the end of the discussion."

"Alright, dear, but please be careful."

Emmett finished breakfast at 6:00 AM on Monday. then picked up his rifle and a sandwich that Esther had wrapped in waxed paper so it could be carried in his coat pocket. As he was leaving, he said, "Esther, I'll park the car on Moon Mountain Road, and walk into the forest from there. I should be home by 6:00 or 7:00 o'clock tonight.

When Don returned home from school at about 3:30 PM he asked, "Mom, has Dad returned yet?"

159

"No, he probably won't return for another few hours, unless he's already gotten a deer."

At 7:00 PM Emmett hadn't returned yet, so Esther gave Don his supper. It had gotten dark, and it was snowing. Esther looked worried.

Don noticed her worry. "What's the matter, Mom?"

"Oh, nothing. I'm just wondering why Dad is so late. He must have gotten a deer at the last minute and had to dress it out before tying it onto the car."

Every half hour that went by caused Esther to become more worried. Don, on the other hand, had been reassured by his mother's earlier opinion that everything was all right, and that his dad had merely been delayed. He spent the evening completely absorbed in listening to his evening radio programs: exciting episodes of "The Lone Ranger", "The Green Hornet" and "Charlie Chan", so his mother's dismay didn't become apparent to him until she made a telephone call at 10 PM.

"Hello, Sheriff's Office? This is Esther Green. My Husband went hunting this morning and is long overdue. He said he'd be home by 7 PM. I'm afraid something's happened to him."

"Ma'am, did anyone go with him?"

"No, he's all alone."

"Where did he go?"

"Moon Mountain Road."

"Did he take along any alcoholic beverages?"

"No, he doesn't drink, and he never stops at bars."

"We'll send someone out to look for him, but we'll have to wait until daylight tomorrow morning."

"Oh, I was hoping you could do something right away. He might have been injured or had car trouble or..."

"I'm sorry, but we can't effectively track him at night, and it would be putting the search team at risk."

"Alright, if morning is the best you can do. Please start as early as you can."

By this time, Esther was completely engulfed in worry, and tears were streaming down her face.

Don was frightened. He'd never seen his mother like this. She looked so small and vulnerable that he forgot his fear and was overcome with compassion. He put his arms around her as he'd seen his dad do so many times when she was upset. "It'll be alright, Mom, Dad's strong and smart. He's probably just had car trouble."

This seemed to comfort her. "Thanks, Son, I feel better now. It's late, you'd better go to bed."

"Okay, Mom. Goodnight. Don't worry, Dad'll be alright."

In spite of the brave facade he'd displayed for his mother, Don was worried and didn't sleep very well. When he got up at 5 AM to use the bathroom, he found Esther dozing in the upholstered chair near the telephone. She'd obviously spent the night there. Since she was asleep, he decided to return to bed without disturbing her.

It was 9:00 AM When Don came out of his bedroom. Esther had decided to let him sleep late and stay home from school. She thought he'd be too worried about his dad to concentrate on schoolwork.

"Mom, is there any word about Dad?"

Esther looked haggard and distraught, and it showed in her voice as she said, "No, Son, nothing."

They sat down to breakfast and ate in complete silence, each lost in their thoughts and worries. Circulating over and over in Esther's mind were the thoughts, is Emmett dead or alive? Is he injured and suffering, alone in the silent, cold, snow-covered forest? Will I ever see his big, strong frame coming through the doorway again?

After breakfast, Esther called the Sheriff's Office again.

"Hello, this is Esther Green. Is there any word yet about my husband?"

"No, Ma'am. We have a search team out looking for him. They found his car, but haven't reported anything else yet."

Then, in rapid-fire succession, Esther asked, without waiting for an answer between questions, "How many people are searching? How far into the forest have they looked? Have they found any tracks?"

The person at the sheriff's office simply said, "Don't worry, the search team is very good at what they do. They'll find him."

"All right. Please telephone me the minute you have any news."

As Esther hung up the phone, Don looked hopeful. "What'd they say, Mom?"

"The search party found his car, but he wasn't in it. Oh God, he wasn't in it," she said, ending in a little sob.

"Don't cry, Mom, he'll be alright."

"But Don, he's been out in this sub-freezing weather all night. He may have been injured, or got lost and cold, and became unconscious and froze, or..." Her voice tightened up and trailed off. She could no longer speak so she went into the bedroom and closed the door so Don wouldn't see her increasing distress.

Now Don was so worried that he shed a few tears himself. He tried to get interested in his "Smilin' Jack" story, but the demons of doubt and fear kept recapturing his consciousness. Later, when Esther called him for lunch, the two picked at their food in silence. Esther's eyes were red from crying, and her face was haggard and drawn with worry. After lunch, they retired to their bedrooms.

About 2:30 PM a car pulled up in front of the house. Esther walked slowly and fearfully to the front window, worried that it would be the sheriff's car bringing the news that Emmett was dead. Instead, it was Emmett's car.

Without meaning to, Esther screamed the words, "My God! It's Emmett!"

Don, hearing the commotion, came running from his bedroom in the rear of the house. "What is it? Is Dad OK?"

"Yes, Son, he's home! Thank God, he's home."

When he came in the front door carrying his hunting rifle, Emmett was immediately encased in hugs from Esther and Don who both rushed over and threw their arms around him. Esther was weeping with joy and Don, who considered himself to be quite grown up, was visibly struggling to hold back his tears.

Emmett, who had been struggling just to stay alive during the previous 20 hours, hadn't had time to consider the impact his ordeal was having on his family. He said, "Aw, you should've known I'd be alright."

His apparently cavalier attitude caused Esther to lose her temper. She released her tight hug, and red faced, she looked him straight in the eye. All the fear and frustration she had been feeling during her many anxious hours came out in one intense, sobbing rant. "Emmett Green! I knew nothing of the kind. For all I knew you were dead. I don't want you ever to go hunting again. Ever!"

At that moment, Don stared at his dad's hunting rifle. It was muddy, and the end of the stock was dented and badly scratched. "What happened to your gun, Dad?"

That's a long story, Son, and right now I need something to eat, a long, hot bath, and some sleep.

CHAPTER 26

THE LONG STORY

Esther quickly prepared a hot meal, and Emmett ate it with deep appreciation born of having had only a sandwich and a can of corn to eat during the past 32 hours. He drew a deep, hot bath, and was lying in the tub with most of his body submerged. His head and shoulders were resting against the end of the tub.

Don knocked on the bathroom door. "Are you OK Dad?"

"Yeah, come on in."

Don opened the door and looked shocked when he saw his dad. "My gosh, Dad, you're as blue as an over-ripe chicken."

"Yeah, Son, I got awfully cold during my little adventure."

Esther came into the bathroom, and said, "Come on, Emmett, tell us what happened."

"Okay, but you'll have to promise not to get upset."

"Yes, yes, now give. What's the story?"

"Well, I drove about 4 miles into the woods on Moon Mountain Road. I parked the car and began hunting at about 7 o'clock. The morning sun was shining, and it felt almost like early spring. I hunted until noon, and then I sat on a log and ate the sandwich you made for me."

Esther said, "Yes, yes, now get to the reason you were gone all night."

"Well, if you'll shut up and listen, I'll tell you." (Emmett was still stinging from the sharp rebuff he'd received from Esther earlier, so he had decided to have some fun by keeping her in suspense as he related the story.) "Let's see, where was I? Oh yes, I parked the car on the mountain road...."

"Emmett Green! If you don't get to the point I'm going to strangle you."

"Okay, calm down. After I ate lunch, I hunted until about 5 PM, but I didn't see a single deer. I'd just started to walk back to the car, when a big buck jumped out of its hiding place and bounded away through the forest. I got off one shot and was sure I'd wounded it; there was blood on the snow. I didn't want the buck to suffer a long, cruel death, and I didn't want to waste the meat, so I chased it. In my excitement, I didn't notice that the weather had turned cloudy and cold. Suddenly, the wind began to blow, then it started snowing. The deer's tracks and drops of blood still showed in the new snow, but it was soon snowing so hard that I could only see about 50 feet ahead. I knew that I must not be more than a few minutes away from the deer because its tracks hadn't filled with snow. I followed the deer a little longer, then I noticed that snow was beginning to completely cover the tracks. I must have only nicked the deer, since it seemed to be getting farther away from me. It was starting to get dark, so I decided to return to the car since I didn't have a flashlight. It was snowing hard, and nothing I saw looked familiar. I couldn't see the moon or stars to get my bearings so I didn't know which direction I was walking. After going a little way, my earlier footprints were completely obliterated by the falling snow. I could have been walking in circles without knowing it. I thought, Oh my God, I'm lost!

So, let's review my situation at this point. It's almost dark, it's snowing hard, it's getting colder by the minute, its…"

Esther cut him off. "Emmett, I'm going to kill you if you don't tell us how you got out of this alive."

"Okay, Esther, okay. Lets see, now, where was I? Oh Yeah, I parked the car on the mountain road."

Esther filled her bathroom glass with cold water, and gave one last warning. "Emmett!"

Considering how it would feel to have cold water poured on him, Emmett continued. "I was good and lost. It must have been about 9 PM. The snowfall had slacked off, and I was stumbling along in the dim moonlight, barely able to see where I was going. The wind was still blowing, and it made eerie creaking and groaning sounds like trees do when one is leaning on another and they rub together. Then, nearby in the blackness, I heard a swish, limbs splintering, and felt the ground jump as an old tree fell near me. Boy, if it had fallen on me… . Anyway, I was stumbling along in the darkness when, without warning, my leg went down through a windfall of two small trees that had fallen over a brook. Snow had drifted over the damn thing. My leg plunged into the ice-cold brook. At that point, I was nearly exhausted, wet, cold and lost, and I thought I was a goner. I knew I had to find the car or I would die, and finding the car didn't seem very likely. Chilled to the bone, I was starting to feel numb and very, very tired. It took all of my willpower to force myself to keep going. By now, it had stopped snowing and dim moonlight filtered down to the forest floor, but I couldn't see any familiar landmarks. At least I could now see my footprints, and most of the time I could avoid bumping into bushes and trees. It must have been about 10 PM when I couldn't feel my feet any more, and unless some kind of a miracle happened, I knew that I was as good as dead."

Esther, who had been holding the glass of water and listening impatiently said, "Quit telling me your life history, and tell me how you survived," as she poured a stream of cold water on top of Emmett's head and down his back.

"Yeow! Okay, okay, I'll get to the point. Please don't do that again."

"Just as I was feeling certain that I was done for, I stumbled onto someone's mountain cabin. My God, what a miracle. What a relief. There was a padlock on the door. I hated to break in, but this was a life or death situation. I used the butt of my rifle to pound on the lock and tear the screws out of the lock's hasp. Inside, there was a stove, fuel, paper, matches, a can of creamed corn, and some blankets. I built a fire in the stove, and opened the can of creamed corn with my pocketknife. Then, after eating the corn, I wrapped up in the blankets and went to sleep. It was about 9 o'clock this morning when I woke up. The fire had gone out, and I was cold, but happy to be alive. I had about $15 in my billfold, and I left all of my cash with a note that I wrote on the back of the corn label giving my name, address and phone number, along with an explanation of what had happened. I included an apology for breaking in, and told the cabin owner to contact me if the $15 didn't cover cost of the corn, and the damage I did to his lock.

The cabin's driveway joined the road where I had parked the car, and I just followed the road for a couple of miles until I got to the car. I was surprised to see the sheriff and one of his men milling around our car. He told me they were looking for a lost hunter who owned the car, and I had to admit that it was my car. It was the most embarrassing moment of my life. I wish you hadn't called them."

"Believe me, Emmett, if you ever go hunting again I'll kill you, and if you get lost you're on your own."

Emmett reached for the faucet and added more hot water to his bath. "Okay. Now you two get out of here and let me soak in peace in this delicious hot water."

CHAPTER 27

MOVING PREPERATIONS

In spite of all the preparations for the upcoming move, Emmett and Esther successfully maintained a calm, settled home for Don, who was absorbed in finishing his first semester in the seventh grade, and selling Christmas cards door-to-door. The family had a traditional Christmas celebration, and attended a church service.

About a week before moving to Portland, Emmett was building a large plywood box. Don came into the shop, and asked, "Dad, what's the box for?"

"It's to put some of our stuff in to protect it from the weather, and from theives during our move."

"Dad, I wish we didn't have to move. My seventh grade science teacher is really good. He's teaching us a lot of interesting stuff."

"I'm sorry, Son, but we have to go. Mom wants me to get a less dangerous job, and the shipyards badly need people with my skills to help repair warships. Don't worry, they have good teachers in Portland."

Emmett didn't know that the Portland schools were overwhelmed with children due to the influx of workers who were there to build and repair warships, not only for the U.S., but also for England and Russia.

Finally, it was only one day before the big move. Emmett attached his two-wheel trailer to the car, and backed it up to the front steps for loading. He had built oak stake-bed sides for the trailer. This extended the height of the trailer bed up to about 5 feet, allowing it to be much more heavily loaded, but making it more top heavy. Emmett had also built a tailgate that could be fastened across the back with large wood screws after the trailer was loaded.

Emmett, Esther and Don all began carrying things, starting with the large plywood box, which was placed in the front end of the trailer. Dishes, silverware, clocks, radios, tools, dress clothes, and other valuables were placed in the box, and the plywood lid was nailed on. Less valuable household items in cardboard boxes were placed on top of the box. Eleven year old Don was now mature enough to really help, and Emmett was quick to show his appreciation. "That's the stuff, Son, keep up the good work."

Finally, furniture and appliances were loaded into the trailer: beds, mattresses, davenport, chairs, dining room table (with the legs removed), washing machine and refrigerator. Emmett began fastening the tailgate onto the back of the heavily loaded trailer.

Don looked puzzled. "What about the electric range in the kitchen?"

"The kitchen stove belongs to the company, Son. It stays with the house."

"Do you think they would miss it if we took it along?"

"That wouldn't be honest, Son. Besides, where would we put it? The trailer is completely full."

"But what will we cook on in Portland?"

"That's my boy, always thinking about food. Don't worry, most rental houses these days come with some kind of gas or electric cook stove."

Emmett tied a large, waterproof tarpaulin over the top of the load. "Well, that's it Son. We'll load the last of the stuff into the car tomorrow morning and get on our way."

Don asked, "Dad, where'll we sleep tonight? All the beds are in the trailer."

"In blankets on the floor."

"Dad!"

"Oh, it won't hurt you. When I was a boy, my family was so poor that we never even had beds."

"Yeah, but one time you told me that you had straw-filled mattress ticking. Can't we go to a hotel tonight?"

"No, son, that would be a waste of money when we can stay in this perfectly good house tonight."

CHAPTER 28

A MOVE MADE IN HELL

Moving day was cold, with a dark gray overcast. At 11 AM, the last items were loaded into the back seat and trunk of the 1937 Plymouth sedan. Emmett placed the family's Cocker Spaniel on some small rugs on top of the load in the back seat. The dog, as in the previous move, was unhappy about being cooped up in such a small space and began whining as the family got into the car.

Don asked, "Dad, aren't you going to open the back window for the dog?"

"No, it's too cold today, and it looks like it might snow. I think I've got a better idea."

Emmett pulled a couple of dog biscuits out of his pocket, and gave them to the dog. The whining immediately stopped. After gobbling down the treats, the dog decided that she wasn't in such a bad place after all, and settled down for a nap.

It had snowed several times during the past month, but the highway to Spokane had been plowed and was clear and dry. However, as Emmett began driving, he saw something that made his blood run cold, and created a knot in his stomach. "Damn it, it's starting to snow. I had hoped it would hold off until we were out of the mountains." He had only driven a few miles when the snowstorm intensified, and visibility was only about 50-feet. Even with the headlights turned on, this was a bad time to be on the highway. As if that wasn't bad enough, the trailer began bucking and darting from side to side at speeds over 25 MPH, and became unmanageable over 45 MPH.

Esther was worried. "Emmett, is the car jumping around because of the snow?"

"No, I think it's because I didn't get the load properly balanced. The trailer is probably tail heavy, but I'm not going to stop and reload it now. It'll be a major job, and I want to get out of the mountains before this snow builds up enough to cause an avalanche and close the road. The narrow, winding road will force us to go slow anyway."

They had only gone a few miles when the road began to get slippery. With the car fishtailing, and trailer bucking and yanking from side to side, controlling the car became nearly impossible, even at 25 MPH. Emmett pulled over to the right and stopped.

Esther looked puzzled. "Why are you stopping here? It's dangerous. The shoulder isn't wide enough to get the car completely off the road."

"Aw, Esther, it'll be all right. I've got to put on chains so I can hold the car on the road. Besides, I don't think there'll be many other cars on the road in this weather, and they should be going slow enough to stop.

Emmett had wisely put the chains on top of the load in the trunk where they were easy to get. He had just started to put on the chains when he heard the faint sound of a heavy truck approaching from higher up on the mountain. He knew the truck would get there before he could get the car moving fast enough on the slippery road to avoid a collision. A truck that heavy might not be able to stop in time.

Fearing the worst, Emmett yanked the front passenger door open, and shouted, "Get out of the car. Get out now, and go up the bank as fast as you can."

Esther and Don heard the fear in his voice. Without hesitation, they piled out of the car and clawed their way up the snow-covered embankment on the right side of the car. Emmett grabbed a large 6-volt lantern-style spotlight out of the trunk. Running to the back of the trailer he aimed the light, swinging it wildly in the direction of the approaching truck. The truck sound was getting louder by the second.

Esther said, "Emmett! Emmett! Get up here. You'll be killed!"

"Oh, be quiet."

"But Emmett, that truck will squash you like a... ."

Her pleading was drowned out by the loud sound of the approaching truck. Even though it was not yet visible through the white curtain of falling snow, the truck was using compression braking, and the sound was deafening.

Emmett frantically flashed the bright spotlight, aiming it back and forth, at about the same height as the truck driver's eyes. Suddenly, there was a sound of truck tire chains skidding on the pavement as the truck's headlights became dimly visible through the curtain of snow. It was 75 feet away traveling at about 20 MPH. Unable to stop, it was gradually moving over into the left lane of the highway. Emmett clambered up on the slippery embankment just before the truck got to his trailer. There was a sudden, short, smashing, squealing sound of metal scraping on metal as the truck whished past and disappeared into a whirling curtain of falling snow.

Emmett inspected the damage and saw that the truck had grazed the left fender of the trailer. It was smashed in just short of contacting the tire. The car, on the other hand, was narrower than the trailer and was unscathed. The truck driver probably hadn't even realized that he had contacted the fender. Esther and Don stayed up on the embankment shivering from the cold and fear, while Emmett put on the tire chains. Thankfully, no other traffic came along. Emmett quickly finished the dangerous job, then shouted, "Come on, let's get out of here before anyone else comes along."

They all climbed into the car as quickly as they could and Emmett drove fully out into the lane, and started picking up speed. Just as they were getting up to 25 MPH, there was a faint rumbling from high up on the mountain. The poor visibility, and steepness of the mountainside, prevented Emmett from seeing up to the top. Emmett looked worried. "My God, That sounds like an avalanche."

The car lurched forward, bucking and swerving, as Emmett quickly accelerated to more than 45 MPH.

Esther grabbed the front edge of the seat so hard her knuckles turned white. Terrified, she shouted, "Emmett, it really isn't safe to go this fast with the car swerving and bouncing around like this."

In a voice filled with tension, Emmett shouted, "I know, but it's better than being buried alive if that sound is an avalanche."

"Are you sure we're going away from it?"

"No, I'm just guessing. It could be either way, but if I've guessed right, we'll be on the Spokane side of it when it closes the road."

"Oh, Emmett, what if you've guessed wrong?"

"Then it won't matter."

The roaring was beginning to sound like a freight train. Emmett frequently glanced at the rear-view mirror, hoping to see some indication that the avalanche was behind them.

Suddenly, he said, "Esther, I guessed wrong, the avalanche was in front of us."

Esther looked dismayed. "Oh Emmett!"

Emmett grinned and added, "The avalanche zone was in front of us, but in speeding up we passed it before it piled into the road. It has closed the road behind us, so now we can go as slow as we wish without anyone crashing into us from behind."

Esther looked disgusted as she reached over and hit Emmett on the shoulder. "You idiot, you almost gave me a heart attack."

The car rumbled along for another 20 miles on its chains until it was well out of the mountains and on the straight, dry stretch of road leading into Spokane. Emmett pulled over to the right side of the lane and stopped with most of the car still in the traffic lane.

Esther asked, "Emmett, why are you stopping?"

"To remove the chains."

"But this is dangerous. We're in the lane of traffic."

"The road is closed behind us, remember?"

"But Emmett, I remember a car going past us toward Kellogg a while ago. What if it turns around and comes back this way?"

"Hell, I didn't think of that!"

Emmett drove the car fully back into the lane and accelerated. Soon after they got up to 25 MPH the other car appeared behind them coming around a curve. Looking in the rear view mirror, Emmett said, "Oh my God, Esther, you were right. Here comes that car. You saved our bacon!"

About 2-miles further along the road Emmett pulled off into a wide place, and removed the chains.

Getting back into the car, Emmett said, "Well, I hope we're past the dangerous part of what so far has been a move made in hell. I guess, now that we are out of the mountains and snow, we can just sit back and relax."

Esther said, "We'll see."

CHAPTER 29

MORE HELL, BUT GOOD FRIENDS

The remaining 30 miles to Spokane were uneventful compared to the previous narrow escapes. The trailer continued bucking and swerving due to its poor load balance, but Emmett and Esther had gotten used to it. Don and the dog, tired from all the earlier commotion, were fast asleep. On the straight dry stretch of road, the family was able to travel at the breakneck speed of 45 MPH until they got to Spokane and had to slow down through town.

"Emmett, why don't you stop somewhere and repack the trailer so it isn't so tail heavy?"

"Oh, Esther, I really don't want to stop. It's 1:30, and it's another 350 miles to Portland. I would need a large paved area, and it would take hours to unload and reload all that stuff."

"Okay, dear, whatever you think is best."

About 30 miles west of Spokane, where the land is flat, and the scrub pine forest has surrendered to sagebrush, strong crosswinds buffeted the car and trailer. This caused the trailer to swerve and buck so much that Emmett could no longer control the car at a speed of 45. He slowed to 35 and could control the car most of the time. However, when an extra strong wind gust hit the trailer, it caused the car to swerve so violently that it went half way into the oncoming lane. Emmett had to slam on the brakes, slowing to 20 MPH to maintain control. Luckily, there was no oncoming traffic.

Esther said, "Good Lord, Emmett, this is too dangerous. We've got to stop somewhere and balance that load."

"Yes, I agree. We'll stop in Lind. It's only another 25 miles or so. Fred Woodmyer lives there now, so we'll stay in a motel there tonight, and visit Fred and his wife, Lydia." Emmett was worried and exhausted; he wasn't usually so pliable when someone suggested something that would keep him from meeting a goal he'd set which, in this case, was getting to Portland that evening.

Emmett had the greatest respect for Fred, who had been his friend and line crew foreman. The two families had spent many pleasant evenings visiting when they had all lived in Spokane. They had taken some day trips together, and Fred's wife, Lydia, and Esther had often gone shopping together.

Emmett drove another 15 miles or so, with the trailer rocking violently from side to side. Suddenly, there was a loud pop followed by violent swerving. The top-heavy trailer tilted dangerously, raising one wheel clear off the pavement. Emmett slowed and steered in a direction to bring the trailer upright. It barely recovered from its precarious tilt in time to prevent it from completely tipping over. The trailer came back down on the raised wheel with a loud grinding and flapping sound.

"Emmett, what was that?"

"Damn it, we've blown a tire on the trailer. I guess it couldn't take the load plus all the wind force and rocking. I don't have a spare for the trailer, and I only have a car bumper jack. It won't work on the trailer."

They headed into a wide place beside the road and Emmett unhitched the trailer. When he released the hitch, the trailer tongue rose up until the rear of the trailer rested on the ground.

Emmett got back into the car. "Yep, the load was tail heavy."

As they pulled away leaving the trailer, Esther said, "Are you going to leave all our stuff here? Someone is apt to steal it."

Emmett replied, "We don't have a choice, unless you want to spend the rest of our lives here. I'm going to see if Fred has a jack that will work and knows where I can get a new tire and inner tube in Lind.

Without the trailer, it only took 20 minutes to get to the Woodmyer's place in Lind. Emmett knocked on the front door and it opened. Standing in the doorway were Fred and Lydia who had seen Emmett coming up their front sidewalk.

With a smile and an expression of delight on his face, Fred chuckled, "Hwoo, hwoo, well look what the cat dragged in. Howdy, stranger."

Emmett smiled as he shook hands with Fred, and said, "Hi. Sorry to barge in on you like this, but we're in the middle of a move to Portland, and our trailer blew a tire. I was such a dumb-head that I didn't buy a jack that would work. Do you have one I can borrow?"

"Sure, Emmett. In fact, I have an old hydraulic jack that has a slow fluid leak, but it works OK. I'll just give it to you, and you'll have it for the rest of your trip."

"Thanks, Fred. Can you recommend a tire store in town where I can get a new tire and inner tube for my trailer, and can you point me to a motel that has a big, paved parking lot where I can re-pack the load in my trailer?"

Fred said, I know a good tire store, but they are only open until 5:00PM, so we'll have to go soon. The motel is not a problem." Then, Fred gave another of his strange little chuckles. "Hwoo,hwoo, the best motel in town is right here at our house, and we'll be insulted if you don't stay with us tonight."

Lydia, in the meantime, had gone out to the car. She and Esther were standing beside the car hugging each other.

Fred drove his own car to the tire store, since Emmett's car was packed full of bedding and other items and had no space for the new tire. The only tires available were recaps, but luckily, the store had one that would fit the trailer After Emmett purchased a tire and tube, Fred drove him to the ailing trailer. Fred's car didn't have a trailer hitch, so after Emmett changed the tire and tube, the men returned to Fred's house. Emmett drove his own car back to get the trailer. Fred went along to stand on the tongue of the trailer. This was needed to provide extra weight on the tongue and bring it down far enough to be hooked onto the car. By the time Emmett and Fred returned to Lind with the trailer, it was dinnertime.

Entering the house, Emmett decided to repay some of the Woodmyers' kindness. "Fred and Lydia, we want to take you out to dinner. Where would you like to go?"

Lydia had already decided on her dinner plans. "Oh, now Emmett, we wouldn't hear of it. I want you to stay right here and have dinner with us. We'll have a good visit and get caught up on what you've been doing."

The next morning, Emmett and Fred removed the tailgate and unloaded all the trailer's contents. Then the men re-loaded the trailer, with careful attention to placing the heaviest items in front and the lighter ones in the rear.

Emmett fastened the tailgate in place, and tied the tarpaulin over the load. "Well, Fred, that should do it."

"My God, Emmett, that's an awfully heavy load. Maybe you should leave part of it here in my garage and come back for it later."

"Aw, It'll be all right. Besides, I don't think the Rationing Board would let me have another increased gas allotment to come all the way back here. Thanks for the offer, Fred, and thanks a million for all of your help. I can't tell you how much I appreciate it."

"Hwoo, hwoo. That's what friends are for, Emmett."

After a nice lunch, prepared by Lydia and Esther, and more reminiscing about old times, it was time to go. The time together had been so enjoyable that Esther had tears in her eyes as Emmett drove away from Fred and Lydia's place. Looking back and waving goodbye, she saw Fred and Lydia standing in their driveway. They were waving farewell, and tears were streaming down Lydia's face.

After traveling for a few minutes, Esther was the first to speak. "Lydia told me that we are the best friends they've ever had."

"Yes, Esther, and I feel the same way about them."

Don, who had been listening, added his two cents worth to the conversation. "I like them too. Lydia's a really good cook." Then, after a few seconds of reflection, he added, "and Mom, you are too."

Esther, feigning disgust, put her arm around Don and jostled him. "You'd better say that, if you ever want me to cook for you again."

CHAPTER 30

HOMELESS

The reloaded trailer traveled smoothly at speeds up to 55 MPH, but it was 7:15PM, dark and rainy by the time Emmett drove into Portland on Sandy Boulevard. There were motor courts, cabins, tourist courts and motels along the street, but they all had colorful neon "No Vacancy" signs that blurrily reflected from the wet street as if to emphasize their message and extract all hope from weary travelers seeking a place to rest. The city was overflowing with defense workers attracted by the government's intense recruiting effort.

Emmett said, "My God, Esther, I didn't think every place in town would be full. We may have to spend the night in the car."

"I have an idea, Emmett. How would you feel about staying with my mother tonight?"

"Does she still live in that old two story firetrap of an apartment house?"

"Yes, I'm afraid so."

"Well, I guess that would be better than the three of us trying to sleep in the front seat of the car tonight."

It was about 8 PM by the time they pulled up in front of the "firetrap". Esther went in, leaving Emmett, Don and the dog in the car. She was smiling when she returned.

"Emmett, Mom has a bedroom with a full bed and a cot. She's willing to sleep on the daybed that she has in her living room, and let us have the bedroom. There's even a warm place in the basement where we can keep the dog. Bring the bedding out of the back seat, and we'll get set for the night."

"Good. I'm tired and hungry, and I'm glad to have a warm, dry place we can get into for the night. I've sure hated having to impose so much on others during this trip, but I'm grateful for their help."

"I know, dear, you're used to being the strong, independent type that we all lean on, but now it's your turn to lean a little."

Emmett, Esther and Don carried the bedding up to the second floor apartment and made up their beds. Esther prepared a supper of canned soup, beans, bread, and margarine from her mother's small stock of food. Her mother was living on welfare, plus $5.00 a month contributed by Esther and each of her four surviving siblings. Esther assured her mother that she would replenish the food stock the next day.

The apartment building had been converted from a fine six-bedroom home built in the late 1800's. After the stock market crash of 1929 the owner could no longer afford to be the sole occupant. He remodeled two of the three upstairs bedrooms to provide a combined living room/kitchen for a rental apartment. There was a hallway from the head of the stairs. It passed between the upstairs bedroom and the apartment's living room/kitchen, and it ended at a bathroom door. All of the woodwork, including doors, was dark varnished oak, and the wallpaper was a floral design with a gray background popular in the late 1800's. The floral design had faded to a dim reminder of its former beauty. A few stained streaks where the roof had once leaked gave mute evidence that the owner was able to afford essential roof repairs, but not wallpaper replacement. A single bare electric light fixture, added after electrical power became available, dimly illuminated the dark hallway. Typical of old houses and tenements, the inside of the building had a vaguely fruity odor, given off by burning natural gas for cooking, mingled with the musty odor of old wood that had been wet and moldy.

The bathroom was equipped with a white claw-footed bathtub and an old fashioned toilet that had been installed shortly after the turn of the century. There was an oak-encased water tank mounted high up near the ceiling on the wall behind the toilet. Hanging down from the water tank was a pull-chain supporting a cylindrical wooden flushing handle at shoulder height. The toilet had a dark oak seat that matched the tank.

Flushing the toilet for the first time was a startling experience for anyone used to a quiet modern toilet. The height of the water tank caused a roaring torrent of water to jet down into the toilet with the force of a placer mining operation. Don made the mistake of remaining on the toilet when he pulled the handle for the first time. Terrified, he jumped off the toilet and halfway across the bathroom.

After visiting late into the night with Esther's mother, Emmett and Esther were exhausted and sank into bed. Don had been sent to bed earlier. He knew this was probably meant to prevent him from hearing adult conversations that might damage his ears or something.

The next morning, after breakfast, Emmett and Esther flew into action. Emmett rented a garage from the apartment landlord and parked the fully loaded trailer in it. He had been worried about leaving the trailer unattended overnight on the street, and he was relieved to see that nothing had been stolen. He was glad that the garage had a strong lock on the door, and no windows.

Later, Esther drove Emmett to the shipyard office of the Ship Electrical Systems company where he was to sign up for work. On the way home, she stopped at a grocery store. She and Don carried the groceries and a newspaper up to the apartment. Her mother, who had her own preferred places for things, put the groceries away.

Esther began scanning want-ads in the newspaper for rental houses or apartments. There wasn't a single ad for a rental. Esther was perplexed. Looking at her mother, she said, "There aren't any ads for rental housing. I wonder if they're only in the paper on certain days."

"No, Esther, there are almost never any ads for rentals. Portland is so overwhelmed with the hoards of defense workers that everything is full, including hotels and motels. If an ad does appear, there's almost no chance of getting the rental before someone who knows someone gets it."

"Oh my gosh, Mom, what are we going to do? I had no idea it was so crowded here."

"Don't worry, the Government is building entire new communities of defense houses here. You'll have to contact the Defense Housing Office to reserve one of them."

Esther used the telephone in the "Firetrap's" downstairs hallway to make the call.

A clerk answered, saying, "Defense Housing Office. This is Melissa."

"Hello. My name is Esther Green. My husband, Emmett, is employed as an electrician repairing ship's electrical systems. We just moved here, and we need to rent a 2 bedroom house."

"Sorry, Mrs. Green, but we don't have any available now. I can put you on the waiting list. That's the best I can do."

"But where are we supposed to live? There are no rentals in this entire city. Do you have any 3-bedroom houses?"

"No."

"One bedroom?"

"No. We don't have housing of any kind available now, but we are building more units out at the Parkside Defense Homes community west of the Saint Johns district."

"How soon can we get into one of them?"

"Perhaps six months. Is your husband a skilled worker?"

"Oh yes, he's extremely skilled. He was a lineman working with high voltage power lines for many years."

"That doesn't sound like the kind of skill needed to work on ship's electrical machinery and circuits."

"Melissa, he's also had extensive formal training in electrical machinery, wiring and instrumentation, and he worked for several years on motor-generators and circuits that supplied direct current to the mines in Kellogg, Idaho."

"Now we're getting somewhere. Have his employer contact us for a housing priority, and we can probably put you into one of the new 2-bedroom houses at Parkside within two or three months."

Esther's voice, which had been edgy with tension, now became smooth and sweet as she turned on the charm that had served her so well in dealing with sales people and office personnel in the past. "Oh, thank you so very much, Melissa. I was very worried that we wouldn't be able to get a place. We have an eleven-year-old son, and right now we are all living with my Mother in her one-bedroom apartment. Thanks again, I can't tell you how much I appreciate the help you've given me. Goodbye."

Esther picked Emmett up in front of the shipyard office that evening. On the way home, she related the day's events. When she got to the part about the housing, Emmett said, "Three months! My God, that means we'll have to impose on your mother to let us stay at her place all that time. And even if she does agree, we'll have to continue cramming all three of us into one bedroom in that old firetrap. And we won't have any privacy with Don sleeping in the same room with us."

"Emmett Green, you inconsiderate, ungrateful clod. My mother has let us stay there out of the kindness of her heart, and…"

Emmett realized that he had stepped over the line into deep manure, and he needed to quickly retrench. He cut Esther off, saying, "I didn't mean it the way it sounded. I only meant that I hate to put your mother out of her bedroom that long. On top of everything else, now we are completely homeless for the first time since I built the house in Philomath ten-years ago. Oh God, Esther, We're right back where we started. I wish we'd never left Philomath."

"Are you done feeling sorry for yourself? We certainly are not back where we started. We have a respectable amount of money saved, and now you have a secure job that's not dangerous."

"Well, Esther, you're at least half right."

"What do you mean."

"We do have some money saved."

"Oh, Emmett, do you mean you are still doing dangerous work?"

Emmett had heard some unfavorable things about shipyard safety from other men who were signing for work. Considering that he might not yet be clear of his previous misstep, he decided to dodge Esther's question.

"Esther, tell me what I have to do to get a house for us."

Esther described the procedure Melissa had told her about. Then, addressing Emmett's concern about imposing, she said, "Don't worry about Mom letting us stay in her apartment. She was pleased with the groceries I got today, and she was even more pleased when I told her we would buy all the groceries and pay the rent on the apartment while we are staying there. She said she'd be happy to continue sleeping on the day bed in the living room."

CHAPTER 31

A NEW SCHOOL AND
A PHYSIC LESSON

Winter break for Portland schools had ended. Esther took Don to the principal's office of his new school to enroll him in the second half of 7th grade.

The office clerk asked, "Did you bring a transcript from his last school?"

Esther pulled a folded paper out of her purse. "Yes, here it is."

Studying the transcript, the clerk said, "It appears that he has been passing all his courses, so we'll put him in the advanced class."

"Advanced class?"

"Yes. We have a mix of kids here from every part of the country. Many of them are just putting in time here because the law requires it until they age out of school, and they haven't been doing well. We've split the class into two parts, the advanced class for students with passing grades, and the other class for problem students."

When Don got home that afternoon, he was excited. "Gosh, Mom, I was worried when the lady in the office said I was being placed in the advanced class. I wasn't sure I'd be smart enough. But after a few hours in class, I realized that they're about 6-months behind my old school. They had an easy math test today, to determine how well the kids remembered what they had learned before winter break, and I got 100% on it."

"How was Science and English, Son?"

"English was easy, but there are no separate science classes. We talked a little bit about science during our discussion of current events, but it was stuff I already knew about, and it wasn't very interesting. I don't think the teacher is very interested in science, or knows much about it." Don continued describing events of his day: new friends he had made and how glad he was that tough, unruly kids, some as old as sixteen in the eighth grade, had their recess at a different time than his.

The next day, when Don got home from school, Esther said, "I have to take Grandma to a doctor's appointment, then pick Dad up at the shipyard. Will you be all right here alone for a couple of hours until we get home?"

"Sure, Mom."

"Now, stay close to home, and don't get into trouble. Take the dog out, then feed and water her."

"Okay, Mom."

After taking care of the dog, Don got hungry and thirsty. He looked in the refrigerator and found several 10-ounce bottles that appeared to be soda pop. They were labeled "Magnesium Citrate." The word, "Citrate", reminded him of citric acid that, as he had learned in his Kellogg science class, is a component of lemonade.

Don thought, Hmm, this looks good. I think I'll try some.

Opening a bottle, he took a sip.

He said to himself, "Wow, this is pretty good lemon flavored pop," then he drank the entire bottle. He was still thirsty, so he drank another bottle.

About an hour later, Don was reading an exciting comic book when his stomach began rumbling and gurgling. He was able to concentrate on the book for another 5 minutes, but then was struck by an irresistible urge to go to the bathroom. He ran into the bathroom and got situated on the toilet as fast as he could, barely sitting down before he explosively emptied out. His guts were writhing and gurgling like a snake that had been force-fed Chinese hot mustard. The aching was awful, and he felt slightly nauseated. About that time, his mom, dad and grandma got home.

Knocking on the bathroom door, Esther said, "How long are you going to be in there? We all need to use the bathroom."

Don suspected the "lemon pop" was responsible for his predicament. He knew he shouldn't have gotten into it, and there would be consequences if he admitted the reason for his trouble. His mind was racing. What to do, what to do. Quick, come up with a believable story.

Finally, he decided on a deception that he hoped would work, and he answered his mother. "I...I think I have a touch of the flu, and I don't feel well." With that, he noisily gave birth to a large cloud of gas.

"Okay, Son, but hurry. All of us need to use the bathroom."

About 15 minutes later, there was an urgent pounding on the door. "Son, we really need to get in there. Did you fall in and flush yourself down?"

By this time, Don felt like he had been turned wrong side out, so he thought it would be safe to leave the toilet for a short time. "Okay, Mom."

Don was just pulling up his pants when he heard uproarious laughter coming from the kitchen. When he came out of the bathroom, Esther asked, "Do you know what happened to Grandma's bottles of Magnesium Citrate physic?"

Caught like a trapped monkey, Don had to admit what he'd done. "I thought it was a new kind of lemon pop."

Esther struggled to suppress her laughter as she scolded Don for his dumb stunt. "The normal adult dose of that stuff is only half a bottle. It's a wonder you're still alive."

"I know that now, Mom. And boy am I sorry. Please hurry and use the toilet. I'm beginning to have to go again."

In the bathroom, Esther was finally able to let out the pent up laughter she'd held back while she had been scolding Don. Emmett and Grandma in the kitchen not only heard her, but also saw Don dancing around out in the hall grimacing, holding the seat of his pants, and crossing his legs. This set off a new round of riotous laughter causing tears to roll down their cheeks. After the others each had a turn in the bathroom, Don spent most of the evening on the toilet. The next morning Don awoke much older, wiser, and glad to have survived the ordeal of the physic lesson. It was a three part lesson he was not likely to repeat: 1) don't get into other people's stuff without asking, 2) don't take drugs that are not prescribed for you, and 3) don't bet your life on chemistry skills you learned in one semester in a seventh grade science class.

Two months later, when winter was beginning to give way to spring, a letter from the housing office for Emmett was delivered while he was at work. Esther wanted to open it, but she and Emmett respected each other's privacy and didn't open each other's mail. Esther felt like she was going to blow a gasket waiting for Emmett to get home so she could see the contents of the letter. By the time she heard his footsteps on the stairs, she was nearly breathless with curiosity and excitement. From the top of the stairs, she said, "Hurry, Emmett. You've got a letter from the Housing Office, and I can't wait to see what it says."

Seeing her excitement, Emmett decided to have some fun teasing her. "Aw, I'm tired. I think I'll take a nap."

"Emmett Green, you open this letter right now!"

"Aw Esther, it's probably just notifying us that it'll be another five or six months before we can get a house."

Esther's face reddened, and a vein stood out on her forehead. "Emmett!"

"All right, all right, don't rupture anything. Give me the letter."

Emmett tore the envelope open and removed the letter. He would have liked to have teased Esther a little more, but seeing the state she was in he decided he'd better not. Without unfolding the letter, he handed it to her.

Esther scanned the letter. "Oh Emmett, this is wonderful news! They're offering us a two bedroom rental house that'll be available in two weeks in the Parkside Defense Homes Community."

Seeing that Esther's anxiety had subsided, Emmett couldn't resist teasing her a bit more. "Living here is so much cheaper. Wouldn't you rather stay here?"

"Emmett!"

"Okay, okay Esther, don't have a hemorrhage. We'll move into the house if you insist."

"Oh, you big tease."

CHAPTER 32

PARKSIDE

Two weeks of waiting for the new house went by quickly. There was a lot to be done, but at least the trailer didn't have to be loaded; it had never been unloaded. The Parkside Defense Homes Community was many miles across town from the school Don had been attending. Esther arranged to transfer him to a school closer to Parkside. This promised to be a challenging change for Don, since he was in the middle of his second semester of 7th grade.

Saturday was moving day. Emmett hitched the trailer onto the Plymouth and parked it in front of the "firetrap". As the family was loading the last of the suitcases, bedding and dog into the car's back seat, Emmett expressed what they all were feeling. "I appreciated your mother's hospitality in our time of need, but I'm sure glad to get out of this place."

Esther said, "Yes, it sure was nice of Mom to let us crowd in on her like that."

Don said, "Yeah, it was better than living in the car." Then after a few moments, remembering the magnesium citrate incident, he said, "But it sure did ruin my appetite for lemon pop."

They climbed the stairs one last time to say goodbye to Esther's mother and thank her for letting them stay with her. As they were leaving, Esther handed her mother $35 toward the next month's rent, food, and magnesium citrate.

Emmett drove to the Parkside Community Office, parked, and went in. Like all the other buildings in the community, it was a low single story building with light gray-green painted plywood outside walls; it looked hastily constructed and temporary. Twenty minutes later, Emmett came out holding house keys, a small map of the community, and a large manila envelope containing a copy of the rental agreement, rules and regulations.

As he got into the car, Emmett handed the map to Esther and said, "I'm sure glad they gave me a map of this place. It's a big community and all the houses look alike to me."

As Emmett drove, Esther navigated. Esther said, "Turn right at the next intersection and go to North Milne Street." After a few minutes, she said, "Slow down, you're going too fast."

"Esther, what's the name of the street just before we get to Milne?"

"Ummm. Daniels."

"Oh Esther, you were too slow. We passed Daniels, and the street we are going past now must be Milne."

"Well, I asked you to slow down. You were going too fast."

"Now I've got to find a place to turn around."

Coming to a driveway, Emmett said, "Here's a place, but I'll have to back out of it into the street. I hope nobody comes around that blind corner ahead."

Emmett pulled into the driveway and then started backing out. At that moment a small, red sports convertible, with an 18-year old boy driving, came barreling around the corner at a speed considerably higher than the Community speed limit of 20 miles per hour. There was a screeching of tires as the car braked and swerved around the trailer which, by now, was far out into the lane of traffic. The car stopped just beyond the trailer, and the driver shouted a few choice expletives, ending with "You idiot, don't you know better than to block the street near a corner?"

Hearing the term "You idiot," Emmett quickly got out of the car ready to fight and said, "Who are you calling an idiot, you careless little bastard?"

Seeing this mountain of enraged muscle coming toward him, the boy put his car into gear and rapidly accelerated, tires smoking and leaving black marks on the pavement. He disappeared down the street at an even greater speed than before. Emmett made a prediction of the obvious. "Sooner or later that kid is going to get into some bad trouble."

Finally, underway again, Emmett drove slowly while Esther again navigated. After they had gone a short distance, Esther said, "There's Milne Street. Turn right. Our house is at 9217 North Milne."

Emmett saw the address on the first house after they turned, and said, "Oh, it's right here on the corner. It looks flimsy, and it sure is small. Are you sure it's a two-bedroom?"

"Yes, Emmett. The Housing Office clerk said it was small when I telephoned the day after we received the letter."

Because of the war, materials and manpower were in short supply, and the houses had to be constructed as rapidly and efficiently as possible. The smallest possible amount of material was used in their construction, and components for the houses were pre-fabricated in factories.

Emmett said, "My God, Esther, they sure didn't waste any materials. The walls look like they were built with 2-by-2 studs instead of 2-by-4's. I hope this house doesn't fall down around our ears."

There was a large plywood auxiliary storage bin at the end of the short driveway near the front door of the house. The bin had a hinged top with a hasp that could be padlocked, and it provided the overflow storage that was needed for such a small dwelling.

Emmett backed the trailer into the driveway, as close to the front steps as possible and he, Esther, and Don unloaded it. Although the house was small, it was well designed. Don and his parents each had their own space and enjoyed some privacy for the first time in three months. The one-bedroom "firetrap" ordeal was over.

The following Monday, Emmett drove his Plymouth to work. Esther walked with Don to get him registered in the seventh grade for the third time in less than a year. That afternoon, Don was 45 minutes late getting home after school. By the time he finally got there, Esther was worried.

"Where have you been, Son?"

"I got lost on the way home from school."

"Lost?"

"Yes. There must be a thousand houses in this place, and they all look alike. I couldn't even find the right street. Finally, I asked a kid how to get to North Milne Street. He didn't know, but he told me how to get to the Community Office. A lady in the Office showed me how to get home. She said this is a common problem, and lots of kids here get lost coming home after their first day in school."

"How did school go today?"

"Not very well. This school is almost as advanced as the one in Kellogg. The school by Grandma's place was far behind, and I didn't learn much there, so I'm about 4 months behind. I told the teacher about it, and she said she wasn't surprised by the difference in local schools because they have been overwhelmed by so many students. I don't have to catch up in science; this school doesn't have any separate science class. I will have to catch up in English, Math, History, and Music. The seventh grade class is so overcrowded, the teacher won't have time to give me much individual help, so I'll have to do a lot of extra studying on my own to catch up."

Saturday finally arrived, and it wasn't a moment too soon as far as Don was concerned. It had been a stressful week for him, trying to catch up while at the same time trying to learn new things. He was delighted to find Pier Park adjacent to Parkside Community, and he decided to take a break from his studies and go exploring.

The park was a beautiful, welcome relief from the Spartan, utilitarian features of the Defense Houses, which were all painted light gray-green and looked alike. The park had a wide expanse of well-manicured grass, and paths that were covered with a soft carpet of evergreen needles and meandered through a forested area that was replete with tall, old-growth trees.

On his way home, Don encountered two boys. One was about Don's age, and the other was an older teen. The older boy, who was carrying a 22-caliber rifle, said, "Isn't your dad the old bastard who cussed me out last week when I almost crashed into his trailer?"

Hearing his dad called a bastard made Don angry. The narrow escape had mostly been the kid's own fault for speeding. However, Don knew this was a dangerous situation, so he played dumb. "I--I don't know what you're talking about."

The older boy spoke to his young companion. "Let's have some fun with this little shit." He reached into his pocket, pulled out a bullet and loaded it into the breach of his rifle, cocking the rifle in the process. Pointing the rifle at Don's head, he asked, "Do you want to reconsider your answer?"

Frightened, Don said, "D-don't point that gun at me. It could go off."

The boy continued pointing the gun directly at Don's head. "Reconsider your answer, kid, or I'll shoot."

Don could see the boy's finger tightening on the trigger as he answered, "I--I Don't know you. I've n-never seen you before. Don't shoot." Don turned his face away, expecting that he was about to be shot as he pleaded, "P-please don't shoot."

Don's heart was racing as adrenaline poured into his bloodstream. Suddenly, there was a loud click. The older boy said, "Hmm, a misfire. I'll have to try again. It'll probably go off this time." He again cocked the weapon and put Don through the whole ordeal again, getting great pleasure out of his terror. Finally, after repeating this action, the boy tired of the game and showed Don the cartridge. The rim had a large number of indents where the firing pin had struck it without causing the bullet to be fired.

With a smug look of satisfaction on his face, the boy placed the cartridge back in the chamber. "See, you little sissy, all your fear was for nothing."

Then Don tried to instruct the boy on something Emmett had once said. "You can never trust a hangfire. It can go off unexpectedly."

That made the boy angry. He said, "Oh, bullshit", and again pointed the weapon at Don, cocking and clicking it time after time. "See, you don't know anything, you little smartass."

Don's mind was racing, desperately trying to find a way to get out of this dangerous situation. Finally, he decided that if he hit this much bigger boy, he'd get beat up, but then the boy would have satisfied his sadistic need to cause pain and might quit clicking the gun. Don stepped up to the 18-year old and hit him moderately hard in the stomach, hoping that his halfhearted attack wouldn't make the bully mad enough to do any real damage. Just as Don had expected, the boy quit clicking his gun, and Don went home with a bloody nose.

Don thought he might have a lot of explaining to do when he arrived home, but neither of his parents was there. He managed to get the nosebleed stopped and get cleaned up before anyone came home. Don didn't want to admit what had happened. He believed that if his mother found out about the incident, she would never let him go to the park again.

Don never saw the older boy again and, in later years, he often wondered what had happened to the careless bully with the gun. Maybe he wrecked his red sports car and got killed, or perhaps he clicked his gun once too often at someone and ended up in jail. Maybe he was drafted into the army and discovered what it was like to have someone shoot at him.

CHAPTER 33

THREE SHIPS AND BIG PROBLEMS

Emmett finished his orientation training and two-month probationary period, and was now fully certified to repair electrical systems on ships. He was pleased to have this job that he believed was less dangerous than his previous one. However, the work often had to be done in cramped, unheated areas in the ship's hold below the water level. Everything was cold and clammy. Condensate, or small amounts of leakage, often dripped on him from above as he worked.

One day, Emmett went to the tool room to get an electric drill and a 1/4-inch bit. He was hurrying back to his worksite when a "brute", a big, muscular, tough-looking man blocked his way. Although Emmett was six foot three, the man towered over him and had great muscles that bulged and tightened his shirt sleeves almost to the splitting point when he flexed his arms. The big guy said, "Green, we've been watching you. You're getting your work done too fast. That's taking work away from other men who could be hired to do the same kind of work, and I've got a friend who needs a job. Knock it off."

Emmett's face reddened as his anger welled up. "Mister, maybe you haven't heard that there's a war on. We need to keep every ship possible in service, and there aren't enough skilled men available to do the work. Your friend must not have the required skills"

"Green, don't be so dense. The company will have to give lots of guys free training in this line of work if they need more electricians than are available. That's better for everyone. You won't have to work so hard, and the new guys will get free training."

"Yeah, but what about our soldiers who won't get the munitions and other supplies they need? You can't just train skilled electricians in a week or two. I'm going to keep on working as fast as I can."

The big guy stepped menacingly forward, but Emmett raised the drill he was holding and pointed the bit directly at the man's stomach. Emmett glanced down at the drill then, gazing into the man's eyes, he grinned coldly. The man got the message and stepped to one side, but he issued an ominous warning as Emmett went past him.

"A lot of accidents happen here, Green. You'd better watch your back."

A couple of days later, Emmett was replacing wiring in the hold of a small cargo vessel called a "Liberty Ship". This type of ship was being built rapidly, often completed in less than 45 days, and there were frequently problems with their welds and electrical systems. The ship had just left on its maiden voyage at sea when welds between several of the hull plates began opening up. The ship barely got back to port where it was immediately placed in dry dock for repairs. Some of the cables that passed through the ship's midsection had been compromised and had to be repaired or replaced. Emmett and other ship system electricians worked on the wiring at the same time welders were repairing the faulty welds. Working on scaffolds in open areas, such as the hold, welders were required to install a large sheet metal spark shield under their worksite to prevent sparks from showering down on men working below.

Emmett was working on wiring near the bottom of the hold when he heard something clinking and clanking down through scaffolding above his work location. Suddenly, a welder's slag hammer whooshed past his head and bounced off the steel deck below. The sharp pointed end of the slag hammer left a deep indent in the deck. Looking up, Emmett saw a welder working 20 feet above him.

Angered, Emmett shouted at the welder. "My God, be careful. That could have punched a hole through my hardhat and killed me."

The welder shouted back in a barely audible voice muffled by the welding helmet covering his face. "Sorry."

Although it appeared to have been an accident, Emmett wondered how the hammer got dropped and why it hadn't landed on the spark shield instead of dropping below. The welder wouldn't have been using a slag hammer during welding while his helmet was down over his face.

The next day, Emmett was assigned to replace some wiring beneath the deck under the ship's galley. He was removing the cover from a junction box when a large cockroach scurried out of a hole in the side of the box. Then, a huge, dark brown spider pounced out of a narrow, dark cable passage beside the box. It grabbed the roach and immediately disappeared back into its shadowy domain.

Emmett threw his arms up in front of his face and jumped back, uttering a surprised "Hunnhh!" Behind him, Emmett heard a deep-voiced laugh.

"Haw,haw, what'd I tell you about watching your back. Accidents happen. You're lucky that thing didn't bite you."

Emmett turned, recognized the "brute" he had encountered a few days earlier, and asked, "What was that thing?"

The brute said, "It's a South American Goliath Bird Eating Spider. They get as big as a dinner plate, and they can give an awful bite that can get infected and require amputation of a bitten hand or arm. This one has apparently developed a taste for cockroaches."

Emmett's eyes narrowed and he clenched his fists. "Did you have anything to do with this? This is the second narrow escape I've had in two days."

The brute grinned broadly and, with an affected tone of innocence in his voice, said, "No, Green, you're starting to sound crazy. What makes you think I had anything to do with it? Accidents happen all the time."

"I haven't forgotten the threat you made about my working too fast. Then, there's this spider. How did a South American spider get all the way to Oregon?"

"Oh, Green, now you really sound paranoid. That spider could have gotten on the ship while it was docked in…"

Emmett cut him off in mid sentence. "Bullshit. This ship started breaking up the first day it went to sea, and barely made it back to port. It's never been docked anywhere but here. If I have any more narrow escapes, you're going to have a bad accident yourself."

Although Emmett had other narrow escapes, they clearly resulted from the kind of work he was doing; none of them happened during the remainder of his assignment on the Liberty

Ship. After that, Emmett and the brute were assigned to different ships, and their paths never crossed again.

A Russian ship had docked, and Emmett was assigned to repair wiring that had been damaged when the ship was bombed and strafed by enemy aircraft. None of the bombs had hit the ship, but plugs were being welded into bullet holes in the walls of the bridge and other personnel spaces all over the ship. During his first day on the ship, Emmett was walking along the deck on the port side when he met two Russian seamen. The first man, who was wearing a fancy uniform, appeared to be the captain. The second was in a plain sailor's uniform.

Emmett thought that, in the interest of international relations, he'd exchange friendly greetings with the men. "Hello. How's it going?"

The captain brushed past, his grim face totally devoid of any friendly emotion.

The second seaman smiled slightly and spoke to Emmett as he walked past. "Captain not speak English. He very sad. He bury many men at sea after planes shoot."

Emmett felt bad about the suffering and death, that had recently happened where he was working. In his mind's eye he saw terrified men scurrying for cover, many screaming in pain as they were killed or wounded by machine gun bullets that ripped through the ship from a swarm of Nazi aircraft as they strafed the ship time after time.

Later, just as Emmett finishing replacing a light switch in the ships galley, the cook walked in. The cook grinned broadly when he saw what Emmett was doing. "Good. You fix light. Now I cook early morning while still dark and cool. I thank you." Then, as he cut a slice off a warm loaf sitting on the counter, he asked, "You like fresh bread?"

It was nearing lunchtime, the bread smelled delicious, and Emmett was beginning to get hungry. "Sure."

The cook handed the slice to Emmett and then started shoveling flour out of a bin into a bowl. Emmett saw numerous live cockroaches being dumped into the bowl along with the flour. The steep sides of the bowl kept the roaches from climbing out as the cook dumped in water, yeast, and other ingredients and started mixing. Looking down at the slice of bread in his hand, Emmett saw cross sections of two cockroaches that had been embedded in the bread when it was baked. As he quickly left the galley, Emmett said In his most polite voice, "Thanks for the bread. I'm going to save it to share with my wife." He had only gone a short distance down the deck when he heard the cook laughing uproariously. Emmett's ruse had failed to fool the cook, who knew how picky Americans are about their food.

When Emmett arrived home that night, Esther and Don greeted him, and he began telling them about his day. "A cook on the Russian ship where I worked today gave me some fresh baked bread."

Emmett took the slice of bread out of his lunch box and offered it to Esther and Don.

As soon as she saw it, Esther said, "No thanks. I don't like bread with that much protein."

Don looked puzzled. "Is that raisin bread?"

Emmett explained. "No. It's cockroaches. That's the way they bake it on the Russian ship."

Don's face wrinkled up as he realized what he was seeing. "Yuck!"

Don's reaction to the thought of eating cockroaches made Emmett and Esther laugh. Then, realizing that it was a joke, Don laughed too.

The next day, Emmett was assigned to repair the degaussing coil on a large troop transport ship. Degausng coils were installed around the entire perimeter of major war ships. They generated a magnetic field that counteracted a ship's natural magnetic disturbance making it invisible to magnetic mines. The coil on this ship had been damaged during shelling from shore guns.

Arriving at the job site, Emmett was greeted by a man about 25-years old. "Hello. I'm Henry Long; just call me Hank. I've been assigned to help you with this job in any way I can. I'm an electrician apprentice. The boss wants this job completed as fast as possible, but there weren't any more qualified electricians available. He hopes my help will speed things up a little."

"Okay, Hank, I'm glad to have your help. Let's get to work."

The two men removed wall panels in different compartments of the ship looking for the location of the trouble. Finally, they removed a panel that felt like it had something heavy resting on it from inside the cable passage between the ship's hull and the cover panel. When they lifted the panel off, exposing the cable passage, a strange object tilted out toward them. Only a single strand of the badly damaged copper degaussing coil was still holding the object.

Emmett was horrified. "My God, Hank, that's an unexploded artillery shell. It must have penetrated the hull somewhere and slithered down the cable passage until it got caught here in the degaussing cable."

Hank reached for the shell. "I'll take it out and throw it overboard."

Emmett grabbed Hank's wrist. "Stop! That shell could still explode. We're lucky it didn't go off when we disturbed it. We'll have to get a naval ordinance man in here that knows how to handle it."

Suddenly, the men's attention was riveted on the heavy shell. The degaussing cable had been ripped open by the shell, which was now slowly stretching the thin strand of copper wire holding it. As the strand stretched, the shell was slowly tilting outward where it would inevitably break the strand and fall to the deck. Horrified, they ran out of the compartment as fast as they could. They were only a small distance down the passageway outside the compartment when they heard a loud clank. The shell had fallen to the deck, but hadn't exploded. Both men had a good laugh about "the little shell that couldn't."

"Emmett, shall I toss it overboard now?"

"No, Hank, we'd still better call the ordinance guys."

After calling ordinance, Emmett and Hank went to a location at the other end of the ship and began removing panels. Each time they removed a panel, Emmett inspected the degaussing cable, declared it OK, then proceeded to the next panel. They were just starting to remove a panel when there was a sound like a muffled explosion from the other end of the ship.

Emmett turned to Hank and asked, "Did you hear that? I wonder if the shell exploded while the ordinance man was working on it."

The two men hurried to the other end of the ship to see if they could help anyone that might have been injured.

Entering the compartment first, Emmett was surprised and said, "There's no ordinance guy here. The shell is still in the same place!"

Then, two things happened; the ordinance man arrived, and a sound like an explosion came from the deck overhead.

Emmett asked, "What was that explosion?"

The ordinance man laughed, and then said, "You guys are really spooked, aren't you? Everything is beginning to sound like an explosion to you. That sound is only the crane loading heavy supply containers onto the upper deck. Don't crap your pants, ladies. Go find someplace where you feel safe. I'll have this shell out of here within a half hour."

Emmett and Hank wasted no time in leaving the compartment as the ordinance man began examining the shell. After they left, Emmett said, "I'd like to see him try to work in a substation with lightning striking all around. Then we'd see some thoroughly crapped pants."

When Emmett got home that night, Esther greeted him.

"What'd you do today?"

"Oh, just the usual routine repair work."

CHAPTER 34

THE BABY

One day in June, when Don was in the eighth grade, he returned home from school and noticed that his mother was putting on weight.

"Mom, your stomach sure is sticking out. I think you're getting fat."

"Son, how would you like to have a brother or sister?"

"That'd be OK, I guess, Mom."

"Well, I'm not getting fat. There's a baby growing inside my tummy."

Don viewed his mother with new respect and awe.

Don, was excited when Emmett got home from work. "Dad, did you know Mom's going to have a baby?"

Emmett winked at Esther as he said, "Naw, you're kidding."

Don had been glancing at Esther and hadn't seen the wink. He was wide-eyed and excited, thinking he was the first give his dad the news.

"Mom said there's a baby growing inside her tummy right now, and it...." Don's excited prattle was interrupted by laughter. Esther and Emmett could no longer hold it in as they realized how much 12-year old Don didn't know about making babies.

Realizing that he had been the target of a joke, Don looked disappointed. "Aw, Dad, you knew all along."

Life in the new home had settled into a routine for the family, except for Emmett's occasional narrow escapes at the shipyard. He carefully avoided letting Esther or Don find out about these brushes with injury or death since Esther was now in what Emmett called "a delicate condition," and Don could never keep a secret from his mom.

On a Monday morning in late October, Emmett was awakened from a sound sleep at 3:00 AM by sharp jabs to his ribs. "Hnnn, huh, what? It's too early to go to work, Esther. It isn't even daylight yet. Go back to sleep."

"Emmett, it's time."

"No, I don't have to go to work until it's daylight."

"Emmett, you big boob, the baby's coming."

Suddenly, Emmett became more awake, but was not yet thinking clearly. "Oh my God, oh my God, Where are my car keys? Let's go."

"Now, Emmett, calm down. I think you'd better get dressed first."

"Oh -- yeah. Where are my clothes? I can't find my clothes."

"Emmett, turn on the bedroom light."

"Oh, uh, yeah."

A sleepy Don, awakened by the loud, excited voices, came to the bedroom door and asked, "What's going on? What's wrong with Dad?"

Esther laughed. "He's not quite awake yet. I'm starting to have the baby, and he has to drive me to the hospital, if he can wake up."

Still looking groggy, Emmett was putting on his pants. "I'm awake, Esther, and I'll be finished dressing in a few minutes."

"Good. I'm glad we won't be losing you to traumatic shock. For a while there, I was wondering if you were going to make it."

"Mom, what's traumatic…?"

"Never mind, I don't have time to explain. Will you be all right here alone while Emmett takes me to the hospital?"

"Can't I go along?"

"No, they don't allow children in the maternity ward, and you'd get bored sitting around in the waiting room."

"Okay, Mom. I guess I'll go back to bed." Don turned and trudged back to his room, disappointed that he couldn't share in the excitement.

Emmett had finished dressing. "Let's go, Esther. What are you waiting for?"

"I have to get dressed. I couldn't do that with Don in here. You'd better comb your hair. You look like a wild man. Have a cup of strong coffee so you'll be wide awake for our drive across town."

Emmett was just finishing his coffee when Esther appeared at the kitchen door carrying a towel. She said "My water just broke. We'd better get going." This made Emmett's heart skip a beat. The two quickly went out and got into the car, and as Emmett started the car, Esther said something she would regret for at least the next few minutes. "My contractions are 10-minutes apart."

Emmett, hearing her remark, felt like 50 pounds of lead had been added to his accelerator foot. He burned rubber out of their parking spot, sped around the corner out of Milne Street, tires squalling, and was up to 40 miles an hour before Esther could say anything.

Hanging on for dear life, and looking terrified, Esther recovered from the initial shock and surprise of rocketing out of the driveway, and said, "Emmett, slow down. This is a 20-mile an hour zone. You're going to get us killed."

"But Esther, I don't want the kid to pop out onto the floor."

"Oh, Emmett, I said the contractions were – unhh, uh, uh, unhhh...."

"Esther, are you having another one?" Emmett inquired, as he drove even faster.

"Unhh, unhh. Emmett Green, damn it, slow down, and I mean slow down now."

Shocked to hear his normally mild-mannered, little wife swear for the first time he could remember, Emmett slowed down to the speed limit.

Esther continued scolding him. "For Pete's sake, you big boob, I said my contractions were 10-minutes apart, not 10-seconds. It'll probably be hours before the baby comes."

After Emmett had driven for another 15-minutes, Esther looked pensive and said, "Oh no, I forgot the suitcase I packed with stuff I'll need at the hospital." She should have realized that saying this would be a big mistake while, in his mind, Emmett was practically in the throes of giving birth himself. The lead foot again came down on the accelerator as Emmett made a tire-squalling U-turn on 4-lane Lombard Boulevard toward home.

Esther, again hanging on for dear life, shouted "No, damn it, we don't have to go back for it now. You can bring it to me later. Now slow down, you idiot, before you kill us."

Fortunately, there was hardly any traffic on normally busy Lombard this early in the morning. Emmett made another tire squalling U-turn back toward the hospital. Then he slowed down to the speed limit, as he felt his panic turn to anger fuelled partially by Esther's criticism, and partially by the anxiety he was feeling.

"Well, Esther, why didn't you say so in the first place. I'm under a lot of stress here and you're confusing me."

"Oh, Emmett, Who's having this baby anyway?"

Later that day, people driving along Lombard wondered what had caused the two sets of U-shaped black marks spanning all four lanes.

Emmett finally got Esther checked into the hospital. The panic and anger he had been feeling subsided as soon as they walked through the front entrance, and he realized that they'd made it with time to spare. It also helped when he remembered that he wasn't actually the one giving birth. He was comforting and reassuring Esther in the labor room when her obstetrician came in.

"Hello, Mr. and Mrs. Green. Esther, the nurse told me that your contractions are about 7 minutes apart. Emmett, you'll have to leave now. I'm going to give Esther something to help her relax. It'll probably be several hours before the baby is born. You should go home and rest -- you look like you need it."

Emmett looked at Esther, and said, "I might as well go home and give Don some breakfast. I'll come back later with the suitcase you need.

"Okay, unhh, uh, unhh, honey," Esther said as she was racked by another contraction.

It was 8:30 when Emmett got home. Don had just finished getting dressed, and asked, "Dad, can you cook?"

"Sure, Son, but I'm a little out of practice."

The truth of that statement soon became obvious. Don summed it up at breakfast with a single question.

"Dad, how did you scorch this egg on the bottom without cooking the top?"

Several days following the baby's birth dragged by, with Emmett preparing breakfasts, school lunches, work lunches, and dinners that lived up to the gourmet standard set by the first breakfast. Finally, the day arrived when Esther and the baby came home. Esther walked through the front door carrying her little suitcase, followed by Emmett carrying the baby.

Don rushed over and wrapped his arms around his mother saying, "Boy, am I glad to see you. Are you able to cook? What time are we having dinner?"

Esther smiled and asked Emmett, "Haven't you been feeding this boy?"

"Yeah, but he's a picky eater. I just couldn't get him to eat much."

Esther smiled as she remembered once eating Emmett's cooking. "Don't worry, Son, I'll cook dinner tonight."

Don again wrapped his arms around Esther, giving her a big hug. "I love you, Mom."

Now that the more important business of food had been discussed, Don could focus on the small bundle Emmett was carrying. Emmett, seeing Don's interest shift, said "Meet your new sister, Lorna," as he proudly pulled the flap of the blanket back to reveal her face.

Don was shocked. He had heard babies described as being beautiful, but he had never seen a newborn before. Here was this little red-faced creature with a shaggy, unkempt mop of curly black hair. Seeing his father's look of pride, Don lied. "Oh, uh, um, I think she's beautiful."

CHAPTER 35

LIFE ON THE HOMEFRONT

Now that the baby had arrived, life in the Greens' household returned to a routine, albeit a much busier one. Emmett had settled into his job at the shipyard. Esther was occupied with the baby and household chores. Don was busy with school, and building and flying model airplanes.

One evening, Esther looked into Don's room and discovered that he had a new interest. He was sitting at a card table with his back toward her. A little wisp of smoke was curling up past the right side of his head.

"What are you doing, Son?"

"Oh, nothing Mom."

"Don't tell me 'nothing,' I can see smoke rising up around your head."

"Oh, that."

"Yes, that."

"Well, Mom, I've taken up smoking."

"What?" Esther felt dread and anger welling up as she quickly walked over to see.

On the table in front of Don were several electronic components: an earphone, some insulated wire and a six-inch square piece of plywood that had six small brass nails protruding from it. A book entitled, "First Radio Book For Boys," was lying on the table beside the components. Don was holding a soldering iron, and was soldering a wire onto one of the nails in the plywood. Smoke was coming from the solder's rosin core, which was being vaporized as the hot soldering iron melted the solder.

Esther, relieved that the smoke wasn't coming from a cigarette, asked, "What's this?"

"I'm building a crystal set," Don replied.

Esther's mood shifted, from dread and anger, to interest.

"What's a crystal set?"

"It's a radio receiver."

Esther was excited as she realized that Don had gone to the public library and obtained a book on an interest that could possibly lead to broader studies and a profession. His interest had progressed beyond the limited number of circuits he could build from the electronics kit that he had received for Christmas in Kellogg.

"Oh, Son, that's wonderful. How does it work?" she asked, expecting that he wouldn't know much about the details.

Chuckling, he said, "I hope it'll work really well."

Esther thought to herself, He really doesn't understand how it works, and he's just building it from illustrations in the book.

Then, sensing his mother's doubts, Don decided to show off his new knowledge. He explained capacitors and resistors that were lying on the table, and how a coil of wire he had wound on a cardboard tube from a roll of toilet paper, together with a variable capacitor, would form a resonant circuit that would tune in individual frequencies of radio stations. Finally, he showed her what he called "a cat's whisker assembly," that he'd purchased at a hobby shop. He explained that a fine wire, called "the cat's whisker", could be moved to contact different locations on a galena crystal in the assembly and find a sensitive spot that would rectify modulated high frequency broadcast signals and convert them into audio frequencies: news, music, and so on, that could be heard through the earphone.

"Wow, Son, I'm impressed. So let me hear it work."

"It's not finished yet, Mom. I still have to solder more components into the breadboard circuit."

"Don't you dare ruin my kitchen breadboard, or you'll never get any more homemade bread!"

"No, Mom, the circuit on this little plywood square is called a 'breadboard' circuit."

"Okay, Son. I'd like to see your radio operate when it's finished."

Esther left the room wondering if Don really knew what he was talking about, or if he was just throwing around a lot of new words he'd learned from the book.

The next day, Esther was disappointed when she peeked into Don's room while he was at school. All the components had been soldered onto the breadboard nails, and wires had been soldered between them. Since Don hadn't demonstrated it, she decided that it probably didn't work and he had just been throwing words around without any real understanding. She was even more convinced, that Don had been blowing hot air, when he got home from school and immediately disappeared into his room without saying anything about his radio.

Later, when Emmett got home from work, Esther confided in him. "Emmett, I'm afraid our son has just been spouting off new words about his radio without... ." She stopped talking when Don entered the room.

"Mom, Dad, I want to show you something."

Don headed into his room with his parents close behind. The breadboard circuit Esther had seen earlier was on the card table.

Esther said, "Son, this looks just like it did earlier today. It wasn't working then or you'd have shown it to me."

"Not quite the same, Mom, The variable capacitor is adjusted differently, and the cat's whisker has been moved. It took me a long time and a lot of adjusting of both components to find a sensitive spot on the crystal at the same time I found just the right capacitor setting to tune in a station."

Carefully picking up the earphone, Don handed it to Emmett.

"Now, be careful, Dad, and don't bump anything or it'll knock the cat's whisker out of adjustment."

Emmett put on the earphone and listened for a few seconds. "I'll be damned, the kid did it!" he exclaimed, handing the earphone to Esther.

Esther listened for a moment, then exclaimed, "Oh my gosh, the announcer just said we have been listening to Portland station KEX."

Don showed a 2-inch length of solder to his dad and said, "This is all the solder I have left, so I need some more to build more experimental circuits."

Emmett handed Don a small amount of money for solder, and chuckled as he said, "Don't spend this all in one place."

The next day, after school, Don rode his bicycle to a hardware store in the nearby Saint Johns district. He planned to buy some rosin core solder for building more electronic circuits. When Don asked for solder, the hardware clerk said, "I'm sorry, but we are all out of solder, and I don't know when we'll be able to get any."

"The war?" Don asked.

"Yes, the war."

Dejected, Don rode his bicycle home, believing that the key ingredient for his new hobby might not be available until after the war.

"Damn war," he muttered under his breath.

Don, along with most of the rest of the population, was really feeling the pinch of shortages caused by the war. But most people didn't complain, at least not in public; they realized that the small deprivations they were experiencing were nothing compared with those being endured by our soldiers.

When Don got home, he said, "Mom, I couldn't get even a little bit of solder today." Then, self-pity welled up in him and he spewed out his frustration. "Everything is rationed: meat, butter, milk, eggs, sugar, gasoline and other stuff too. We can't even get enough gas for a trip to the ocean, and I'm hungry for steak, pies, cakes and real butter. This new white stuff called 'margarine' doesn't taste like butter, even when you mix the color capsule into it."

"Well, Son, remember that a lot of men are getting wounded or killed in the war. Those who manage to survive usually have only Spam for meat, and their eggs and milk are always the dried, powdered kind. They often have only field rations to eat."

Don wrinkled his nose as he remembered once having powdered milk and powdered eggs.

"And remember, Son, if this war goes on for five more years, you'll be drafted into the army and that's what you'll be eating. So appreciate what you've got now."

Don looked thoughtful. "Yeah, OK Mom." He hadn't realized how well off he was, and how much worse it could be in the future. He was still thinking about it when he headed into his room to do his homework. At dinner that night, Esther served beans cooked with small bits of ham. Don ate his dinner with new appreciation. "Gosh, Mom, this sure is good."

Two days later, as the family sat down to dinner, Emmett got a wry grin on his face, "I've got a surprise for both of you. Don, you said that you needed some solder. I was able to get a couple of feet of rosin core solder from a guy at work today. It's in my coat pocket."

Don said, "Oh boy," and started to leave the table.

"Now just a minute, Son, you'll want to hear the rest of this. I think I've found a bigger house for us. The owner advertised it for sale in the paper today, and I looked at it on the way home. It's on Peninsular Avenue, not far from here, and it's only about three blocks from Lombard Street where the electric bus line runs."

Portland Electric buses in the 1940's ran like electric trolleys, except they could be steered since they had rubber tires and ran on the pavement instead of tracks. Two long poles extended upward from swivels on top of the bus. On the top ends of these poles were electrodes that slid along on overhead wires to power the bus. Clean and quiet, the buses used no fuel. However, they were an irritation to drivers since one of the electrodes would often slip off its wire. When this happened the bus stalled and blocked traffic until the driver could get out and put the electrode back onto the wire.

Don was excited. "Wow, Dad, I'll be able to take the bus to movie matinees downtown."

"I don't know about that, Son. You'll be entering high school next year, so we'll think about it. Your school would be about three miles from the new house, and you would have to ride the public bus to get there."

"That's O.K. Dad, I won't mind taking the bus to school. In fact, I think it'll be kind of fun."

Esther looked especially happy. "Oh, Emmett, it would be so nice to live in our own home again, and move out of this tiny place into a larger one. We'd be able to put the baby into a room of her own. The little noises she makes at night have been waking me up."

"Yes, and its got a basement where Don can spread out his experiments and build models."

Don grinned broadly. "Wow, Dad, I'm really looking forward to living in the new house."

"Now hold on, Son, we don't have it yet. We have to negotiate a deal with the owner."

CHAPTER 36

THE DEAL

The next day was Saturday, and Emmett took the family to see the house that was for sale. The owner, Mr. Dominea, cordially invited them in. After they completed a tour of the house, Esther whispered into Emmett's ear, "It's wonderful. Let's buy it."

They returned to the living room where Mr. Dominae was reading a newspaper. As they approached, he got up from his chair, and asked, "Well, what do you think?"

Esther and Emmett were good "horse-traders," and knew how to bargain. Esther spoke first. "This house is beautiful. I really like it."

Then Emmett stepped into the conversation with his bad-guy act. "Well, I don't know. There are cracks in the basement floor that will have to be patched. The stucco on the exterior also needs patching, and the roofing looks like it will have to be replaced before long."

Mr. Doninae had done a little horse-trading himself, and he said, "Another party looked at the house this morning. He made an offer, but it was below my asking price."

Esther lost her horse-trading sense and looked alarmed as she asked, "How much did he offer?"

Mr. Dominae smiled confidently, as he realized that he'd struck a nerve, and he said, "That's confidential."

Don could see his dreams of a basement workshop and nearby bus line evaporating.

"Dad!"

Emmett, the only one of the horse-traders who had bought and sold real horses, maintained his cool demeanor. He had overcome his shyness that had been so evident when he was bargaining for an apartment in Spokane. He started toward the door as he said, "Well, OK then."

Now it was Mr. Dominae's turn to worry. The war had been going well for the allies, and there were rumors that it might end soon. He knew that if it suddenly ended, thousands of defense workers would be laid off, and the bottom would drop out of the housing market in Portland.

"Now, just a minute, Mr. Green, why don't you make an offer?"

Emmett could see that his tactic had worked, and he could probably get the house at a lower price. However, he thought he'd better set the hook a little deeper before he tried to reel in this fish. He said, "I didn't think making an offer would be of much use. I can't pay your asking price."

"Make an offer, Mr. Green. The other party hasn't been able to get financing yet, and he might not be able to get it."

Esther said, "Emmett!" (She hadn't quite caught on to Emmett's game, and she feared that he was really considering walking out on the deal.)

Don said, "Dad!" (He had no inkling about what was going on, and he didn't realize that he was learning important negotiating tactics from his father.)

Emmett had been able to save a respectable amount of money while working at well-paying jobs and living in either free company-supplied or low-cost rental housing during the past five years. He also had heard the rumors that the war might end soon, so he knew he had good leverage for negotiating the price.

"Mr. Dominae, your asking price is $9300. I can pay cash right now, and I'll give you $7300 if we can move in within two weeks."

Mr. Dominae stroked his chin for a minute, then replied, "I won't sell the place at that price, but I could let you have it for $8500 cash."

Emmett started toward the door.

"Dad!"

"Emmett!"

Mr. Dominae looked alarmed. "Now hold on for a minute. Your wife and son really want this place, so I'm willing to lower the price a little more."

Now Emmett smiled inwardly, but he was careful not to show his satisfaction outwardly; he knew his fish was well hooked, but that the deal was still fragile at this stage. He said, "I'll split the difference with you. I can give you $7900 and that's my final offer."

Mr Dominae had been thoroughly worked over by this expert horse-trader whose skills had been forged in the fires of poverty, and he looked tired as he said, "Well, that's below the offer made by the other party, but 'a bird in the hand ...' you know."

Emmett asked, "Then it's a deal?"

"Yes. I'll have the papers drawn up in the next couple of days. Before you leave, I'll need a $300 earnest money payment. We will need to sign two copies of an earnest agreement form, one for me and one for you."

Esther had recovered, from her earlier fears of losing the deal, and she returned to her usual horse-trading mode. "Mr. Dominae, be sure to add a statement in the earnest money agreement that the deal is contingent on you moving out within two weeks."

"All right, Mrs. Green. It's going to be difficult to move that soon, but I can do it. Mr. Green, can you have the balance of the money in my hands within one week?"

Emmett thought for a moment before he spoke. "Yes, but I want to put it in escrow contingent upon the title search clearing and our being able to move into the house within two weeks. That way, if anything goes wrong I won't have any problems in getting my money back."

"That's fine with me, Mr. Green, but you will have to pay the escrow and closing costs,"

Now, Esther entered the game again. "I don't think it would be fair for us to pay all the closing costs. Will you pay half of the closing costs if we pay half the closing costs and all of the escrow cost?"

Mr. Dominae looked surprised as he said, "Well, I agreed to the $7900 price thinking you would pay all the closing costs."

Emmett glanced at the door in such a way that Mr. Dominae would see him do it.

Seeing Emmett's threatening glance at the door, Mr. Donimae quickly added, "But, if we can agree to a move-in date three weeks from now instead of two, it will make life a lot easier for me, and I will agree to pay half the closing costs."

"Esther said, "That will be fine."

This was actually the schedule she'd hoped for, since it would coincide with Don's graduation from the eighth grade. The new home was too far from Don's elementary school for him to walk, and there weren't any buses that went directly there from Peninsular Avenue.

Emmett held out his hand, and asked, "Deal?"

Mr. Dominae looked relieved as he shook Emmett's hand, and said, "Deal."

It had been exhausting, but all the horse-traders were happy with their completed deal. On the way back to Parkside, Emmett, Esther and Don were excited and ecstatic. They reveled in discussing the plans they had for living in the new house. As a life lesson for Don, and because they were so excited about it, Emmett and Esther re-hashed the horse-trading methods they had used in making the deal.

CHAPTER 37

THE TELEGRAPH, AND VICTORY

Emmett, Esther, Don, and baby Lorna moved into the new house. There was enough space that items in storage could now be placed in the house. Don had his basement workshop, and Lorna had her own room.

One day, as Emmett was getting home from work, Don asked, "Dad, would it be OK if I set up a telegraph between our house and Dick's house?"

Not realizing the danger this activity would put the boys in, Emmett replied, "Sure, Son, but what will you use for wire? It's about 600 feet to Dick's house, and you'll need two wires."

"I don't know, Dad. Bell wire would be nice, but I have only about 100 feet of it."

Emmett thought for a moment, then said, "I saw a burned out solenoid coil in the trash at the shipyard. It contains lots of fine wire. I'll get it for you if it's still there tomorrow."

"Thanks, Dad."

The next day, the two boys went to Don's basement workshop and began building two telegraph sets. Their design was similar to that of a telegraph Don had built when he was in Kellogg. Excited, the boys sawed a scrap of plywood into two 6" wide by 8" long pieces to serve as bases, and cut strips of metal from a tin can to make the transmit/receive switches and armatures that would buzz. Don and Dick worked together to mount components for each telegraph on its plywood base. They drove a large nail into each plywood base, then wrapped the nail with a coil of bell wire to form an electromagnet. After mounting the armature, so one end was over the electromagnet, Don connected a 12-volt AC toy train transformer to the coil. The armature jumped and started to buzz. Don smiled with satisfaction.

Dick's jaw dropped, and his eyes widened as he shouted, "It works!"

"Of course it works, Dick. Didn't you think I knew what I was doing?"

"I had my doubts."

The boys made telegraph keys from wide strips of tin can metal. Don made two knobs, by cutting short pieces off of an old broom handle, and fastened one on top at the end of each key to form an insulated grip. He then mounted the keys and transmit/receive switches on the bases, soldered a few short wires between the components, and the telegraph sets were complete.

Late afternoon, when Emmett got home from work, two exuberant boys rushed up the basement stairs to greet him.

Don breathlessly asked, "Did you get it Dad?"

"Get what?"

"The burned out solenoid."

"Sorry, Son, I forgot it."

"Aaaww, daaad."

After a short pause, just long enough for the disappointed, dejected boys to start walking away, Emmett said, "Just kidding, Son. Look in my coat pocket."

"Oh boy. Thanks, Dad."

Don reached into his dad's big coat pocket and pulled out a 3-inch diameter, 6-inch long solenoid coil.

Emmett decided he'd better try to soften any potential disappointment. "Son, I don't know if the wire is any good. Remember, this solenoid was defective, so don't expect too much."

"Okay, Dad."

The boys could hardly contain themselves as, with trembling hands, they removed the outer insulation that encased the wire coil. Inside, they found enamel insulated copper wire that looked similar to a small amount of #35 hair wire Don already had. Don was happy to see that the only thing wrong with the solenoid coil appeared to be a break in the wire just inside the outer insulation cover.

"Wow, Dick, this wire appears to be in good shape. Let's string it between our houses right now."

"Okay, Don."

Just then, Esther called down the basement stairway. "Don, It's time for dinner, and for Dick to go home."

"Aw, Mom." Don was disappointed. He didn't have any sense of time when he was working on an interesting project, and it seemed to him that his mother always seemed know when to call him to cause maximum disruption of his fun.

The next day, the two boys unrolled wire from the solenoid coil as they strung it between the houses. They started at Don's bedroom and ran the wire out under his window, high up in a nearby tree, over the top of two garages between the houses, up to the top of Dick's house, and then down under the bottom of Dick's basement bedroom window. A second wire was strung in a similar manner. The wire was so thin that the window could be closed on it without leaving a visible crack at the bottom. Their hands shook with excitement as boys connected the wires to Dick's telegraph set.

"Dick, close your telegraph's receiving switch. I'll run over to my place, connect power to my set, and send you a message."

"Okay, Don."

Don returned home and connected the 12-volt transformer to the power input wires on his telegraph set. His hands were shaking and his heart was pounding with excitement as he depressed his telegraph key and -- nothing happened! He tapped his key several times in rapid succession. Nothing happened. No buzz from the telegraph. Nothing.

"Oh crap," he said as he tapped the key a few more times in disbelief.

"I wonder if Dick heard anything on his end," Don said to himself as he ran to his friend's house.

As Don entered Dick's room, he asked, "Dick, did you hear anything over here?"

"No, nothing. Isn't it working?"

"No."

Dick's face reddened. "For crying out loud, Don, I thought you knew what you were doing. All this work was for nothing."

Don was embarrassed. His mind was racing, trying to figure out what was wrong. Since the telegraph was essentially the same design that he'd used in Kellogg, it ought to have worked. The only difference was the wire between the two telegraph sets.

"Dick, it might be a break in the wire, or the wires might be shorted together somewhere between our houses."

"Maybe, Don, but how can we tell? There's nothing obvious or we would've seen it when we strung the wire, and we don't have any way to make measurements on the wires."

Before the boys could decide on a course of action, Dick's mom appeared at the top of the stairs and called. "Dick, it's time to eat dinner."

Dick looked discouraged as he asked, "Do you think it's any use?"

"Sure, Dick, I'll figure out what's wrong and we'll get it working."

Don's earlier enthusiasm and confidence had been temporarily replaced by embarrassment. Although discouraged, he'd inherited some of the stubbornness and determination that had propelled Emmett from poverty to prosperity in spite of the challenges he faced.

That night, Don lay awake for hours trying to figure out what to do. Finally, at about 1:00 AM, he decided to connect the 115-volt house current to the telegraph. He got up and removed a power cord from an old lamp in the basement. By 2:00 AM he had connected the power cord to the telegraph. Realizing that Dick was probably asleep, he decided to not test the telegraph until morning. Also, he still remembered his painful encounter with electric shock when he stuck a fork into an open hotplate coil in the Spokane apartment eight years earlier. He knew house current was potentially dangerous, and that he might have need of emergency services. He was an inexperienced 13 year old and was willing to take the risk, but he didn't want to do it at night.

The next morning dawned bright and beautiful. Don had been so excited that he hadn't slept at all. Finally, when his clock reached 7:30, he couldn't wait any longer. As he plugged the power cord into an outlet, he was flushed with excitement. His heart was pounding as he paused for a moment thinking about all the things that could go wrong. Then with a mixture of ignorance, curiosity, excitement, anxiety and fear, he reached out with a trembling hand and pressed his telegraph transmission key.

"Buzzz!" He almost jumped out of his skin when the sudden buzz pierced the silence of the morning. It appeared that the telegraph worked. However, there was a nagging question; had it buzzed in Dick's room 600 feet away? Don sent several more signals, then closed his receive switch. This caused the telegraph to buzz continuously. The buzzing continued for a few seconds, then stopped. Had Dick switched his receive switch to transmit? Had something burned out? No! A perfect Morse code signal slowly buzzed out "A-O-K---C-O-M-E---O-V-E-R." Then Don's telegraph started buzzing continuously, indicating that Dick had closed his receive switch. Don switched his receive switch to transmit and tapped out "O-K", then unplugged the power cord, and started to leave for Dick's house.

Esther was in the kitchen preparing breakfast. "Where are you going, Don?"

"To Dick's house."

"It's nearly time for breakfast, so stay here."

"Aw Mom, I told Dick I'd be right over."

"I didn't see you use the telephone. How did you tell him?"

"Telegraph."

"What?"

"Dick and I built telegraph sets and connected them between our houses. We sent messages this morning."

"Oh, that's nice. But don't leave."

"Awww, Mmomm. Okay, I'll send Dick a message that I'll be over after breakfast."

Don went into his room and began to send another message. His dad came into the kitchen to see if breakfast was ready, and he noticed the kitchen ceiling light dimming slightly in a rhythmic pattern that looked like code. Immediately, his mind shot back to the telegraph Don had mentioned a few days earlier. Hurrying into Don's room, he found him slowly tapping out "C-A-N-T---C-O-M-E---N-O-W-.---M-U-S-T---E-A-T---B-R- ... "

"Oh, hi, Dad."

"How come the lights are dimming, Son?"

"I don't know, Dad. It happens when I send a message to Dick."

"Oh my God, Son, do you have it plugged into our 115-volt house current?"

"Yes, Dad. I'm following in your footsteps. Dick and I finished the telegraph sets and installed the wire from here to his house. For some reason, my 12-volt train transformer didn't have enough power, so I tried house current and it worked."

"Are you sending the signals through the wire from the solenoid coil I gave you?"

"Yes."

"Son, that wire is too fine to carry a current high enough to dim the lights."

Emmett traced the wires to the point where they went under the window, raised the window, and saw something that horrified him. There were little wisps of smoke rising from two blackened streaks in the wooden windowsill under the telegraph wires.

"Son, look at this. You could have burned the house down. I'm afraid your days as a telegrapher are over."

"Awww, Daaad."

"I'm sorry, son, but this is just too dangerous."

"Okay, I'll send Dick a message that we can't do this anymore."

"No, Son. His windowsill is probably smoking too. You might burn his house down if you send any more messages."

Emmett unplugged the power cord and pulled the fine wires loose from the set to ensure that the telegraph system was out of operation. Then he sat on Don's bed facing the would-be telegrapher.

Emmett's face became serious. "Son, I don't want you to follow in my footsteps. The work I've been doing for the past 10-years is too dangerous. I've had many narrow escapes, and I survived only by the grace of God. I had to do this kind of work because I quit school after the eighth grade to help support my family. This is the only kind of work I can get to make enough money for us to live well and send you and Lorna to college so you'll have a better life."

"But Dad, you've made a good living at all of your jobs."

"Yes, Son, but with a good education in a profession, you won't have to do such backbreaking work and risk your life every day. You'll be able to make even better money than I have."

Don didn't fully appreciate the importance of the life lesson he'd just gotten from his dad. Dejectedly, he said, "Okay, Dad, I'll dismantle the telegraph system."

For the next year, life in the new home settled into a routine. Don rode the city bus each day to high school and completed his freshman year. His high school was so crowded, and teachers were in such short supply, that classes were taught in two shifts. Don was in the first shift, which started at 7:30 AM. Even with two shifts, study hall was so crowded that students had to sit three to a desk. Each desk had originally been intended for only one student. It had a built-in folding bench seat and a hole in the upper right-hand corner of the light-colored varnished Maple desktop for an inkwell. With a single student at a desk, the hinged part of the top could be lifted up to reveal a space underneath for storage of the student's books and supplies. However, under these crowded conditions one student had to sit on top of the desk, and two sat in the seat back-to-back facing the aisles, so the storage space inside the desk was useless. Students were expected to bring from their locker only the books and materials they would need for each day's study hall session. Any surplus had to be placed in the limited space on the floor under the desk, or in the student's lap.

On August 14, 1945, stunning news rocked the nation. The Japanese had surrendered! Pandemonium erupted everywhere in Portland; people banged on pots and pans, set off fireworks and danced in the streets. Men grabbed girls and kissed them, car horns honked, church bells rang and startled dogs barked. People ran down the street yelling, "The war is over," some people cried, some laughed, bugles and trumpets blasted and boat and train whistles tooted. It was as if all the pent up fears, worries and frustrations from the past several years were released at once in a cacophony, a mad symphony of hysterical sounds and actions.

When Don heard the commotion coming from every direction, he tuned in a local radio station in an attempt to find out what was going on. An announcer was just saying, "We interrupt this program to bring you an important news bulletin. The Japanese Government has surrendered." His voice was choked with emotion as he continued. "I repeat, the Japanese Government has surrendered."

"Victory! Thank God, we won!"

When Emmett got home from work, he looked worried.

"Esther, I'll have to get a job that doesn't depend on the defense industry. We'll have to sell this house before the shipyard starts laying people off."

"Oh Emmett, I haven't read anything in the paper about impending layoffs."

"No, but you will in the near future. I want to get ahead of the mobs that will be looking for work and selling their houses, when that happens. I've heard about a possible job opening in Springfield, and I'm going to look into it."

"All right, Dear, whatever you think is best. But I worry about how much this will upset Don. He likes his school, has made good friends here, and he loves his basement workshop."

"I've got that covered, Esther. When Don told me that he wanted to follow in my footsteps, I decided to arrange for him to get a taste of the world of hard labor. I've talked to my brother, Oliver, and he's agreed to hire Don to work with him for a few weeks. That way Don won't have to fret for the next several weeks about having to leave here. It will also keep him from being underfoot while we sell the house and prepare to move."

"But Emmett, Don is too young for that kind of work; it's too dangerous."

"Oh Esther, he's almost a year older than I was when I had to quit school and go to work full time in logging. Besides, my brother said he would keep an eye on him."

"But… ."

"He's going and that's that. He has 4 weeks before school starts, and the work experience will do him more good than harm."

"Yes, Emmett, if he lives through it."

Esther stormed off to the bedroom as Emmett went into Don's room to give him the news.

"Son, I've got good news for you. Your uncle Oliver wants you to work for him the rest of the summer. He'll pay you 50-cents and hour, so you can earn about $60.00 before school starts."

"Oh boy, Dad. Then I can buy that gas-powered model airplane I've been wanting."

CHAPTER 38

LOGGING, MOVING, AND DEAD MAN WALKING

The next morning, Emmett drove Don the 80 miles to Oliver's house on a small farm in Philomath. Don was greeted by Oliver's wife, Jeanette, and son, Leroy, while Emmett took Oliver aside and spoke to him quietly.

"Oliver, now that the war is over, the shipyard will be laying off most of us. I hope to sell our house before that happens, and I think I can get a job in Springfield. I don't want to tell Don about it until it's done. There's no reason for us to upset him for the rest of summer while we sort all of this out. I believe a clean break from Portland would be better than weeks of anxiety would be for him."

"Okay, Emmett, I'll keep it under my hat. By the way, I can't afford to pay Don much. We've had to pay a lot for logging rights, and I'm strapped for cash."

"Don't worry about that. I told Don that you would pay him fifty cents an hour, but I'll reimburse you for whatever he earns. I mainly just want him to get some work experience, and be out of the way while we sort things out."

Oliver and his family lived in a 2-bedroom cabin next to a railroad track that bisected their farm. The cabin had running water in the kitchen, and electric lighting, but no water heater or indoor bathroom. A wood-burning stove was used for cooking and for heating water in containers placed on top of the stove. Baths were taken either in an improvised outdoor shower stall under a cold-water hose or, on cold days, in the kitchen in a large washtub of warm water. An outdoor privy met the family's toilet needs. Many flies, wasps and spiders had taken up residence inside, and the smell was overpowering.

Don slept on a cot next to a wall of a bedroom he shared with Leroy. In the morning, Don heard a strange buzzing noise behind the wallpaper near his ear. Leroy, saw Don looking at the wall and explained the noise simply by saying, "Hornets nest." During the weekend, Don went to church with Oliver's family, and later Leroy gave him a guided tour of the farm. The highlight of the tour was a steam powered train rumbling past the house.

Leroy grinned as he said, "Watch this."

As the train approached, Leroy's Scottish Shepherd ran alongside the engine yapping and barking as dogs often do when chasing automobiles. Leroy waved at the engineer who waved back, then pulled a valve handle that released a hissing cloud of steam shooting out the side of the engine. This frightened the dog and it ran to Leroy, tail between its legs.

Leroy said, "This dumb dog does that every time. He never learns - - I think he's brain damaged."

On Monday, Don went to work in the woods at 6:00 AM as a whistle punk, the easiest, safest job in his uncle's logging operation. Leroy was already working there as a skilled Caterpillar tractor operator, loading logs onto the trucks and clearing brush.

There was a Donkey, which was a gasoline-powered winch system about the size of a large pickup truck, for dragging logs up the mountainside to a loading area. This system included a main reel, a smaller drag reel, and control levers with which the operator could apply power and braking to each reel independently. These two reels controlled a thick main cable, and a thinner drag cable. Logs were dragged up the mountainside using the main cable. If a log hung up on an obstacle, it was dragged backward a short distance with the drag cable so it could be freed.

Attached to the main cable was a slip-loop of cable called a "choker." A "choker setter" cinched the cable loop tightly around each log. The choker setter had the most dangerous job in the operation, crawling under and over the logs to set the choker. He was in constant danger of having a log roll and crush him, or having his fingers cut off if the main cable started pulling while he was still setting the choker. After he finished setting the choker, he shouted, "Ho!" once to start pulling the log up the mountainside.

The whistle punk was needed because the noise from the Donkey's engine prevented the operator from hearing the choker setter. Stationed a considerable distance from the Donkey, the whistle punk could hear shouts from the choker setter and relay them to the donkey operator by squeezing a switch that honked an automobile horn mounted on the donkey engine. A simple set of signals was used to relay the commands: one honk meant "pull the log forward", two meant "stop," and three meant "drag backward."

The woods were beautiful, and Don was fascinated with the variety of sights and sounds. In the chill air of the morning, a woodpecker rapped out a tattoo on a nearby tree, while squirrels chattered and scolded. Sometimes a thin veil of fog swirled amongst the trees high on the mountain as a passing cloud crept silently through the forest. When the weather was warm and dry, a deep, fluffy layer of red-brown dust carpeted the logging roads. Don was amazed to see his feet submerge in the dust up to his ankles the first time he walked to the whistle punk station.

One afternoon three weeks later Don was enjoying the sights and sounds around him and daydreaming. He wasn't paying attention, and he accidentally honked the Donkey horn once, the signal to start pulling the log up the mountain with the main cable. He knew that the choker setter was probably in a vulnerable position. Don didn't know the cancellation signal. In an instant, several thoughts flashed through his mind: if I immediately send two honks to stop, the Donkey operator may think that the original honk plus two more means pull backward; if I wait to send the two, the operator will start pulling forward before I can send the stop signal. Desperately, Don sent a large number of short blasts. It worked. The cable didn't move. What a relief! The choker setter could have been killed.

Just as Don was feeling relieved, thinking he'd gotten out of trouble, the choker setter came storming up the mountainside yelling, "Listen, kid, you could have killed me. You stay awake, and pay attention to what you are doing or I'll make you wish you had."

Just as the choker setter was leaving, an angry Donkey operator showed up. "What's the matter with you, kid? You've got to be careful, or you could get someone killed."

That night, after they got home, Don's uncle spoke earnestly. "Don, you only have a week left before school starts. The men have complained about the incident today, and the choker setter has lost confidence in you. I'm going to have to let you go. I'll call Emmett tonight and ask him to pick you up."

Don hadn't learned the lesson about backbreaking work that Emmett had in mind, but he had learned two other lessons just as valuable. First, your reputation is a fragile thing. Second, unskilled jobs that can be filled by almost anyone without training are not secure; there are plenty of unskilled people around to fill them. One little mistake, and you can be fired.

Emmett wasn't able to make the trip to Philomath the next day, so Don's uncle drove Don back to Portland. When they stopped in front of the house on Peninsular Street, Don saw a trailer hooked onto his Dad's Plymouth backed up to the front steps. The trailer was almost full of their household goods. Don went into the living room, and was alarmed to see that it was empty. His voice strangely echoed in the hollow room as he called out.

"Mom?"

Esther came out of a bedroom carrying an armload of bedding,

"Mom, what's going on?"

"We're moving, Son."

Don felt angry and sick as he said, "Again?"

"Yes, Son, Dad got laid off from the shipyard. We barely got the house sold before the prices began to drop. The buyers are retired, so the layoffs won't affect them."

"But, my friends, my school, my... ."

"I'm sorry, Don, it couldn't be helped. Dad got a job with Mountain States Power as a lineman in Springfield, Oregon, about 100-miles from here. We bought a small two bedroom house there, and this is the last trailer load of stuff we have to move."

Don was visibly upset. He pouted for a few minutes, then Emmett came into the room and handed him a box of his model airplane materials and equipment.

"Here, Son, find a good place for your stuff in the load."

Don felt sick as he carried the items out to the car. In one devastating crunch, he had learned that most of the things he cherished were gone. His basement workshop, friends, the vacant lot next door where he had flown his model airplanes, his school... . Just as he arrived at the car, Esther came out with an armload of bedding and placed it on one side of the back seat.

Don noticed that the other side of the back seat had been left vacant.

"Go ahead and get in, Son. You sit here," Esther said, pointing at the vacant side of the seat. "Emmett is bringing the last load of stuff to put in the trailer, and we'll be leaving in a few minutes."

Still holding his box of stuff, Don got into his space on one side of the back seat. Emmett fastened the tailgate on the trailer and got into the driver's seat. Esther got into the passenger's seat carrying Lorna, and Don looked longingly out the car window at the home he would never live in again.

It was getting dark by the time they pulled away from the house. Suddenly, Don asked, "Where's Pat?"

Esther answered. "Oh, we took the dog in a load this morning and left her tied to a doghouse in the backyard of our new house."

As the car droned along through the darkness down Highway I-99 toward Springfield, Don had plenty of time to pout and build resentment. Finally, they arrived at the new house. Even though it had an attached garage, it looked a lot smaller than the Portland house. This didn't help Don's deteriorating disposition.

Emmett was backing the trailer into the driveway when Don asked, "Does this house have a basement?"

"No, Son."

"Where will I work on my stuff?"

Emmett thought for a moment. "I'll build a workbench across the end of the garage."

Don felt more resentment and anger as he thought about working on his projects in the garage, freezing in the winter and roasting in the summer, but he said nothing. He knew his Dad wouldn't tolerate any complaining.

Even though it was after 10 PM, Emmett insisted on unloading the trailer. He had to report for work the next morning. The new house was so small that many items in this last trailer load would have to be stored in the attic. Before Don got out of the car, Emmett gave him instructions.

"Don, I want you to help carry things from the trailer and put some of them in the garage. I'll tell you which ones. Later, I'll go up in the attic. You'll carry things from the garage up a ladder and hand them to me."

Although Don wasn't saying anything, his body language and general demeanor shouted the resentment and anger he was feeling as he sullenly carried things. When the last item had been brought from the trailer, Emmett set up a stepladder under the attic access opening in the common wall between the house and garage.

Emmett climbed into the attic opening. "Okay, Son, start handing stuff up to me."

Don responded by slothfully carrying things up the ladder; he was obviously seething with self-pity and resentment. Emmett laid each item aside until several had accumulated, then he disappeared into the opening as he carried the items deeper into the attic. The attic wasn't floored, so Emmett had to carefully pick his way, stepping only on the ceiling joists which were 16-inches apart. Finally, there were only a few items left on the garage floor. Emmett was carrying a load deeper into the attic, when Don heard a sudden splintering, crashing sound through the attic opening. Then he heard his dad shout.

"Shit! Oh my God! Don, go get your mother. Hurry!"

Don wondered what had happened. When he ran into the house in search of his mother, he saw a strange sight. His father's entire leg was dangling out of the hallway ceiling. Esther emerged into the hallway from the bathroom.

"Oh my Gosh, Son, what happened?"

"Dad put his foot through the ceiling. He wants you to come to the garage right away."

Esther looked up at the new dangling-leg ceiling fixture and shouted, "Emmett, are you OK?"

There was no answer. Esther ran to the garage, and shouted toward the attic opening. "Emmett, what happened?"

"Aw, my damn foot slipped off the joist and went through the ceiling. I can't pull my leg back up through the hole because the plaster and lath are pushed downward around my leg. They dig into my leg when I try to pull it up, so I'm trapped. You'll have to pull down on the lath to release my leg."

Don and Esther carried the stepladder into the hallway under Emmett's leg. Esther climbed up and pulled down on some of the lath, but there were too many individual strips and she couldn't release their cruel grip on Emmett's leg. Don saw the situation, and finally realized how serious it was; his dad was really trapped. He climbed up onto one of the cross braces on the back of the ladder and, together with his mother, pulled down on many of the lath strips. Emmett was finally able to pull his leg back up through the hole in the ceiling. Don carried the ladder back into the garage and placed it under the attic opening. He chuckled as he waited, expecting his dad to emerge from the opening laughing, or at least smiling.

Emmett appeared at the opening looking drawn, gray faced, and exhausted. He sat with his legs hanging over the bottom of the opening. One pant leg was torn. Little spots of blood had soaked through the material where sharp points of broken lath had punctured the skin. As Emmett sat there, his chest convulsed as he silently wept, tears streaming sown his face. Don had never seen his dad like this. Suddenly, he realized that his dad, this superman, who always seemed able to do anything and everything, had finally reached his breaking point. It was 12:30 AM, and Emmett had been loading, driving and unloading all day. Don was overcome by waves of guilt for his earlier behavior, and he felt intense compassion for this man who had always worked so hard to provide for his family. In an attempt to make amends, he lamely asked, "Gosh, Dad, what can I do to help?"

Emmett regained his composure. "I don't need a sullen, pouting kid helping me. Go to bed."

"But, Dad."

"Go to bed."

As he got into bed, Don was deeply sad about his lack of cooperation that day. He'd learned several lessons: his dad wasn't superman, everyone has a breaking point, and it can be difficult to undo hard feelings that you've caused.

The next day, Don registered as a sophomore at Springfield Union High School. Emmett reported for work at Mountain States Power Company's dispatch yard. Esther needed the car for errands, so she drove him to the yard. As Emmett got out of the car, he and Esther noticed a number of sad-faced men walking toward the dispatch building. As one of the men walked past the car, he shouted to the others, "Look over here. New dead man walking."

Another of the men came over to the car. "Hi. You must be Emmett Green."

"Yes, and you are?"

"I'm Bob Clark, the foreman of the crew you are joining. Don't mind those guys. You're replacing a lineman that they all liked. He was electrocuted two weeks ago, and the guys in the crew are still hurting."

Esther looked horrified. "Oh, Emmett."

"Aw, Esther, it'll be all right."

CHAPTER 39

NEARER MY GOD TO THEE

Emmett settled into his new job. The crew's resentment of this new guy who'd replaced their friend had faded after a couple of weeks. Emmett quickly established a reputation for being a hard worker who was willing to do jobs no one else wanted to do.

One day a linemen from another crew, Tiny Atkins, walked over to Emmett and said, "Green, you're working too fast and making the rest of us look bad."

Emmett thought he was joking and chuckled as he said, "Well, maybe all of you should work faster."

Tiny's face turned red. "Damn it Green, I'm serious. You're stealing work from other men the company would hire.

Anger surged within Emmett's gut, but he forced himself to be polite; he was still trying to gain full acceptance by the men in the company. "Sorry, Tiny, I didn't think about that. I'll try to slow down a little."

Tiny's face returned to it's normal color. Seeing this, Emmett decided to remind him of something. "But remember, Mountain States Power is in competition with Municipal Power here and is having a tough time holding on."

Tiny reddened again. "Oh bullshit, Green. Mountain States has plenty of money, and we're entitled to get some of it without working our butts off."

Emmett walked away as he said, "We'll see."

A few days later, it was raining. Insulators on a 6000-volt line had cracked, and the resulting current leakage was causing intense radio interference in the Springfield Police Department.

Bob Clark's crew was assigned to replace faulty insulators on three poles near the police station. Ordinarily, this would have been an easy job, but one of the insulators was at the top of a pole on a busy street corner. However, because of intense competition with Municipal Power, Mountain States didn't want to inconvenience customers by cutting power on the line during the work. Municipal's lines were on one side of the street, and

Mountain States' lines were on the other. There were 6000-volt lines running in different directions at slightly different heights on the pole. The rain made the dangerous situation even worse.

Arriving at the job site, Bob and his men looked up at this electrical death trap, then looked at each other.

Bob spoke first. "Okay, which one of you is going to climb up into this mess?"

No one spoke.

"Come on, I need a volunteer."

Dead silence.

"Then, I'll have to assign someone. One of you smokers give me three matchsticks and we'll draw straws."

One of the men had reached into his pocket, and was starting to fish matches out of a waterproof container. Emmett said, "Oh hell, put your matches away. I'll do it."

The other linemen looked relieved, and they looked at Emmett with new respect.

Emmett knew he was going into a life and death battle. He slowly and carefully put on his climbing equipment.

The other men were concerned about this new brother, and kibitzed with potentially life-saving suggestions. "Emmett, that wrench is sticking too out far and could contact a wire. You'd better tuck it in." "Emmett, that screwdriver is too long and floppy. You'd better get a shorter one." As Emmett started climbing, the other linemen and their grunts took tools they would need and started walking to the two other poles that had leaky insulators.

Emmett unfastened his safety belt preparing to climb past the first level with its cross arm supporting three 6000-volt wires. He held onto the pole and began climbing upward. When his hands encountered some water trickling down the pole to the ground he received a mild electrical shock through his leather gloves. Surprised, he momentarily let go of the pole. As he began to fall backward, he grabbed the pole and endured the shocking sensation while he again fastened his safety belt around the pole. The belt had been treated to keep it from absorbing moisture, so it wasn't conductive.

Bob yelled, "What happened. Why did you let go?"

Emmett yelled, "Damn current through the water streaming down this pole had enough voltage gradient between my hands and feet to give me a shock." Then he dropped the end of a hand line fastened to his tool belt. He yelled to the Grunt below. "Send up rubber gloves and guts."

After putting on the rubber gloves and placing guts on the first level of wires above him, Emmett pulled the hand line up into a tight skein and hung it on his tool belt. With his hands now safely insulated by the rubber gloves, he again unfastened his safety belt and climbed up through the space between the wires. The cross arm and three wires on the second level were about 4-1/2 feet above and ran crosswise to the ones below. Emmett had to crouch and move a quarter of the way around the pole to place guts on wires of the second level. He had to repeat the climbing, crouching and moving around the pole to reach the insulators on the top level. When he arrived, he could hear the leakage current from the 6000-volt line sizzling through a cracked insulator just a couple of feet from his head. He fastened his safety belt around the pole then, digging his climbing hooks securely into the pole, he leaned back against his belt. Still wearing the rubber gloves, he carefully threaded his hand line down between the wires below. It had stopped raining; he was thankful for that small relief.

Emmett yelled, "Send up two more guts, an insulator, a standoff stick and a new tie wire." He installed the guts and replaced the leaky insulator. Then he slowly and carefully climbed down, unclipping his safety belt, crouching, and moving around the pole in reverse order from his earlier climbing procedure at each level. He removed and dropped the guts as he descended. By the time reached the ground, it was about two o'clock in the afternoon. Bob Clark said, "You must be tired after all that. It'll be all right with me if you rest in the truck for a while at our next job location."

"Naw, a little hard work never hurt anybody."

Bob looked surprised. "Well, Emmett, at least stay on the ground. I don't want you working hot wires while you are tired." Then, Bob turned to the rest of the men and said, "Okay, men, pack it in. A couple of leaky insulators have to be replaced in Glenwood."

At dinner that evening, Emmett related the events of the day. Esther got tears in her eyes as she realized how easily she could have lost him on that perilous day.

Esther said, "I think we owe God a prayer for watching over you today. Let's bow our heads. Don, that means you too. Oh God, we thank you for this food, and for bringing Emmett safely home today. Amen."

Don, who hadn't really thought about the danger his dad faced every day, and especially on this day, had an epiphany and in a voice hoarse with emotion said, "Yes, thank you God."

A month passed without Emmett having narrow escapes any worse than the usual ones faced by power linemen in 1945. It was now the peak of Oregon's rainy season. Although there had been talk of building flood control dams on the Willamette River, none had been built. The river was above flood stage, and a strong windstorm hit Springfield during the night. At 4:30 AM the electrical power failed. Fifteen minutes later Emmett's telephone rang. He had been awakened earlier by the wind and rain buffeting the house, and he knew that a combination of soaking rain and strong wind meant that trees would be falling into power lines.

Picking up the phone, Emmett said, "Hello. Yes, OK, I'll be there in a half hour."

Esther awakened and asked, "What is it?"

"Go back to sleep, Dear. I have to go to work. Springfield's main feeder line across the Willamette River is down."

"I'll get up and fix you some breakfast."

"No, there isn't time. The entire city is without power. There are lines down everywhere, and all the crews are being called out."

"All right, I'll get some candles so you can get dressed, and I'll pack you a lunch."

"Thanks, Esther. God only knows when the crew will have time to go to a restaurant."

Esther quickly put on her housecoat, lit candles, and rushed to the kitchen. Fifteen minutes later, Emmett kissed her good-by and she handed him a full lunch box. When she heard the car start, she closed her eyes and prayed. "Please God, keep him safe.

Amen." She often said this prayer when Emmett was leaving for work, especially when he was going out on emergencies. Something had saved him from many narrow escapes. Maybe her prayers had helped; they certainly hadn't done any harm.

About 30 minutes later the line truck, towing a small outboard motorboat on a trailer, drove along an access road on the west bank of the Willamette river near Springfield. The truck stopped near a downed power line. A 150-foot Douglas Fir tree had fallen into the line and had broken the wires near the west bank. Fast-moving flood currents had swept the ends of the wires downstream, pulling them far out into the river.

Bob Clark got out of the truck and surveyed the damage. Turning to the men, he said, "The best way to fix this is to cut the wires free at the H-structure on the other side, and splice new wires across the river." He looked around at the men, decided on a plan of action and said, "Emmett, I want you to string a pilot line across the river, and use it to pull three new power lines across. Splice the new wires onto the old ones at the H-structure. Take Morrie along to grunt for you. We won't connect the new lines to the power on this side until you've finished, so you won't have to use hot sticks."

Emmett and Morrie loaded the necessary tools into the boat, and attached the end of a pilot line from a reel on the truck to one side of the boat. Emmett started the 12-horsepower outboard motor. The raging flood current was flowing at about 15 miles an hour. In the middle of the river, the boat struggled against the current and was buffeted by large waves.

Emmett said, "My God, Morrie, I don't know if we're going to make it."

"Yeah, this damn boat is too small."

A moment later, a wave washed over the transom, and the boat quickly sank. Emmett was wearing boots and a fully loaded tool belt. Pulled down by his equipment, he sank at an alarming rate, buffeted and tumbling under the swift, turbulent water. By the time he unfastened and dropped his tool belt, he was far under the muddy floodwater and not much light shown through. His ears ached from the pressure at that depth. He realized that he was again in a life-or-death struggle, and said a brief, silent prayer in his mind. "God, please help me get out of this alive and back to my family again. Amen."

Emmett started swimming with powerful strokes in what he hoped was an upward direction, but a little voice in his head told him to pause and let a small amount of air out of his mouth. He was horrified to feel the bubbles go past his chin instead of his forehead. Lacking a view of the surface, he'd been swimming downward in this murky dark brown world. Turning around, he started swimming in what he hoped was an upward direction, but he was slowed by his heavy boots and was starting to need air. Removing the knee-high boots wasn't an option; by the time he unlaced them he wouldn't have had enough oxygen left in his lungs to make it to the surface. As he continued to swim through the murky darkness, his chest convulsed involuntarily trying to take a breath through his tightly closed lips. His lungs and stomach were aching from lack of air, his arms and legs were getting weaker, his heart was pounding. He was feeling light headed, and he was fighting to keep from inhaling water. He thought, my God, am I dying?

Suddenly, he saw a bright light; he had broken through the large waves at the surface. Air! Wonderful, life giving, delicious air! Gasping in a great lungful of it, he inhaled some water too and it made him cough and gag. He managed to get several more breaths before the current carried him to a strange-looking patch of water. The surface of the river there had a raised appearance where water was apparently being forced upward higher than normal. When water flows rapidly over large, submerged boulders, it causes this apparent flow upward from below. As the current carried Emmett to the downstream edge of the raised area, he felt himself being pulled down by undertow. He was able to take a large breath just before he went under again. Now, underwater, the current reversed in a vertical eddy, carrying Emmett a few feet upstream around the boulder and spitting him up to the surface again. Gasping and coughing, he managed to get a little air before being swept a few feet downstream where he was again sucked under by the undertow. On the third time through this cycle, Emmett was tiring, and he was getting weaker from lack of oxygen. He saw wooden chicken house floating past 15 feet further out in the flood current, but he couldn't get to it.

No matter which way he tried to swim, he was swept down stream, sucked back under, then spat out on the upstream side of the boulder to begin another cycle. He thought of Esther, and the plans he had for Don's and Lorna's educations. He was desperate to survive. In his mind he heard himself silently praying. "God, help me. Help me!" The fifth time he surfaced, he noticed everything was gray and devoid of any color. He thought, My God, I'm dying.

Then something struck Emmett's left shoulder. It was a floatation ring thrown from a River Patrol boat. Coughing and gasping for breath, Emmett grabbed the ring. Using the lifeline attached to the ring, a patrolman pulled him over to the boat and helped him climb aboard.

Morrie sat, shivering on a bench along one side of the boat, wrapped in a gray wool blanket, drinking a steaming hot cup of coffee. One of the patrolmen wrapped a blanket around Emmett. The blanket had been stored in a cabinet next to the engine compartment, and it was deliciously warm. This made Emmett realize how cold he was, and he began to shiver. The patrolman handed him a cup of hot coffee.

"Here, this'll help warm you up. We saw you two struggling in the water when we came around the bend. Sorry it took us so long to get to you, but we got to your partner first and grabbed him while we had the chance. We saw you go under, but we weren't sure where you'd resurface so we had to approach slowly to avoid running over you."

Emmett warmed his cold hands around the steaming cup, and sipped its contents as he silently prayed. "Thanks, God, for helping me stay alive again. From now on I'll try to be a better Christian. Please help me survive in this job and provide for my family. Amen."

CHAPTER 40

THIRTY SEVEN

The River Patrol boat dropped Emmett and Morrie off on the riverbank near Bob Clark's crew. Bob got on the radio and arranged transportation to the dispatch yard for the two men so they could drive their cars home, get cleaned up, and rest. The other linemen and grunts were pleased when the River Patrol captain offered to haul two crewmen and pull the pilot line across the river with the powerful patrol boat.

Emmett arrived home at 11 AM, wet from his "little swim," as he had jokingly called it when talking to his fellow crewmen. He was thirty-seven years old and had survived in his dangerous profession for 11 years. In the 1930's, Emmett had told Esther that 13 years was the average time a man lived after he began working as a lineman. She had no up-to-date information about this, and the danger of Emmett's job was constantly on her mind. Seeing Emmett arrive home early from work and soaking wet, Esther suspected he'd had another near-fatal accident and she said, "Okay, what was it this time?"

Emmett's face was tired from forcing a smile as a show of bravado for his crew. He knew Esther would see right through his false front, so he told her the whole truth about his "little swim".

"Oh, Emmett, please find another line of work. I'm worried sick that I'm going to get a visit from your foreman someday to tell me you've been killed."

"Aw, Esther, this is the only job I can do that pays enough for us to have a decent life and give our kids a college education." Then, grinning, he said, "Besides, my life insurance would let you live in style."

Tears welled up in her eyes. "Emmett, dear, I don't care about the money. I love you and I want to grow old with you."

Emmett realized the insensitivity of his last remark, and he put his arms around her as he said, "Okay, Dear, I'll try to find a safer job. By the way, I'm taking you and the kids to church on Sunday."

Esther recovered from the wave of sadness that had engulfed her, and she said, "Made a deal with God, huh?"

Emmett said, "Uh huh." That night he lay awake for a while trying to think of a safer job in which he could make a good living. He couldn't think of one.

Emmett's next two years were almost free of life-threatening narrow escapes. Then, in 1948, a power pole was set down too far back on a trailer and caused the trailer tongue to fly up and nearly tear Emmett's ear off. His ear hung by a thin strand of flesh. The other men's faces reflected the horrible sight of Emmett's, dangling ear. Blood was running down into his shirt collar, soaking his shirt and undershirt. He felt numbness rather than intense pain where the blow had landed, but he knew from the men's facial expressions that something was drastically wrong. He asked, "What's wrong," as he reached up to feel the side of his head. "What's this", he asked as he felt an unfamiliar object dangling from his head.

Emmett started to pull the object around where he could see it better.

Bob Clark shouted, "Stop! Don't pull on that."

Emmett realized that the loosely dangling object must be his ear, and he started to feel sick as he visualized himself with only one ear. His face took on an unnatural pallor.

Worried that Emmett might be going to go into shock, Bob said, "Don't worry, Emmett, I've seen worse. The Doctor can sew that back on, and you'll be as good as new."

On the way to the Doctor's office, Emmett confided in Bob. "I think I've about used up my 13 years of staying alive in this profession."

Bob knew that Emmett had started line work in the 1930's when 13 years for a lineman were as 9 lives are for a cat.

"Emmett, I think your information is out of date. There have been many safety improvements in line work since you started in the 30's."

"Maybe so, Bob, but I can't shake the feeling that my time is almost up."

After Emmett's ear was stitched back on, Bob sent him home to get cleaned up and to rest. When he walked into the kitchen,

Esther first saw the bloody shirt, then she saw that his ear had a
number of neat, black stitches holding it onto his head.

"Emmett, I swear to God that if you don't get into another line
of work before you get killed, I'm going to kill you myself!"

Emmett didn't say anything, but just went to the bathroom to
get cleaned up. What could he say? It had all been said before.
He didn't know any other kind of work he could do that would
pay enough.

Two weeks later, a bad snowstorm raged through Oregon's
Coast Range of mountains. Snow and ice had accumulated on
tree limbs and had broken many off. Falling trees and large limbs
had knocked power lines down and caused numerous outages.
Emmett received a telephone call at 2 AM during the storm.

"Hello."

"Emmett, this is the dispatcher. We want you to meet your
grunt, Morrie, here at the dispatch yard, and take a pickup truck
with line repair equipment to the base of a mountain near Gunter.
There's a break in the line near the top of the mountain. When
you get here we'll give you a map showing the location. All the
line crews are being called out. Trouble is so widespread that Bob
Clark's crew has been split into two-man lineman-grunt teams to
cover several small jobs at the same time. The 25 people that live
in Gunter have been without power since about midnight. We
hope you'll be able to restore their power. The line fuses have
blown, and there are no customers between the fuses and the
break, so you can work the line cold."

"Okay, I'll be at the yard in about 25 minutes."

At the dispatch yard, Emmett and Morrie loaded a pickup truck
with equipment and supplies, then Morrie drove the truck while
Emmett studied the map with a flashlight. When they got to the
narrow mountain highway, they were relieved to see that a
snowplow had removed most of the snow from the road.
However, as they approached their destination, they ran into a
snowstorm and had to install tire chains on the truck.

Arriving at the mountain location the engineers had marked on
the map, Emmett aimed the truck's spotlight up the mountainside.

He stared at the stunning beauty revealed by the bright beam that stabbed through the blackness. "My God, Morrie, look at that."

Snowflakes brilliantly sparkled like diamonds passing through the beam of the spotlight. The mountainside was heavily wooded with Douglass Fir trees and underbrush, and it sloped upward at an angle of 30 degrees. In this frozen wilderness, it was so quiet that the men heard the soft, whishing sound of snowflakes falling onto the deep snow. When they got out of the truck, they stood in wonder and listened to the sound as they experienced the breathtaking beauty and cold, deadly peacefulness of it all. They knew that many dangers could be lurking on the mountainside in its steep, sparkling, pristine whiteness. Morrie, who was only 21 years old and still living with his parents, hadn't faced anything like this before and wasn't anxious to face it now.

"Emmett, how are we going to get through all this brush in the deep snow and darkness?"

"With a lot of hard work."

"Crap, Emmett, I don't think it'll be worth it. Let's just sit in the truck and wait for morning."

"Oh Morrie, Don't be such a pansy. Folks in Gunter don't have power, and many of them are without heat. Remember that we're being paid double time for this work. We owe it to the company to give it our best shot."

"But, all that brush... ."

"It'll give us something to hang onto while we climb up the slope."

"Oh hell, Emmett. Okay, you're the boss, but I still think we should wait until morning."

Emmett went around to the back of the truck and put on his tool belt. He wedged his climbing hooks upside down on his back under his tool belt, then picked up a hand line and gave it to Morrie. Emmett could see that Morrie was getting ready to complain about having to carry the hand line, so he said, "I wouldn't ask you to do anything I wouldn't do myself," as he picked up a 500 foot coil of number 6 wire (weighing about 40 pounds) and hung it on his shoulder. Then he placed two 11,000-volt insulators in the large breast pockets of his Carhart coveralls. He picked up another insulator and gave it to Morrie. Without saying anything, Morrie placed the insulator in one of his coverall pockets. Then, as he looked at Emmett, Morrie began to laugh.

"Morrie, what's so funny?"

"Look at yourself. The two Pyrex insulators in your breast pockets make them stick out in front, and you look like a well endowed female."

Emmett looked disgusted. "Morrie, you need to find a girlfriend."

The men donned fur lined leather gloves and hardhats with cold-weather liners and built-in battery powered headlamps, Emmett picked up a machete, and they set out on their climb. They had only gone 15 feet up the slope when they ran into an impenetrable wall of brush. Selecting the least dense place, Emmett swung the machete vigorously, chopping a path through. The snow was about 2 feet deep, and progress was slow, even in the areas where the brush was sparse. Just as Emmett had predicted, the brush gave them something to hang on to while climbing up the steep slope. After two hours of grueling work, struggling through the deep snow and brush, they arrived at the mountaintop. The power line was located in a narrow cut that had been cleared through the forest. A Douglass Fir tree weighing about 2 tons had fallen onto the line, snapping all three wires as if they had been mere threads.

The men left most of the equipment at the base of a pole near the break, then struggled through the snow to the fallen tree. They hoped to pull enough wire from under the tree to avoid having to make a trip back down the mountain for more wire. Just as they arrived at the tree, there was a thundering crash, and the ground shook under them. A large tree had fallen across the tracks they had left in the snow.

"My God, Emmett."

"Yeah, Morrie."

Both men realized that if the tree had fallen 30-seconds earlier, Emmett's widow and Morrie's parents could have been getting a grim visit from foreman Bob Clark.

Emmett said, "let's get this damn job done and get out of here."

The men pulled as much wire from under the tree as they could. Emmett cut off wire that had been snarled or hopelessly pinned under the tree. Morrie hurried to get the coil of new wire left at the base of the pole, and brought it to Emmett.

An hour and a half later, Emmett was at the top of the final pole and had completed a Western Union splice on the last wire. As he climbed down the pole, Emmett shouted, "Okay, Morrie, this job is done. All we have to do now is replace the blown fuses."

It was about 8:30, and the gray dawn had given way to a day with heavy, dark clouds threatening more snowfall. The men walked and slid down the trail they had broken through the snow and brush earlier, and in less than half an hour they got back to the truck.

Consulting the map, Emmett saw that the fuses were located on a pole about five miles back along the road. After traveling about three miles they were out of the snow zone and on bare pavement. At 55 MPH the truck fishtailed around on the road, and made a terrible rumbling sound.

Morrie slowed the truck to a stop and said, "Damn it. We'll have take the chains off before we go any further."

Emmett was 16 years older than Morrie, and he was already nearing exhaustion from lack of sleep, climbing poles, splicing wires, carrying the bulk of the equipment, and chopping through the brush up the mountainside.

"I guess I'm getting too old for this stuff, Morrie. I'm already tired out, and I need to save enough energy to climb the fuse pole. Will you remove the chains while I rest?"

Morrie had expected Emmett to help remove the chains, and he was surprised to hear this response from a man who had always seemed tireless. Then he saw Emmett's ashen face and realized that he should have been a more willing helper. "My God, Emmett, of course I can."

Emmett was fast asleep when Morrie got back into the truck a few minutes later, so he drove carefully to their destination trying not to awaken Emmett. When they arrived, Morrie carried the equipment to the pole. Then he gently shook Emmett awake, and said, "It's time for you to replace the fuses."

Emmett awoke and quickly jumped out of the truck. He put on his gear and climbed the pole. Twenty one year old Morrie watched with new respect as this "elderly" 37-year old man immediately sprang into action without complaint. He thought to himself, I hope I'm in condition that good when I'm that old.

When Emmett and Morrie got back to the yard, the dispatcher scolded Emmett. "What took you guys so long? We've had angry complaints from residents in Gunter because they didn't have power until almost 10 AM." Emmett just turned and walked away, leaving Morrie to explain the tribulations they had faced.

Morrie gave an enthusiastic explanation, only slightly embellished, about their exploits that night. The district superintendent overheard this. His facial expression showed that he was impressed. Mildly rebuffing the dispatcher, the superintendent said, "Emmett is the kind of dedicated leader we are lucky to have in this company."

Emmett arrived home at 10:30 a.m. At noon, Esther prepared a nice lunch, but when she went into the living room to get him, she found Emmett fast asleep in his chair.

"Poor guy, he's all tuckered out. I'll just let him sleep," she said to herself.

At dinner, Emmett said, "Esther, I'm getting too old to do this kind of work. When I was young, I could have done twice as much as I did today without getting so tired."

"Well, of course you're too old. It's a wonder you've even survived this long with all the near-fatal accidents you've had. I wish you'd get into a less dangerous job where you didn't have to go out in all kinds of weather and at all hours of the night. I've been offered a job at Lerner's clothing store in Eugene, and I'm going to accept it."

"But Esther, I don't want you to have to work outside of home, away from the kids. And you'll have to commute to Eugene."

"It's only 4 miles to Lerner's, and the kids don't need me at home all the time anymore, with Don finishing high school and Lorna in the first grade. I can work part time so I'll be home most of the time when the kids are. And when I'm not here, Don can baby sit Lorna. Besides, I think I'll enjoy working at Lerner's."

"Well, OK, if you think you'll enjoy it."

A few weeks later, Bob Clark's crew was assigned to replace an insulator and install a guy wire on a pole that was supporting an 11,000-volt line. It was an old line, and it passed through several wooded areas. The customers it served included some stores and a cold storage plant. They had been telephoning and writing to Mountain States Power Company, complaining bitterly about frequent power outages caused by equipment failures and falling trees. Bob decided to work the line hot to avoid the inevitable complaints from customers if their power was interrupted again.

Both grunts were absent from Bob's crew that day, so two of the linemen served as grunts. Emmett had performed several climbing jobs earlier that day and looked tired, so Bob asked him to serve as a grunt while one of the other linemen climbed the pole.

The lineman on the pole attached a guy wire which then dangled loosely from the pole just below the cross arm. He attached a hot stick to the live power line, then removed the bolts from the clamping shoe that held the line onto the insulator. Using the hot stick, he pushed the line far out beyond the cross arm. He fastened the base of the hot stick to the power pole and clamped a gin pole in place to help support and stabilize the line before he replaced the insulator.

Meanwhile, Emmett and another lineman dug a hole and buried the guy wire's heavy concrete Dead Man Anchor in it. Emmett was pulling the dangling guy wire over to the anchor as the lineman on the pole was using the hot stick to pull the line over to the new insulator. Suddenly, the line slipped out of the clamp on the end of the hot stick and fell onto the guy wire Emmett was holding. Wooden pegs that attached the rubber heels onto his special lineman's boots were better insulation than metal nails, but they couldn't withstand 11,000-volts.

Emmett felt a tremendous jolt, and his world turned black. The current made his leg muscles contract with such force that he landed unconscious on the opposite side of the road from the pole.

Bob Clark and the second lineman, who was serving as a grunt, ran over to Emmett and saw that he wasn't breathing. As the lineman got ready to administer artificial respiration, Bob thought, My God, Emmett told me just a couple of weeks ago that he thought his time had run out. It looks like he may have been right. What a shame. Emmett was being considered as a foreman to replace me when I retire at the end of the month.

Bob's pessimism was well founded: the artificial respiration method used in the early 1940's wasn't often successful.

CHAPTER 41

DEAD OR ALIVE, THE GOAL

The lineman on the pole struggled to re-clamp the hot stick and lift the line off the guy wire. Bob was standing beside the lineman who was on his knees rolling Emmett over preparing to administer artificial respiration. Suddenly, Emmett gasped, took a large breath, and stirred. After a few seconds, he asked, "What happened?"

Bob yelled, "My God, he's alive!"

The high voltage had evidently made Emmett jump free from the wire in time to save his life.

Then Bob said, "Emmett, What's my name?"

"Bob Clark."

"What company do you work for?"

"Mountain States Power."

"Who's the U.S. President."

"Harry Truman."

Bob turned to the men and said, "Thank God. There doesn't appear to be any brain damage. Divine providence and perhaps his boots saved his life." Then Bob said, "Emmett, I'll call for an ambulance to take you to the hospital."

"Naw, Bob, I'm OK. Just a little shakey."

"Are you sure you don't need an ambulance?"

"Naw, it isn't worth all that fuss. I'll be OK," Emmett said as he shakily struggled to his feet.

"Alright, Emmett, but let me know if you start feeling any unusual effects. We'll get you home as soon as we finish up here."

Emmett began to feel pain in his right index finger. There was a quarter-inch charred burn on it. Then he noticed that the bottom of his right boot was smoking. He sat on the front bumper of the line truck, took off the boot, and saw that a dime-sized black spot that had been burned into the bottom of his right foot. He thought to himself, My God, I've become the Smoking Man I saw in the training movie so many years ago.

Looking at Bob, Emmett said, "I've got to quit. If I continue in this line of work, I'm going to get killed."

"Now, hold on, Green. Don't be hasty. Management is considering offering you a foreman's position to replace me when I retire next month. You would then be part of management, and you'd be prohibited by the company's union contract from doing any climbing or grunt work. It's the safest job in line work, and it pays well."

"Okay, Bob. But I don't think I can survive another minute as a lineman."

"You have a lot of unused vacation. Why don't you take some time off, rest, and think things over while you wait for management's decision?"

"Thanks, Bob. I'll do that."

The crew replaced the defective insulator and installed the guy wire. After leaving Bob and the crew at their next job location, the line truck driver took Emmett to his car in the dispatch yard's parking lot.

As Emmett got out of the truck, the driver asked, "Are you sure you're OK to drive home?"

"Yeah. Thanks, I'm feeling better all the time. It has been nice working with you guys. I'm going to miss you."

When Esther arrived home from her job that evening, Emmett was already there. Normally, he didn't get home until after she did. She looked at Emmett and asked, "For crying out loud, what happened this time?"

Emmett jokingly said, "I've been smoking." Then he showed her the hole in his finger and explained what had happened.

"Emmett Green, that's not funny! You get a safer job or else...."

Emmett interrupted her. "I gave my boss notice today. I've quit my job as a lineman."

"Huh?" Oh Emmett, I'm so glad you won't be doing that dangerous work any more," she said as she wrapped her arms around him.

However, even as she gave Emmett a hug, Esther wondered if she had been too hasty in insisting that he quit the only skilled job he knew. She worried that he might be unhappy after changing to another kind of work, and that he might blame her for badgering him into it.

Emmett explained what his foreman said. He also told her he was taking a two-week vacation.

Esther was relieved. "Oh, Emmett. A foreman! That would be wonderful. You would be able to stay in line work without being in so much danger."

Emmett used his vacation time to work in his vegetable garden, catch up on maintenance chores around the house, and plan a new dream house he was thinking about building for his family.

Three days before the end of his vacation, Emmett was cleaning out the garage. Esther excitedly brought him a letter that had just arrived from Mountain States Power Company. He started to stuff the letter into his back pocket.

"Emmett Green! You open that letter right now. I want to know whether they are letting you go, or are offering you a job as a foreman."

Emmett smiled as he tore the envelope open and said, "I thought you wanted me to quit line work at any cost, so why do you care what the letter says?"

"Oh, quit teasing me, you big oaf, and read the letter."

Emmett unfolded the letter and read, in part, as follows:

"Dear Mr. Green:

We are pleased to offer you a position as Power Line Crew Foreman to replace Bob Clark who is retiring. If you accept, you will receive an immediate pay increase of 20%. All of your benefits will continue at their present level, except that you will be granted an additional week of vacation per annum. If you decide to accept this offer, you will start working with Bob next week for one week of transitional training. Please let us know within three days whether you will accept this offer. ..."

Esther read the letter past Emmett's shoulder. She threw her arms around him and started squealing and jumping up an down like a young school girl. Emmett put his arms around her, but just stood there smiling. Esther let go and stood back. Grasping both of Emmett's hands and looking up at his smiling face, she asked, "What's the matter, Emmett, aren't you really happy about this?"

"Of course I am, but the garage door is open. What will the neighbors think if I jump around and squeal like a school girl?"

"Oh Emmett, you never show any emotion if you can help it. Besides, no one would ever mistake a big brute like you for a school girl."

Emmett held onto both of Esther's hands and started jumping around and squealing in a falsetto voice. Esther reddened as he demonstrated how ridiculous and out of character this behavior was for him. Seeing her embarrassment, he stopped and asked, "Satisfied?"

"Okay, Emmett, I admit that calm satisfaction looks a lot better on you than excited school girl does."

"Do you know what this promotion means, Esther?"

"Tell me."

"We are now in a good enough financial position that we can send the kids to college, build our dream house, and maybe even buy a new car without the risk of ending up in the poorhouse."

"Oh Emmett, we've finally accomplished our long-dreamed-of goals. Thank you, dear, for your hard work and the risks you've endured to get us here."

"I didn't do it alone. Your support: tolerating interruptions in our lives; sleepless nights and worry about the dangers in my work; taking care of the kids and running our household has made it possible for me to give it my all. You've stuck with me through thick and thin, and we make a good team. With God's help, dear, we've accomplished this together."

CHAPTER 42

EPILOG

Emmett and Esther each lived to the age of 92 years, and remained happily married for 70 years until Emmett had a heart attack and died in 2000. Esther passed away in 2002. Don and Lorna both graduated from college. Don became an Engineering Physicist and Lorna became an English Teacher. The legacy of Emmett and Esther's love, devotion to family, hard work and frugality continue to reverberate through their descendents in the form of love, family harmony, concern, and helping each other.

Made in United States
Troutdale, OR
08/12/2023

12017775R00144